DESPERATION MOON

BY

KEN DOUGLAS

A BOOTLEG BOOK

A BOOTLEG BOOK
Published by
Bootleg Press
2431 NE Halsey, Suite A
Portland, Oregon 97232

Bootleg Books may be purchased for educational, business, or sales promotional use. For information please e-mail, Kelly Irish at: kellyirish@bootlegpress.com.

First Bootleg Press Trade Paperback Edition.

November 2003

10 9 7 6 5 4 3 2 1

ISBN: 0974524611

Cover by Compass Graphics

For the three women in my life

LENORE MARIE

VESTA IRENE

&
TIFFANY ANN

Mom, the great gal I married and my darling
daughter

Where would I ever be without them?

///

DESPERATION MOON

CHAPTER ONE

RICE STARED INTO THE MIRROR behind the bar. Death stared back. Even filtered through the smoky haze, he saw it, clear as if it were lit up. He ran his fingers under his eyes, starting at the bridge of his nose and moving outward, stretching the sagging skin, pulling it tight around his large skull. A year from now and it would be worm food. He dropped a hand to the ashtray and picked up his cigarette.

He held the filter between thumb and index finger and studied the glowing ash. No fear of cancer now. He sucked his lower lip between his teeth as he pondered the ultimate question. What would it be like? Would he see that light? He smiled, thinking about the twenty-dollar whore he used to live with on Pico Boulevard all those years ago. The last woman. The only family he'd ever known. Would she be there, framed by the light? Would she have that same crooked smile?

He took a drag off the smoke, then exhaled, now studying the back of his hand. The liver spots stood out like tea stains on paper. He coughed, barely getting his hand to his mouth in time. A second spasm, then he was fighting to control the coughing jag.

"You okay, guy?" the bartender said. He was big, bald, with beefy hands. His Hawaiian shirt, half tucked in, was wrinkled, old and as seedy as the bar. But still, the bar did well with the college crowd, as it was only two blocks from Second Street in Long Beach's fashionable Belmont Shore section. Two blocks from the pickup drag, but only a buck for a beer. Buck for a mixed drink, too.

Rice gasped for breath. "I'm okay now."

"You sick or something?"

"Or something."

"What?" the bartender said. Inquisitive bastard.

"Malaria. Picked it up in Viet Nam, comes back every other year or so and gives me a couple a bad weeks. Doctors said I was cured, but I still get the attacks. What do they know, doctors?" Rice told the lie so often it flowed from his lips like truth.

"Tough. Should you be drinking?"

"Doctors said I was cured."

"Yeah." The bartender laughed. "I was in Desert Storm." He slapped another Bud on the bar. "On the house."

"Thanks." Rice shivered as a cold spell rippled

through him. Bothers different people different ways, AIDS. Made Rice shiver, made him cough.

"You sure you're okay?" The bartender picked up a towel and started washing glasses.

"I am now." Rice took a short swallow. He wasn't much of a drinker. "Not bad."

"Just a Bud."

"Been a long time for me." Then, "If you could live anywhere you wanted, you know, a place to grow old in, where would it be?"

"No contest," the bartender said. "St. Martin in the Caribbean. The wife and I go every year. Always wanted to retire there, but the way prices been going up in the islands, I'll be staying in California, and I won't be getting close to the water either."

"I'm fifty-six years old," Rice said, "and I got a chance to spend the rest of my days on the Riviera, soaking up rays and learning French. Never been. It's like a dream—me, the beach and all them young girls sticking their titties in my face." Rice held back a cough. He wanted to say more, but he'd said too much already.

"Hey, can we get a couple more over here?" a big man a couple stools down said. The bartender frowned. Godzilla and his buddy were hotshots working the babes. They'd hit on everything that had come in the door. The girls smiled, tossed their hair, took a drink, then left the men for richer and more sober pastures. Godzilla was starting to get loud.

"Just a second." The bartender laid a couple more Buds on the bar and the big man took a long pull on his beer. His buddy took a quick swallow. From the looks of him, he'd had enough. Tough having a friend like Godzilla.

"What you looking at?" Godzilla said, meeting Rice's eyes in the mirror. Rice ignored him as he ignored his own image, instead darting his eyes to the door reflected behind his right shoulder. Rice watched Clay slide in and approach the bar, smooth as a panther.

"Gonna answer me, asshole?" Spittle flew from Godzilla's mouth as he slurred the words.

"Watch your lip." Rice spoke barely above a whisper, but the man heard and was leaving the barstool. Rice wrapped a fist around the beer bottle when Clay came up from behind with a karate kick of some kind into the man's solar plexus.

Godzilla grunted as he sagged to the floor. Now his friend was off the stool, but Clay's gun was out and in his face quicker than a snake strike.

"Police," Clay said. "Sit back down or join your friend on the floor."

The man sat.

"Fucker." Godzilla started to push himself up, but Clay kicked him in the gut and had him flat again.

"You gonna be good? No trouble?" Clay said.

"Yeah," Godzilla said and Rice was impressed. Two shots to the gut, either of which would take the breath away from a normal man, and Godzilla was still talking.

"Alright," Clay said. "I just came in for a cool one. Otherwise, I'd run you two in."

"No trouble," Godzilla said.

"If you're gone quick we'll forget about this," Clay said and in seconds they were out the door.

"Aren't you out of your jurisdiction?" Rice said.

"They don't know that." Then, "You're early." Clay had a voice like an E string on a good guitar.

Rice loved to hear him talk, maybe that's why he'd been taken in by his bullshit.

"You too," Rice said.

"I like to stake out the territory."

"What's it all about?" Rice wanted to know. "I thought we agreed. No more meetings till it was over."

"Let me get a drink." Clay turned to the bartender, "Gin and tonic." Pussy drink, Rice thought, but he'd never say it. He could've handled Godzilla and his friend, but Clay was sober and knew his way around a fight.

"You didn't have to do him while he was down."

"I enjoyed it," Clay said.

"Some things ain't right." Rice took another sip of his beer as Clay picked up his drink and started for one of the dark booths on the other side of the pool tables. For a second Rice thought about walking away from the whole thing, but he didn't want to blow his shot at the Riviera.

"Got quarters?" Rice laid two ones on the bar.

"Sure," the bartender said and he got change from the cash register.

"Thanks." Rice scooped the quarters up.

There were three booths on the back wall in the dimly lit bar and two pool tables between them and Rice. Clay was sitting in the middle booth. A couple was making out in the booth to his right. They were all liquored up and going at it hot and heavy. Soon they'd be in a back seat out in the parking lot. Two guys were playing on one of the tables, three guys were standing around watching. They were all young, in their twenties, out having fun on a weeknight, wives probably at home watching the tube, or maybe they were together, stitching and bitching about their men.

Rice went to the empty table and fed it a couple of quarters and listened to the balls drop. "Might as well shoot a game." He racked them up.

"I haven't played in years." Clay slid out of the booth.

"Seven for me, since the last time I went away."

"Lag for break," Clay said.

"My quarters." Rice settled the cue ball and made the break. Two solids found pockets.

"We have a slight problem," Clay whispered. "And you're the solution." He bent over the table, took a shot out of turn and missed.

"Don't keep me in suspense."

"My mother's stomach started acting up in Florida."

"So?"

"She's bringing my wife's niece, Kelly, back three days early."

"So?"

"Carole's been staying with me. It's part of my alibi, remember?"

"So the niece alibis you instead."

Clay laid the pool cue on the table and turned to Rice. "Look, what we got going is as perfect as it can be. It works for all of us on a lot of levels. This is just a new complication, but we can turn it into an opportunity."

"I'm listening." Now Rice laid his stick down. It didn't look like the game was gonna get finished.

"Kelly's grandmother and my wife are involved in a custody battle that goes to court in a couple of weeks. Who wins is fifty-fifty. Under the circumstances I think it would be better for all concerned if Granny wins."

"I'm not following you, Clay."

"I want you to snatch the kid. Tomorrow night."

"No."

"The front door will be unlocked. Just drive up, walk in, grab her and take off. You can take her to the house out by the airport."

"You're not hearing me. I said no. Like you said, it complicates things."

"Not really. Granny's worth a fortune. She'll pay a half million easy to get her back. That doubles your share, and that would really make the rest of your life worth living."

"You can't be serious."

"She'll pay right up. Day after, guaranteed." Clay picked up his stick and took another shot. He missed again. "I never was any good at this." He set the balls back the way they were and did it again. This time he made it. Rice hated cheats. "Your shot," Clay said.

"Sure." Rice took the stick. It had been a long while, but it was like riding a bike. He could run the table easy, instead he chose to miss a straight in shot. No point in pissing Clay off.

"Think of it," Clay said, "two perfect crimes back to back and we walk away winners with nobody the wiser."

"Twice the chance we get caught."

"You want out? It's okay. The big guy'll do it."

"No, I'll do it."

"That's more like it. Carole's gonna be at the movies, 7:00 to 10:00. My mother's gonna drop the kid by at 8:00. I'll put a video in at 8:30, then I'll go to the store for some snacks or something. You come in right after I leave and make the snatch."

"You gonna call the cops, anything like that? You know, to try and make it look good."

"You kidding?

"What about your wife?"

"By the time Sara gets back from Australia, the kid will be with Granny in Hawaii and we'll be counting our money.

CHAPTER TWO

SARA SLID THE CAR around the overturned Jeep, squinting against the high noon desert sun. Sweat poured off her brow, stinging her eyes. Her clothes were wringing wet, sticking to her body. It was almost too hot to breathe. Summer in December. The seasons were upside down.

"Look out!" Lisa yelled.

"I see him!" Sara yanked the wheel to the left to avoid the man that was suddenly in front of her. He jumped right. Then she was into the slide. She cranked the wheel more to the left, into the direction of it, downshifting, gently riding the accelerator as the Mitsubishi Montero hydroplaned over six inches of fine red bull dust, like driving over baby powder.

She turned back to the right, red dust flying from all four tires, losing traction again, correcting, driving blind, then back on the track, shooting out of the cloud. She shifted down into third as she hit the brakes, then second. She stopped the car and turned to look back.

"I'm okay," the driver yelled, "get going." Sara flashed a thumbs up signal, shifted into first and was off.

"The track goes straight out for the next ten kilometers," Lisa, her younger sister, said. Sara heard the stress in her voice. More than usual. Sara sensed Lisa didn't believe her about the black eye. Lisa commented about it when she picked her up at the airport, listened to Sara's explanation, then didn't bring it up again. Sara, caught up with her own problems, had let Lisa's doubts fester till the tension between them was getting in the way of their teamwork. It was stupid. She knew better.

She floored the Montero, shifting through the gears a hair before redline. She kept her eyes forward, afraid to blink, trying to keep her mind on the race.

"Gully coming up, half a click," Lisa called out, reading from the rally instructions.

Sara downshifted into fourth, tapping the brakes as she went into third, standing hard on them for the briefest time as she went into second, left foot flying between clutch and brake pedal, the right keeping the accelerator on the floor. She took her foot off the brakes inches before the front tires hit the gully and they floated over it. Then she was back on the clutch, shifting through the gears.

"Perfect." Lisa's voice cracked above the roar of the engine. "But you have to do it again in half a click."

Sara downshifted again. "I hate Australia," she said. "One minute, dust half a foot deep, then this." Gullies made by long dead waterways rippled through the dry, caked desert floor. And up ahead, more dust. There was no getting rid of it. It was in her hair. It stuck to her body, mingled with her sweat. It coated her teeth.

Double clutching, she slammed the Montero into second, but she misjudged her timing and jumped on the brakes a fraction of a second late. Clay, Kelly and the coming adoption battle were all on her mind, messing with her judgment. "Hang on!" The front tires cleared the gully, but the rear wheels hit hard, knocking the wind out of her as she fought to keep control.

"Flat," Lisa said.

"Yeah." Sara pulled well off the track. She stopped the Montero and caught her breath as Lisa jumped out. A few seconds later, breathing normally now, she followed her out of the car.

"What were you thinking about?" Lisa said as she opened the rear door. She pulled out the tire iron and tossed it to Sara.

"Kelly," Sara said. She squatted and started loosening the lug nuts. "I keep trying to think positive, telling myself, no way is the judge gonna take her away from me."

Lisa pulled one of the spares and the jack out of the back. By the time Sara had the lug nuts loose, Lisa had the car jacked and was ready with the spare. "I'm sure the judge will do what's right for Kelly," Lisa said.

"Kelly belongs with me and Clay." Sara slipped the tire on and started tightening the lug nuts.

"Let's just concentrate on the race," Lisa said.

"You're right." Sara finished.

Lisa grabbed a bottle of water from the back, rinsed her mouth out, spit, then took a long drink. "Here." She tossed the bottle to Sara, then started throwing the stuff into the back of the car. Sara tossed the bottle in after and in seconds they were back on the road again. The operation took less than five minutes.

"Straight out two clicks, no problems, then a sharp left," Lisa said as Sara sped through the gears.

"Got it." Sara accelerated until they were sailing along at a hundred-and-sixty kilometers per hour.

Two kilometers later Lisa yelled, "Slow down! Dust ahead, too slow to be another racer."

"Camels," Sara said. Generations ago camels were introduced to Australia, but apparently the Aussies didn't get along with them. Now they roamed free, as at home in the Great Australian Desert as in Arabia.

"A herd," Lisa said.

"Photos!" Sara slowed to match the speed of the desert beasts as she punched the horn, scattering the camels.

Lisa grabbed the camera bag and pulled out one of the cameras, bringing it to her eye as she pulled off the lens cap.

"Hurry, you're gonna miss the shot," Sara said as Lisa started shooting, the motor drive gobbling up the film as fast as the Montero's tires were gobbling up the dirt track.

"Think I got some good ones," Lisa said.

Then they were through the terrified animals and Sara started to pick up speed, anticipating the sharp left. She downshifted, lightly riding the brakes into the turn. Once through it, she went back up through the gears.

"Only twenty-five hundred kilometers to Darwin," Lisa said.

"Let's hope they're easier than the last four thousand." Sara had been driving since before sunup and she was getting tired. Each day was harder.

"How you holding up?"

"I hate getting old." Sara was twenty-eight. "And I wanna get in before dark tonight."

"I want a bath," Lisa said.

"They say there's showers at the next campsite."

"I heard. Pretty exciting," Lisa said.

"Up ahead," Sara said, looking off into the distance.

"Yeah, dust cloud," Lisa said.

Sara kept her eyes on the speeding cloud. There was a car in front of it. She'd be able to see it when the track curved ahead. "I got the car. See it?"

"Got it," Lisa said.

"Can you get his numbers?"

"Got 'em." Lisa picked up the mike and yelled into it. "Two-fifteen, Two-fifteen, pull over, car behind wanting to pass."

The dust cloud slowed and Sara locked the picture of the road ahead into her mind. "Ready?"

"Yeah," Lisa said.

Sara accelerated into the cloud. She was driving blind, the fine red dust all she could see. She started losing traction on the left side. "Where's the road?"

"Right, right, right!" Lisa yelled. Then they

blasted out of the haze and Sara pulled the car back up onto the track.

"I hate that."

Then up ahead, another dust cloud. Sara tightened her grip on the wheel. The track made a thirty degree turn to the right and she saw the numbers on the side of the auto ahead as Lisa grabbed the mike.

"One-two-four, One-two-four, pull over, we want to pass." This time the dust cloud didn't slow and give way.

"What's wrong with him? Call again." They were closing fast and Sara didn't want to drive into the dust without the driver in front knowing she was coming up behind him.

"One-two-four, do you copy? We are on your tail, wanting to pass. If you don't pull over we will push."

"His radio's out. Hold on, here we go!" Sara eased down the accelerator and headed into the cloud. "Can you see anything?"

"No, yes, take it easy. Now!"

Sara nudged the car in front.

"He knows we're here," Lisa shouted. "Look out, he's losing it. Come on fella, get it back. He's got it, Sara. He's pulling over now." Then, "There's a gully right around here!"

They slammed into it. The Montero bottomed out. Hard. The engine blew before they completed another kilometer, leaving Sara no choice but to pull off the dirt track. She looked at the gauges. "Shit, shit, shit! No oil pressure."

"I messed up. Sorry," Lisa said.

"I should've stopped when we hit," Sara said,

calming down. "If I'd been checking the gauges, I would've seen the pressure drop." She opened her door to get out.

"No!" Lisa grabbed Sara's arm and pulled her back into the car as One-two-four flew by, covering them in a fine red haze.

"Asshole didn't even stop to see if we're okay," Lisa said.

"Takes all kinds."

"What do you think's wrong?" Lisa said.

"Let's see." Sara popped the hood latch, then got out of the car. There was still dust in the air, but most of it had settled. She raised the hood, then looked underneath. "Looks like the oil filter smashed into the front differential when we bottomed out. Oil's sprayed all over the place."

"What now?" Lisa said.

"The sweep car will pick us up and we'll get a tow."

"It's my fault," Lisa said. "If I'd only called that gully before we went into the dust—"

"Plenty of blame to go around. If I'd paid better attention to the gauges, we'd still be in the race." She closed the hood and closed her eyes. Damn, she'd wanted to win.

"Sorry, Sis. I know what it meant to you."

Sara still had her hands on the hood. She felt the heat radiating from it, almost too hot to touch. She took her hands away and faced her sister. "Ah, well," she said, "to quote Mick Jagger, 'You can't always get what you want.'" She smiled and tasted the bitter scent of defeat. She knew the smell was imagined, but she suffered it anyway. Silence, she thought, the loser's companion. She hated silence.

"I wanna talk about it now." Lisa's whisper cut through the dry desert quiet. "Now that we're out of the race."

"What?" Sara stared across the red desert sand. She sighed. Her body felt like it was vibrating, as if she were still in the car, speeding and bouncing over the dirt track, but the constant roar of the engine was gone now. There was no wind, not a wisp of a breeze. Sweat slipped down the back of her neck. She made a comb with her fingers and pushed her sticky hair back.

"So, you gonna tell me, or what?" Lisa said.

"I told you it was an accident. We took the boat out for a sail the day before I left. We anchored out by Grissom Island and some friends called and invited us over to their boat. I was standing behind Clay in the dinghy, holding the potato salad, when he pulled back on the starter cord. Elbow met eye and I was on my back."

"Battered women always have such great explanations," Lisa said.

"Oh, stop it," Sara said. "If a man hit me, I'd slice his balls off, and you know it."

"What about if it was Clay?"

"Clay knows it too." Then, "Look, racer coming. Must be Two-fifteen, wonder what held him up." They tabled their conversation as they watched the cloud approach. "Another one behind it," Sara said.

"Toyota," Lisa said. Two-fifteen was approaching fast. It slowed and Sara saw the Asian features of the driver and navigator as Lisa waved them on.

"It's that girl singer from Japan," Sara said. "It didn't click who it was when we passed them back in the dust. I had no idea they were this close to the lead."

"Apparently she's not just a pretty face," Lisa said as the Toyota roared past.

Then the next car was upon them. It was the Jeep they'd stopped for earlier. Lisa was waving him on, but he stopped anyway. "We're okay, keep going," Sara said.

"You're sure?" The driver said. Sara nodded. He had a toothy smile with sparking blue eyes. Sara didn't know him. His navigator waved as they went by. Sara recognized him from races past, but didn't know his name. Then it was quiet again.

"Okay, maybe Clay didn't do it on purpose, but he's capable of it and you know it," Lisa said.

"He is not." Sara sighed again. "Clay would never hit a woman."

"He's been brought up on charges twice before for brutality and this time it seems especially bad. I've seen him so angry at you that it scared me."

"So we argue. We always work it out." Sara heard herself saying the words, but she was beginning to wonder if it was true. Clay was getting harder and harder to get along with.

"What about the brutality? Just because he's a cop doesn't mean he can beat suspects so bad they have to go to the hospital."

"They were criminals resisting arrest," Sara said.

"That last one was sixty-seven years old."

"He had a knife."

"Big deal, Clay's got a black belt. He could've got the knife away without half killing him. Sooner or later he's going to hit you. I see it in his eyes."

"No, he'd never do that," Sara said. "He loves me and I love him. We've got some problems, but we're working them out. And he's seeing the department shrink about his temper problem."

"Voluntarily or did the department make him?"

"Come on, Lisa. I don't want to talk about it any more."

"It's just that he seems to be getting worse," Lisa said. "There's got to be a reason."

"Okay, I'll tell you, but you have to promise to keep it secret."

"My lips are sealed."

"Swear."

"Cross my heart."

Sara stared out across the vast plane. She saw a dust cloud off in the distance. Too far to hear the roar of its engine as it charged toward them. She sighed and the sound of it seemed to wake up the desert quiet. She felt the sweat trickle under her arms, the sun on her face. There was no shade, save that made by the car.

"It's Clay's fault we can't have kids. He's got a low sperm count."

"Like he's shooting blanks?" Lisa said.

"Yeah. We've known since April. I'm sure that's why he beat up that man and it's for sure why his temper's running out of control. He feels like he's less a man because he can't reproduce. But he'll get over it and everything will be back to normal, you'll see."

"Hey, I'm sorry," Lisa said.

"It's alright. Thank God for Kelly. She's taking a lot of the sting out of his anger. He's the perfect angel around her. He really loves her."

"I know how bad he wanted kids. It must have been quite a blow to his ego. No wonder he's been acting the way he has been. He must be mad at the world."

"He's getting better." Sara wiped the sweat from her brow with the back of her hand, then she sat down with her back to the car, seeking what little shade there was.

That night, after being towed to the campsite, Sara packed her bag. She had one suitcase and the heavy camera bag. She'd just bought the cameras, two Canon fully automatic jobs. One had a wide angle zoom, the other a telephoto. Off road racing had been good to her. She wanted to remember it.

"Gonna miss all the after race parties," Lisa said, intruding on her thoughts.

"That's okay, Sis, the great Australian Safari road race extravaganza can roll on without me. I'm sure you'll have enough fun for the both of us." She laughed, but it was forced.

"Only one more race for us," Lisa said. "I'm gonna miss it."

"Me too, but Kelly needs a full time mom."

"What if you lose the case? What if she has to go and live in Hawaii with Estelle?"

"It won't happen," Sara said. "Not a chance. No way would a judge take her away from a stable family to live with an old woman."

"She's not that old," Lisa said. "And the way you say it makes her sound like Cinderella's mean stepmother. She's not. She's a nice woman who loves her granddaughter. She's fighting for the child she loves, just like you."

"Whose side are you on?" Sara said.

"I'm on Kelly's side. She's my niece too, don't forget. And I think it would be a lot better for Kelly if you two could work something out between yourselves. This court battle isn't doing anybody any good."

"It's all Estelle's fault."

"She's not your enemy."

"She is right now."

"So, how are you going to make a living?" Lisa said. Sara hated it when she did that, changed the subject before it was closed.

"I'm gonna buy in at Condor. Carry Ann needs the cash and I'll need something to do."

"That's why you've been taking the flying lessons?"

"Yeah, I didn't want to say anything till I was sure. I'm sure now."

"But buying into a flight school, going to the same job every day. I don't know."

"I'll be able to schedule my hours around Kelly's school. I want to be home when she's home. It's important. All I want is to be a good mother to her. Truth, if we hadn't taken the sponsor's money, I might have bailed on the last race."

"We could've returned it," Lisa said. "We can afford it."

"No, a deal's a deal. Besides, they've been good to us, we couldn't have just walked out on them." She looked up at the night sky. Millions of stars blanketed the heavens. She was cold as she stared up at the Southern Cross. This was the kind of sight that the average person never lived to see.

"Danny says he can have the car ready to ship in a couple of weeks. They'll have it in Rabaul by the end of next month, fit and ready to race."

"I'll be there," Sara said.

"I wish you could stay," Lisa said. Racers, reporters, mechanics and groupies were gathering around the picnic tables for the nightly barbeque, but Sara wouldn't be joining them. She was leaving shortly on a press bus to Alice Springs, then a flight back to Sydney, then home.

"So do I, but I've been away too much this year already. I want to be home when Clay's mom brings Kelly back from Orlando. Besides, Papua New Guinea doesn't sound like my kind of place. Bad enough we have to race in the jungle, if one of us has to live there for six weeks, it might as well be you. After all, you're the navigator."

CHAPTER
THREE

SARA'S PLANE LANDED in Los Angeles at 8:45 in the morning. With her running shoes, faded Levi's and plain white tee shirt, she blended right in with a group of college kids as she passed through customs. How nice to be that age, she thought. Nothing on your mind but studies and the next vacation.

It was 10:00 by the time she climbed into the shuttle bus to Huntington Beach. The van had three bench seats in back. There was a forty-ish looking couple in the rear seat. He was dressed twenty years younger than his age with a batik shirt and surfer shorts, the kind that came almost down to the knees.

She was wearing cut off Levi's and a tee shirt knotted at the waist, exposing her stomach.

"Good morning," he said as Sara climbed into the middle seat.

"Morning," Sara muttered.

"Been away long?" The man had a laugh in his voice and a deep tan, like he worked out of doors, a construction worker maybe.

"Just a little over a week."

"Five years for us. I'm Seth, this is Rebecca."

"I'm Sara."

"You coming back from a short vacation or a business trip?" Seth asked. He had a Santa Claus twinkle in his eye and a sincere smile. The kind of man who was interested in people, a talker, but Sara didn't mind. Then she saw the phone.

"Business trip, can you excuse me, I have to make a call." Then to the driver, "How do you use that?" She pointed to the phone in the middle console up front.

"Got a credit card you can make a call," the driver said. He was a young black man with close cropped hair and manicured nails.

"Important call?" Seth asked as Sara punched out the number.

"Kind of," she said. Then "It's ringing." She turned away from the couple in back.

"Tucker and Sweet." The girl on the other end of the line sounded like she was too young to work in a law office.

"Desmond Tucker please, this is Sara Hackett." Sara felt a tingle at the back of her neck. The news was going to be bad, she just knew it.

"Sara."

"Hello Desi, I just got back."

"I thought you were going to be incommunicado for another week," he said.

"Yeah, me too." Sara sighed. She'd known Desmond Tucker all her life and his bedtime-soothing voice had always put her at ease. "I slammed into a gully and managed to blow the engine. Lisa's going with the car to Papua New Guinea. I came back early to see if there was anything I could do to help the case."

"You should've called. There's nothing you can do." Desmond always gave it straight out. Good news or bad, he never pulled his punches.

"You said you were going to try and talk to the judge, maybe try and get an idea how he might rule."

"Yeah, I did, but he's a tight lipped bastard. We're friends, but there's no way he'd come right out and tell me what he's gonna do."

"I don't understand," Sara said.

"We have dinner and drinks, couple three times a month, just a couple of old bachelors." They weren't really bachelors, they'd both lost wives to cancer within weeks of each other. Their mutual tragedies had forged a bond between them. "Usually, if he's going to rule for me, we have more than one drink."

"I thought you said we had a case. You said you're the best lawyer in the state for a custody battle." Sara clenched the phone in a white knuckled grip.

"Hey, I said there was nothing *you* could do. I didn't say it was over. Wainwright's a family oriented kind of guy. Knowing that, put yourself in his place. He's seeing a loving grandmother fighting an aunt who's running all over the world risking her life driving fast cars. On top of that, she's married to a policeman. It's not that he hates cops, but he's way liberal, kind of thinks most cops lie on the stand. Once he finds out you've quit racing and sees you and Clay all lovey dovey in court, I'm betting he'll rule in your favor."

"You really think so?"

"I've known Jim Wainwright all my professional life. He never really knows what he's gonna do until he does it, but I think we have better than an even chance."

"So what should I do?"

"Absolutely nothing. Live your life, let me sweat the legal stuff."

"Okay, sorry I bothered you."

"You're never a bother, now I gotta go. Say hello to Clay for me."

"Bye Desi." She turned the phone off and handed it up to the driver as they were leaving the airport.

"Divorcing?" Seth, the man in back, asked.

"No."

"Then why the custody battle?"

Sara turned and met his open smile. He seemed like such a nice man, someone who liked to listen, so instead of feeling annoyed at the personal questions, she found she wanted to tell him.

"My brother and his wife were killed in an auto accident last year. Their daughter's been living with me. My sister-in-law's mother thinks she should be living with her, in Hawaii."

"Sounds like you should work it out between yourselves."

"Yeah, life should be so simple. Sometimes I wish I could just take Kelly and sail away."

"It's not always that easy, sailing away," Seth said.

"It could be for me. I've got a forty-five foot sloop all set for cruising and I've been saving my money. It has always sort of my dream."

"But somehow, you don't know how, stuff just always seems to get in the way," Seth said.

"Yeah, exactly, my career, then my marriage, now Kelly."

"If you're gonna go, you just gotta go. There will always be a reason to postpone taking the boat away from the dock for the last time."

"You sound like you know what you're talking about."

"We just finished our second circumnavigation, been living eleven years on a fifty-foot ketch. *Island Girl's* her name."

"But you just came in on a plane."

"True, the boat's on the hard in Trinidad. We flew in because we've just become grandparents for the first time."

"You don't look that old."

"Living on a boat keeps you fit," he said. His wife nodded. No way did she look old enough to be a grandmother. Estelle, now she looked like a grandmother. Not this woman.

"So how old are you?"

"I'm fifty-one," Seth said. "I can't tell on Rebecca."

"Going on thirty." Rebecca laughed, stuck out her lip and blew the hair out of eyes. "Seth's right, there's a million and one excuses for not leaving. One day you just gotta do it."

"But how do you support yourselves?" Sara said. "Are you independently wealthy or something?" She figured they must be, you had to be if you wanted to live on a boat like that.

"No," Seth said, "we sold our house when the last kid—we had three—left for college. We bought a boat and took off. Mostly we earn our way. Rebecca does canvas work, makes awnings and bimini tops and does sail repair. I fix diesel engines, boat refrigeration and any other mechanical thing that can go wrong on a boat. We live pretty close to the wire."

"So you were able to support yourselves when you left?"

"Heck no," Seth said. "We didn't have a clue. We had enough money saved to maybe make it for a couple of years. We learned."

"Then you learned fast." Sara was fascinated. These people had done what she'd been dreaming of ever since she was a little girl and her father taught her how to sail.

"Yeah, we had to."

"I can fix anything on a boat," Sara said, "glass, ferro-cement, aluminum, steel or wood. I can fix or make sails, dodgers and biminis. I can do the electronics, twelve volt or one-ten. Refrigeration is a piece of cake. I eat diesel engines for lunch. I can do it all, plus I have a good boat, paid for, and a nice bank account, but I've never been able to just chuck it all and leave. I guess I don't have your courage."

"You can really do all that?" Seth said. Sara heard the amazement in his voice.

"Sure, I was always a tomboy growing up. I loved engines and my dad loved to show me how to work on them. He raced cars for a living and I guess I inherited his love for the sport, my sister too, because that's what we do."

"So how's that fit in with boats?"

"My parents loved sailing. When dad retired they were gonna take off and sail around the world. I guess I inherited their dream too."

"Did your father retire? Did they go?" Rebecca asked.

"Dad retired six years ago, but they didn't go sailing." Sara stiffened up when she thought of the plane crash, so unfair. "They died in New Zealand. They were on a helicopter flight to the top of a glacier on the South Island. Something went wrong and the chopper flew into the side of a mountain. Eight tourists and the pilot, dead in an instant."

"Your parents and your brother, that's hard," Seth said.

"Sometimes life reaches out of nowhere and kicks you in the butt," Sara said. "It can be rough, but there's nothing you can do about it, you just have to deal with it."

"So is it your parent's boat you have?" Rebecca said.

"Yeah, their boat, fitted and ready to go. Maybe someday."

"You're still young," Rebecca said.

"I'm getting older everyday." Sara looked out the window. They turned onto the San Diego Freeway. The traffic was running smoothly. She'd be home in less than an hour.

"So what's holding you back now?" Seth asked.

"My husband's a cop. He enjoys day sailing, but the thought of being out there after dark, with no land in sight, terrifies him. He won't admit it, but I can tell. He's a real macho kind of guy, but he gets green as soon as the sea starts to kick up."

"Sounds like you got the wrong husband."

Rebecca laughed.

"Then there's my career. Well, no, I gave that up when I decided to take Kelly, my niece. But I could never just take her and go off on *Wave Dancer*, that's my boat. Kelly's grandmother would have a cow."

"Dump the cop, take the niece and grandmother down to *Wave Dancer* and pull up the anchor." Seth laughed, but Sara could see he wasn't joking.

"I love my husband," Sara said.

"Then I guess you won't be cruising anytime soon and that's sad," Rebecca said, "because if you can adapt, it's the best kind of life there is."

"Yeah, that's what I've heard." Sara sighed as the driver shifted the van over into the fast lane. She closed her eyes and tried to imagine it, living on *Wave Dancer*, cruising in Hawaii or the Caribbean. That dream died on her wedding day, but in fairness to Clay, she'd known it before she'd taken the walk down the aisle. Clay was firmly rooted in Southern California and he was a man with dreams of his own.

"We're here, ma'am," the driver said. Sara opened here eyes. Seth and Rebecca were gone. "You were really out, didn't even wake up when I dropped the others off."

"I guess I needed the nap. I didn't get any sleep on the flight."

"We'll you're home now. You can get all the sleep you want."

"Yeah." Sara paid him and gave him a generous tip. A slight breeze rippled by as she started up the walk to her front door. She fumbled through the film in her purse and fished out her keys. As usual the house was neat and tidy, not a speck of dust anywhere. Clay was a neat freak.

In the kitchen she opened the refrigerator and reached in for a can of Coke and stopped herself. It was fully stocked. Fresh milk, fresh fruit, orange and grapefruit juice. She'd only been gone a little over a week, but she'd expected nothing in there but soft drinks and beer. Clay was a voracious eater. Usually he devoured whatever she'd managed to stock up in three or four days, then ate at restaurants until she returned.

She pulled a Coke out from behind the milk, popped the top and took a long swallow. It was heaven going down. There was a pad with a pencil on a string stuck on the refrigerator. She thought about leaving a note, but decided not to. If she surprised him with his favorite meal, Marengo chicken, chicken cooked in a garlic, tomato and sherry sauce, he'd be like a kid on Christmas Eve, happy and lovable.

She finished the Coke and trashed the can in the basket under the sink. Then she stashed her baggage in the den. It would spoil the surprise if he stumbled over her suitcase and camera bag before she returned.

She saw two rolls of film sitting next to the electric coffee maker and she scooped them up. She planned on going to the photo place to develop her race photos before she did her shopping, so she might as well develop Clay's film too.

She entered the three car garage through the kitchen. The spot closest to the door, where Clay parked his Jeep, was empty, so she had an unobstructed view of her baby. A fire engine red '67 Austin Healey. The top was down. She smiled and ran her hands across the hood as she passed it on the way to her Montero, a souped up street version of the one she raced.

She started to get in the Montero, but changed her mind. She wanted to feel the wind on her face, so she tossed her purse into the Healey and got in. She started the car, then punched the automatic garage door opener that was clipped to the visor. The rumble of the Healey's engine rippled through her as she waited for the door to open. Then she roared out the driveway, punching the door opener as she crossed the sidewalk. She was at the corner before it closed.

She loved her car. It defined her. They'd spent the first year of their marriage restoring her. Sometimes the hunt for parts was as frustrating as it was expensive, but now she was showroom new and stock to the core.

"Hey, lady. Nice car."

Sara looked, it was an older guy in an old Porsche Speedster in the lane next to her. He waved, downshifted and took off. Part of her wanted to give chase, but the Porsche was a faster car and he looked like he knew how to drive. Besides, the last thing she needed was a ticket for speeding down Beach Boulevard.

Lady, the guy actually called her *lady*. Funny, she still thought of herself as a girl. She laughed. Then she thought about that couple on the shuttle van, Seth and Rebecca. *If you're gonna go, you just gotta go.* That's what he'd said. She was still thinking about them when she pulled into the parking lot at the Goldenwest Mall.

"Hey, Sara Hackett, how's it going?"

"Hey yourself, Spider," Sara said as she entered the photo store. She'd known Jim Horner since he was a baby. He was fifteen, forgetful, worshiped comic books and had changed his name last year. He was a Spiderman freak and he pitched a fit if you called him anything else. Sara didn't mind, but she knew it drove his parents nuts.

"You're back early. Dad said we wouldn't see you for another week." Beth and Bob Horner lived with their children, Spider and Sophie, down the block from her.

"I crapped the car out halfway through." She dumped the film out of her purse. "Can I pick these up in a couple of hours?"

"All of it?" He counted the rolls. "Twenty. Not for anyone else, but for you, sure. Just don't tell my boss I put you to the head of the line."

"Our secret," she said. "Thanks, Spider. I was gonna go to Lucky's, then come back, but I think I'll wander around the mall for awhile. What time is your lunch break? I'll treat at Taco Juan's."

"One o'clock. Is Lisa back, too?" He had a crush on her sister, but Lisa was eight years older than he was and thought it was cute.

"No, she's going with the car to Papua New Guinea. She won't be back till February.

"I'll be over her by then." He smiled. "Seriously, I've got a girlfriend now."

"She won't be jealous of us?" Sara laughed.

"See you at one." He laughed back.

"It's a date," she said. Out in the mall, she wandered about the stores. Window shopping. There was nothing she wanted. Nothing she needed. She picked a bench across from the food court and watched people come and go. She pushed herself up at 1:00 and went back to the photo store.

"Only got a little over half of them done," Spider whispered. "Boss came in with a lot of stuff he wanted real quick. I'm gonna have to cancel our date." He passed over the photos. "Pay when you pick up the rest."

"Won't you get in trouble?" She saw his boss, a gangly kid of about nineteen behind the large developing machine.

"Naw, just don't skip out on me." He smiled.

"Right, that's me, Sara Hackett, public enemy number one." They both laughed.

Back in her car, she took a pack of the photos out of the bag. It was the shots Lisa had taken as they blasted through the camels. She was using the telephoto and she'd got some great shots of their terrified expressions as they fled from the car in a hail of red dust. She put the pack back in the bag, started the Healey and headed down Westminster toward Beach.

Ten minutes later she pulled into the Lucky's Supermarket parking lot. She parked between two vans and pulled up the convertible top. It was Friday and the lot was almost full. She was lucky she didn't have to park on the street.

She started to get out, but she saw a ragged homeless man by the entrance. He wore a sign around his neck. 'Work for Food.' She watched him for a minute. Maybe he'd go away.

She fished another pack of pictures from the bag. They were of the first day. She was flipping through them, looking at pictures of eager racers standing next to their gleaming cars. They were taken on a bright sunny day. The cars looked new and fast, the racers proud. The last photo on the roll was one of her and Lisa standing in front of their Montero.

She took a careful look at the image of herself.

That shiner stuck out like a dent in a new car. She'd tried makeup, but that only seemed to make it worse, so in the end she'd decided to leave it alone.

She shifted her attention to Lisa. She was smiling. Her long blonde hair glistened in the sun as it flowed over her shoulders. Lisa's hair was so fair and hers so dark. The sisters were separated by four years and different mothers. Sara's mother had died when she was only two. Sara had inherited her dark hair and green eyes, as Lisa had received the blonde hair and blue eyes from her own mother. But it was everything else that was so amazing. In almost every other feature they were identical. It was uncanny.

She put the photos back in the packet and glanced over at the entrance. The vagrant was blocking it with his hand out as a woman fumbled in her purse for some change. Sara took out another pack of pictures and frowned. They weren't hers. Spider had given her someone else's photos by mistake.

Sara looked at the top photo. It was a picture of a teenaged girl, fourteen or fifteen. She was wearing a sun dress as she walked along the beach. The breeze whipped her long auburn hair behind her as she faced into the wind. She looked happy. She also looked like she didn't know she was having her picture taken.

Sara felt like a voyeur as she looked at someone else's picture. She should put them back in the pack and mind her own business, but something about the way the photo was taken intrigued her. Because of the way the background was blurred, Sara could tell it was taken with a high powered telephoto lens. Probably a five hundred millimeter. Expensive stuff to go shooting unsuspecting teenagers at the beach.

She flipped to the second photo. The same girl.

And she was in the third, the fourth, the fifth and the sixth. Different locations, but the same girl. Quickly Sara shuffled through the pack. The girl starred in every picture except the last one.

Like the others, the thirty-sixth photo was taken with a long telephoto, but its subject was different. It was a head shot, and she could tell by his bull neck that he was a weightlifter. He was a hard looking man. Close cropped black hair that matched his black eyes. He was staring at the camera, but it looked like he was staring out of the photo and into her soul. She didn't think she ever wanted to meet him. Unlike the girl, this man knew his picture was being taken and he didn't like it.

"Brrr," Sara put the pictures back in the bag. She'd take them back to the photo store as soon as she finished shopping. The homeless man was still there, accosting another woman. One of those, the kind that preyed only on women. She pulled a dollar out of her purse. It was easier.

She handed the dollar to the man without a word. He didn't even say thanks. She was his favorite kind of customer. In the store she grabbed a shopping cart and strolled the aisles in search of the ingredients for her Marengo chicken, but she couldn't get the images of the girl and that hard looking man out of her mind. She wished she'd never opened that pack of pictures.

She paid for her groceries , started for the parking lot with the bag wrapped in her arms. She saw the two vans, but the space between them was empty.

"Shit!" Her car was gone and for a reason she couldn't define, she imagined that dark man with the bull neck and the black eyes, grinning while he drove it, top down, speeding on the freeway.

CHAPTER FOUR

PAIGE RADOSLAW SAW THE MAN with the big neck and the beady eyes right after their mother dropped them off at the beach. She'd seen him the other day, too. At South Coast Plaza Mall. He must be one of those guys that thought girls went for that icky bodybuilder look. She wondered why he wore his hair like that. Maybe he was in the Marines or something.

"See that guy over there," she said. They were standing by the bike trail in front of the Huntington Beach Pier. She stepped back as a kid maneuvered his ten speed off the concrete path and onto the grass to go around a pair of girls leisurely skating along on their Rollerblades.

"Where?" Peter was twelve, three years younger than her. He was handsome, hyper and skinny, with blond hair that touched his shoulders, and he had the bronze skin of one who spent his time in the sun.

"The guy that looks like a bulldog over by the hot dog cart." There was a group of people surrounding the vendor. The man she was talking about was standing among them, waiting his turn to order.

"The creepy guy in the black sweat shirt? The body builder?"

"Yeah."

"What about him?"

"I saw him at the mall yesterday."

"So?"

"So, Dad said we should be on the lookout for people like that. You know, men we see too much."

"Jeez, Paige, are you paranoid or what? He's not a kidnapper. No way could he know we were gonna be coming here. Besides, there's no one after us. Never has been, so chill out."

"Those cops dad hired said we should stay on our toes all the time."

" 'Cuz they're like dad, super paranoid, like you're getting. Lots of people in California have money. It's not like up in Montana. No one cares about us here and you know what? No one cared about us up there, either."

"Okay, gimme a break. I only brought it up 'cuz I saw him two days in a row."

"You probably see lotsa people two days in a row. He just stood out 'cuz he's so big and ugly."

"More than that. There's something about him."

"He kind of looks like one of those cops," Peter

said. "But that guy has a normal haircut and a normal neck. It's just a coincidence, that's all."

She turned and snuck another look at him. He did kind of look like one of her father's security people, just a little. Maybe that's why she'd noticed him in the first place. Peter was probably right. She was just being paranoid.

"Hey, there's Sueno. I'm gonna see if I can borrow his board."

"You know what Dad said about surfing," Paige said, being a nag and hating it.

"You're just jealous 'cuz I can surf and you can't take flying lessons."

"It's too hard learning with Dad. I need a real teacher." She clenched her fists. She didn't think it was fair, but she didn't want to get angry about it.

"Act like you're interested in the company. It always works for me. Spend a couple of days following him around and he'll be eating out of your hand."

"Not if he finds out I let you surf."

"But he's not gonna."

"You brat." She laughed.

"Hey, I gotta go." He took off, chugging through the sand toward his friend.

"I'll watch from the pier," she called.

He turned and gave her a quick wave and shouted back, "Today's the day." She wondered what he was talking about as she wandered toward the pier, weaving her way through surfers and sunbathers on this warm December day.

She found a good spot on the rail. A slight tingle ran up her spine and she turned around. Bulldog Neck was on the other side of the pier munching his hot dog. Still coincidence? Must be. But she'd feel better if Peter were out of the water and they were someplace else.

She pushed him out of her thoughts and looked out over the ocean. Surfers were shooting the curl. The sun was floating halfway between noon and sunset, reflecting off the water, forcing her to squint as she tried to make out Peter among the dozens of youths waiting to catch a wave. It was Christmas vacation, but it almost seemed like summer. A skinny man next to her was eating a taco. He was leaning over the rail, looking out to sea. There were three Japanese tourists on her other side.

She looked out toward the surfers and saw him. Brazen and lanky as he stood up on a huge wave. He had more daring than brains, but she loved him anyway, despite the fact that he was her younger brother.

"Hey, Peter!" she yelled out. There was no way he could hear and she knew it, but she couldn't help herself. "Hey, Peter!" She waved her arms over her head.

"Which one's Peter?" the man with the taco asked.

"That one." She pointed.

"He's good. How old?"

"Twelve. He's my brother."

"He'll be back for the surfing championships."

"You think?" Paige said. Peter was standing straight up, no bend in his waist at all. His arms were out to his sides, balancing like a man on a high wire. He looked like he was born to surf.

"Sure. He's good. What's his name?"

"Peter, Peter Radoslaw." Peter's ride was almost

finished, but he was still standing as the wave carried him to the beach.

"Then you're Paige, Cyril Radoslaw's daughter."

"How do you know that?" She looked around, wary. Peter was paddling back to catch another wave.

"Radoslaw's not a very common name. I work for your father. Computer research."

"Really." She looked away from the ocean to the man next to her. He had puppy dog brown eyes, big and round, but his teeth were yellow, like he smoked too many cigarettes. His baby fine hair was brown going to gray, blowing around the sides of a huge bald head and he looked kind of funny, the way the wind was whipping his hair like that. He was wearing faded jeans, not Levi's, and a tattered, but clean blue and green Hawaiian shirt with an ancient backpack hanging over his right shoulder. He looked harmless.

"I've been working for him for three years now, ever since he moved his company to California. My name's Rice Sibley." He smiled and showed more of those yellow teeth. His breath smelled like peppermint, despite the taco in his hand.

"Paige Radoslaw, pleased to meet you, Mr. Sibley." She held out her hand.

"Call me Rice. Nobody at Radoslaw Systems uses a last name." He shifted the half eaten taco to his left hand and took her right in a firm, but gentle grip. It wasn't one of those macho, high school grips, but it wasn't a weak girl grip either.

"That's right." Paige sighed. Her father always said you could tell a lot about a man by the way he shook hands. She felt a slight tremor from Mr. Sibley before he relaxed the grip.

"You look relieved." He was still smiling. He

seemed okay. He was probably just a little nervous, meeting the boss's daughter and all. Her dad could be pretty intimidating.

"Yeah," Paige said. "My Dad's kind of a paranoid person. He's always after us to be on our guard."

"Cyril Radoslaw paranoid?" He laughed. "We have the tightest security on the planet. Plus he makes us change our passwords every Thursday before we go home for the weekend." Radoslaw Systems was on a four day work week. "And we have to have our badges checked every time we come to work, no matter how well those guards know us. Sometimes I feel like I'm working in a fishbowl."

"That's my dad." Now she laughed. "It's 'cuz when he lived in Poland everybody ratted to the Communists. Sometimes kids even told on their parents. And if you had any money at all, everybody was after it. He's been in America since before I was born, but he still hasn't got Poland out of his head."

"Maybe that's not so bad," Rice said. "If it keeps his children safe and his software secret till he's ready to release it, then maybe paranoid's not a bad thing to be."

"I guess," she said. "But when we were little, in Montana, he had to know where we were all the time. I mean every licking sticking second. It's not quite so bad here. Oh, we still get lectures from him and his security people, and we still have to be home on time, but we have a lot more freedom. He doesn't expect us to call him every hour and report in."

"You had to do that, call in?"

"Oh, yeah. It took Dad a long time to get used to America. Maybe if we had moved to Southern California when we were little it would have been different."

"How so?" He tossed the rest of his taco over the side and they both watched it as it fell toward the sea.

"Here we have tons of friends. They're in the house all the time. There's always something to do. And now that he's so successful, he's got other stuff on his mind besides us."

"And you didn't have friends in Montana?"

"Not so many. And it was real cold during the winter. I think that reminded him of Poland, and anything that reminds him of Poland makes him paranoid."

"Isn't that why he moved up there to begin with, because the weather was similar to what he was used to? At least that's what they say."

"Yeah, I guess. Thank God he met my mom. She was a California girl up there on a skiing vacation. It took her thirteen years to get him to move down here." He smiled, showing those yellow teeth again. He was kind of old, but he was nice. "Do you come here a lot?" she asked.

"All the time. I love the beach and the kids. It makes me feel young again. I used to surf here every weekend."

"Why'd you stop?"

"I don't know. I guess I grew out of it." He sighed. "Look at that! He's straight out of 1962." Rice pointed to an ageing surfer who was paddling his board alongside the pier, out toward where the kids were waiting to catch their waves. He was wearing a loud yellow Hawaiian shirt with faded yellow shorts that went down to his knees. She saw the traditional ring of hibiscus flowers around each leg. The flower rings were bright pink.

"He's big and fat, but he sure looks graceful." Paige wondered how that could be so. The surfer was lying on his stomach as he paddled his long board. She bet it was heavy. The man was ancient. Thick gray hair flowed over his back. He looked like a white whale as he lay on the board, but his arms moved through the water like a seal's flippers.

"He's a surfer from the old school, that's for sure," Rice said. "It brings back memories. I used to wear baggy pants just like that."

Paige looked at the surfer's pants. "I think they're cute."

The Japanese tourists next to her were watching the old surfer, too. She looked around. A lot of people were watching him. The usual noisy buzz that drifted along the pier had quieted. People were tapping others on the shoulder and pointing. Did people know him? Was he famous?

She turned back to the surfer. He was shrinking in the distance, but she'd noticed something else strange. The kids out beyond the pier were sitting on their boards. None of them were trying for waves. They looked like they were waiting. Passersby stopped to see what everybody was staring at. Some of them didn't get it, because he was too far out now.

The surfer paddled among all the kids on their tiny high tech boards. A couple paddled aside to make way for him as he maneuvered his big board around. He was little more than a speck out there now, but there was no hiding the drama that was unfolding.

A wave was building behind the group of surfers. Apprehension filled the crowd. Did these people all know him? Was it possible? The surfer let the wave roll under him and more surfers, the ones farther away, sat on their boards. It was as if they were communicating via mental telepathy. Like dolphins.

The surfers on the beach were standing now. The ones without hats had their hands up to their foreheads to shield their eyes. The winds aloft were scooting wispy cirrus clouds across the sky, but none dared cover the sun. It was as if they too, knew something special was about to happen.

Another wave formed behind the surfers. This one bigger than the last. It was the kind of wave all these kids loved to ride, but none tried to catch it and the old surfer ignored it. Paige found herself holding her breath. Goosebumps peppered her arms as if she'd been too long in a cold bath. More people were watching now. It was almost like something holy was about to take place.

Paige ran her eyes along the beach. Mothers and children were watching the surfers standing next to their boards. They must be wondering what they were staring at. Two policemen walked among the crowd. They were looking out at the surfers on their boards, too.

"Look at that!" Rice said.

Paige turned. "Holy cow!" It was the mother of waves. Any other day all those kids would be paddling to beat the band, struggling and straining to catch that wave. But today only one man moved his board into position. He was standing even before the wave was under him. Too early. Surely the wave would trash him. But it didn't. He rode up and over it as graceful as a swan in flight.

And then he was in it, shooting the curl as the great wave wrapped around him. And as if a spell had been broken, people started to cheer. Some were waving. Some stamping their feet. People were going nuts.

"Holy Moses!" Rice yelled.

The Japanese were shouting a slew of short syllables. They were as enthusiastically caught up as everyone else.

The surfer was lost in the tunnel of water swirling around him, then he shot out of it and was riding the crest, hair streaking behind him. The bright Hawaiian shirt, unbuttoned, flapping like a flag. He was too far for her to make out his expression, but he was standing back like a man that would be grinning. He was going to ride that wave all the way to the sand.

Then he turned and was shooting toward her.

"He's going to shoot the pier!" Rice said.

It was happening so fast. She gasped. It felt like her heart stopped. He was coming straight for her. She didn't know how fast, but it seemed fast. Real fast. Fast fast. Nobody shot the pier. It was too dangerous. Besides, it was against the law. You could get killed.

The roar was deafening. People were screaming like they were at a rock concert. He was close now. She saw his face clear as her own in a mirror. He was grinning. His white beer belly stuck out from his body. It almost looked like he was pregnant. She wondered if he could button that flapping shirt. He held a hand up, waving as he shot under the pier.

She dashed to the other side, afraid that he'd smashed up on the pylons below. She sighed when the crowd cheered even louder as he shot out from underneath, heading toward the beach and the waiting police officers.

He was going to jail now. But so what? A man like

that wouldn't care. It would just be another adventure.

"Who was that?" Paige asked as she watched the cops lead the man away.

"Johnny Tanner," a young man with hair longer than Peter's said. "He used to be the best surfer in the state, but he got a job, got married and quit coming to the beach about thirty years ago."

"It looks like he just made a comeback," Rice said.

"Yeah," the man said, "those kids out there must have been expecting him."

"It was spooky," Paige said.

"Look," someone said.

Paige looked out to where the surfers had been waiting. Several of them were up on a wave, but one of them was in the lead and he was following the same course as the old surfer had only moments before. Paige felt her heart leap. It was Peter. And she knew what he was going to do.

"No, Peter. Please no," she murmured.

He was going to shoot the pier. It was just the kind of stunt he'd pull. If he got hurt she'd never forgive herself. She should have put her foot down that first time he'd borrowed a board last summer. Instead she'd been his silent partner. For over a year they'd kept it from their parents. Peter's surfing. Dad would have a cow. Mom would scream the roof off.

"He's going for it," someone yelled. Johnny Tanner and his stunt were forgotten as all eyes were on the skinny kid who seemed to be hanging over the front of his tiny board.

The wave wasn't as big as the one Tanner had ridden, but it looked plenty big to Paige, and Peter seemed to be going faster.

"Hail Mary!" Rice said.

"He's just a kid," someone else said.

He was so close now. He looked up. Their eyes locked. Then he was under the pier and Paige shivered. She was sure he was going to be killed. But then a quiet roar welled up from the crowd. Quiet, because many of the watchers were sighing rather than cheering. Paige was one of the sighers.

She looked toward the beach. The cops were halfway to the street. Johnny Tanner was with them. They'd been watching Peter's performance. One of the police officers started back toward the water as Peter rode the board right up onto the beach. Then he was off it and running toward the pier. The cop started after him, but gave up when he realized it would be no contest. Once the kid was among the crowd, he'd be safe. No one would give him up for shooting the pier and the cop knew it.

She lay back against the rail and heaved a second sigh. He'd made it. Now he'd brag till Mom picked them up. But she'd rather hear him boast about his feat than watch as the paramedics scraped him off those pylons. Still he was going to be awful hard to take for the next two hours.

"If your father saw that, he'd throw a fit. You should hear him talk at work. He acts like you two are made of glass."

"You're not going to tell him?" she pleaded.

"Hey, not me. I'm no snitch." He smiled.

She returned it. "My folks are really weird. Peter was kind of a sick child. Actually right up till we moved away from Montana. So they don't want him doing anything dangerous, like surfing. But Mom drops us off at the beach all the time. What does she think he does here? He's only twelve. If he wants to surf, he's gonna surf, especially if there isn't anyone to tell him no."

"You could," Rice said.

"I'm his sister, not his mother."

"You could tell your folks."

"No way. I'm no snitch, either."

"Good show, kid," someone yelled out.

Paige looked toward the end of the pier. Peter was coming toward her wearing a grin a block wide. He was dripping wet in only his bathing suit. He looked like the picture of young health. She thought about how he used to look, like a starved and skinny dog too sick to come in out of the rain. California had been good for him.

"Hey, big sister. Did you see that?" he called out.

"You stupid. I should ring your neck." She ran to him and gave him a hug, not caring that he was getting her tee shirt and shorts all wet. "Don't you ever do something that stupid again."

"No way," he said. "Once was enough."

"Were you scared?" she said, breaking the hug.

"No, I wasn't scared."

"I woulda been," Rice said from behind Paige.

"Oh, Peter, this is Rice. He works for Dad."

"Glad to meet you Mr. Rice." Peter held out his hand like a man.

"Just Rice." He shook it. "I caught your ride. Pretty impressive."

"I won't be doing that again anytime soon. Pretty hairy."

"I thought you said you weren't scared," Paige said.

"It was hairy, but I wasn't scared. Not too much

anyway." He laughed and Rice and Paige laughed along with him. Then he said. "Hey, Sueno and some of the guys have done some of that wall art on the seawall. Ya wanna go look at it?"

"Sure," Paige said. It was something to do.

"What wall art?" Rice asked.

"The bike trail goes along the bottom of the cliff all the way to Bolsa Chica Beach," Paige said. "The cliff has been held back with a brick wall and lotsa artists have painted murals on it."

"Like graffiti?" Rice said.

"No. It's all approved by the city or something. It's gotta be art," Paige said. She looked up. Some dark clouds were moving in from the west. It looked like they might get a little rain.

"So it's not really a seawall," Rice said.

"Sure it is," Peter said.

"No, a seawall holds back the ocean. This wall you're talking about is holding back the land."

"So what would you call it?" Peter said. "A cliff wall?"

"I don't know, but I'd like to see it. Do you mind if I tag along?"

"If it's okay with Paige, it's okay with me."

"Sure," Paige said.

"Great," Rice said. He reached into his pack and pulled out a cellphone. "Gotta call my wife and tell her I might be a few minutes late. Go on. I'll catch up."

Rice caught up with them before they reached the end of the pier, where they turned left and started toward the bike trail. Peter stopped along the way and picked up his sandals and shirt. Five minutes later they were at the fork in the bike trail. The right fork went up and along Pacific Coast Highway, the left stayed on the sand and went straight below the cliffs all the way to Bolsa Chica. The bottom path was hard dirt, so not many bikers took it. Sometimes the life guards used it and other times an oil truck might be seen on it. This part of the beach was generally deserted because there was no access from the highway and it was a long walk along the trail.

"Look, I know that man," Paige said. It was Nick Nesbitt from KYTV news. Paige had met him only last week when he'd done a story on her father. He was with a cameraman. "Hey, Mr. Nesbitt. Remember me?"

"Paige Radoslaw, the most beautiful girl on the coast," Nesbitt said.

"What'cha doing?" Paige asked.

"A story on the wall art. Kind of a puff piece for a slow news day."

Nick Nesbitt looked weird to Paige, sweating under his makeup. They talked for a minute or two, then said goodbye. Paige looked around for Rice. He'd sort of stepped back when they started talking to the newsman and she thought that was kind of strange, because usually everybody wanted to meet TV people.

"How far down is this masterpiece?" Rice asked after about twenty minutes.

"My friend said it was about halfway," Peter said.

They took a long time looking at all the murals along the way, because Paige loved the art on the seawall. She always had.

"Someone's coming," Rice said. Paige looked at the cloud of dust swirling behind the black van as it sped along the dirt track coming from Bolsa Chica.

"It's that man," Peter said as the van slowed. "The one with the bulldog neck."

Paige looked up.

Rice grabbed Peter from behind.

"Run, Paige!" he screamed.

CHAPTER FIVE

SARA WAS HALFWAY ACROSS the parking lot when the heavens opened. She picked up her pace, stopped and stood in the rain, staring at the empty space. No, she silently moaned. Not the car. Not that. She'd been so careful with it. Not parking it on the street. Keeping it in the garage at night. Using the Club. Clay was gonna be furious. She stomped her foot. She'd forgotten to put the Club on the steering wheel. How stupid. Her poor car.

She was getting soaked. It was probably kids, she hoped. If so, that was a two-edged sword. She'd get the car back, but they'd drive the hell out of it with the top down, so it'd be good and soaked.

She trudged back to the store. She was going to have to call Clay at work. He hated that, but this was business. Police business, and Clay was a policeman. So much for the surprise Marengo chicken.

The homeless man was still waiting at the door. He saw her approaching and pushed himself off of the wall. "Can you spare a little to help a poor man out?"

"Here." She thrust the bag of groceries at the startled man. She was through the entrance and inside the safety of the dry store before he could respond.

"Hey," she said to a box boy, "can you get me Greg?"

"You want the manager?"

"I thought that's what I just said."

In a few seconds she was facing a balding man in his middle forties. Greg looked tired, as if the burden of life weighed on him. He must be putting in long hours, she thought. He was wearing a gray business suit with a tie that stood out from across the room. It was blue and gold and wide. A big cartoon sun with a bright happy face smiled out from the center of it and under it were the words, 'Good Day Sunshine.' A Beatles tie. He smiled. "Hey, Sara, what's up?"

"Your tie." She smiled back. "It's nice. I was pretty angry, but I like the Beatles. It kind of helped."

"I'm glad. What's wrong?" Greg had been flirting with her for over three years. She appreciated the attention, but all he ever got for his efforts was a smile.

"Can I use your phone? Someone stole my car out of your parking lot." She glanced at a giant wall clock behind him, the kind that used to be hanging behind every teacher she ever had from grade school to high school. It was 2:15. There was a good chance Clay would be at the station.

"Sure, follow me." He led her through the store and into a small office. "Just dial 911." He pointed to a phone on a small desk.

"I know the drill." She picked it up and punched the buttons. More than three. She saw the curious expression in his eyes, but he didn't say anything.

"Robbery-Homicide." A young woman answered on the first ring.

"Is Detective Clay Tredway there?"

"No, ma'am. He's out at the moment."

"Can you tell me when he'll be in?"

"No, sorry. We generally don't give out that kind of information."

"My car's been stolen."

"Oh well, then you called the wrong number, this is Robbery-Homicide." The woman had a cheery Southern accent and for some reason it grated on Sara.

"Well, normally I would do that, ma'am," Sara said, imitating her. "But my husband is a police officer. And he loved that little ol' car more than anything in the whole wide world and I thought that he'd like to be the first to know."

"Sorry about putting you off," the woman said. "You did ask for a particular officer. I just figured it was someone you might have met on the job. I didn't know it was your husband. Sorry."

"That's alright," Sara said. "Now can you tell me where he is?"

"You don't know?"

"I just got back in the country. I went straight to the Lucky's to get something for dinner and when I came out the car was gone."

"Darn."

"What?" Sara said.

"He won't be back till next week. He's taken some vacation time. Can I help?"

"What vacation time? Clay didn't say anything about taking any time off."

"I don't know anything about his personal life, ma'am. I'm new. Why don't you give me your name and I'll send someone right over."

"Sara Hackett," she said.

"I thought you said you were married?"

"I don't use his name. People do that now. It's allowed."

"Sorry, I was out of line again."

"I'm in the manager's office of the Lucky's Supermarket on Beach. Can you have them send someone over or should I call 911?"

"I'll take care of it, seeing as you're a member of the family. Oh, and I'm awful sorry about your car."

"Thanks." Sara hung up.

"I didn't know your husband was a cop," Greg said. "I bet they work overtime getting that car back."

"Oh, they will," Sara said. "That car was our pride and joy. We've got a lot of hours into restoring it."

"One of those," he said and Sara nodded. It had never occurred to her before, that although she was on a first name basis with him, all they really knew about each other was what took place in the store. He flirted, she smiled, that was it.

"Yeah, one of those. She's a fully restored Austin Healey MK 3000. The last year they made 'em. She's original to the core, right down to the electronic overdrive. It's a heartbreaker. I feel like crying." She was talking, but she was thinking about that vacation. Why in the devil would he take time off? Was he sick? Was it something serious? Something he was trying to hide from her?

"I hope you get it back." Greg seemed genuinely concerned.

"So do I."

"Look, if you need anything, if there's any way I can help, let me know."

"Thanks, Greg."

"I mean it, call me. There's nothing I wouldn't do for you." He smiled.

"Can we wait out front?" she said. "It's kind of stuffy in here." She wasn't sure, but it seemed like he was going beyond flirting. It seemed like he was out and out coming on to her. She shook the feeling aside. After all, he'd just learned her husband was a cop. It had to be her imagination.

"Sure." He led her back to the front of the store.

She looked out into the rain as a black-and-white pulled up. She stepped out and stood in front of the covered entrance. The homeless man was hurrying across the parking lot with his arms around that grocery bag, running from the law. She waited till the car pulled up to the front of the store. Two uniformed officers got out.

"Are you Sara Hackett?" the one riding shotgun asked. They both looked so young.

"Yeah," she said.

"Can you tell us about the car?" Sara did. A detective car pulled up as he was finishing his report. "We'll get right on this," he said as Jerry Dunn and Dick Spencer got out of the white unmarked.

Jerry was tall, just over six feet, with broad

shoulders, a square jaw, and an athlete's build. He had dark hair and dark eyes. He looked like a soap opera stud. Dick on the other hand was fair-haired, blue-eyed and thin. He almost looked underweight.

Sara started to wave, but checked herself as Jerry's dark eyes met hers. She shivered under his gaze and didn't understand why. They were friends, good friends.

He broke eye contact and turned back to the uniformed officer. "You got all the details?"

"Yes, sir."

"Then handle it."

"We're gone." The uniform climbed into the passenger seat as his partner was starting the car. The black-and-white peeled out of the parking lot, leaving Sara alone with two of Clay's best friends.

"So, Jerry," she said, "some new girl you have working over to the cop shop tells me that Clay took some time. Mind telling me what it's all about?" She was more concerned about Clay now than the car.

"He said he needed some time to get his head together. He's probably at home right now."

"He wasn't there when I came home. The fridge was full too. What's that all about?"

"I wouldn't know. Maybe he's eating out more." He smiled, but it was a weak one. He was keeping something from her.

"It was different food, Jerry."

"Come again."

"Not the same stuff that was in the fridge when I left. That means Clay went shopping. He never does that."

"What are you getting at?"

"I don't know, Jerry. You've been his partner

longer than we've been married. If there's something up with him, you know what it is. So what gives? And why didn't you just let the black-and-white finish up with me like they would've for anybody else? I'm a cop's wife, not a VIP."

"We look after our own. You know that. Besides, it's the Austin Healey. Clay loves that car. We gotta do everything we can to get it back."

"You're changing the subject, Jerry. I'm getting worried now. Is he sick or something?" she said. Dick Spencer took a step back, as if he didn't want anything to do with the conversation and that worried her even more.

"No, look it's nothing like that," Jerry said. He took her by the arm and led her out of earshot of the others. "Look, we can't talk too much about it here, but we finally made it."

"What are you talking about?" Sara whispered.

"Well, let's just say that Clay bumping into Cyril Radoslaw at Macworld last year was the best thing that ever happened to us." Clay was a Mac nut. A year ago last January he went up to San Francisco to the Macintosh convention, where he met the software giant. Against all odds they became fast friends.

"I don't understand."

"We're going to work for Cyril, me and Clay, at over three times what we're making now."

"You're quitting?"

"Turned in our thirty day notice last week. Clay had two weeks vacation time coming so he took it. He figured he might as well get the paid time off since he earned it."

"So how come he didn't tell me? Why all the secrecy?"

"He wanted to surprise you."

"Really?" She gazed into his deep brown eyes. But she couldn't tell whether he was telling the truth or not. Cops had a way of hiding their feelings. Even from wives and friends.

"Look, we can't stand around here all day. You wanna come over to my place? Janet would love to see you. Besides, I wouldn't feel right leaving you alone here."

"No, I wanna go home and digest all this. Can you drop me?"

"I don't think that's a very good idea."

"Why not?"

"You've just had a traumatic experience. You should be with someone until you get over it," Jerry said. Dick got into the passenger seat of the unmarked. He picked up the mike.

"Jerry, I had my car stolen. It happens to lots of people every day and they all deal with it. I'll survive. I just want to go home." She wasn't whispering anymore.

"Gotta go," Dick yelled. "Couple of mutts with a sawed off in a stop-and-rob down the road. We're the closest."

"Damn." He dashed to the driver's side. "Call Janet. Please. Have her come and pick you up."

"Alright. I'll call her," Sara said.

"Atta girl." Then he closed the door and in an instant the unmarked was speeding down Beach, water flying from around its tires.

Sara watched till it was out of sight, then she looked up at the sky. She shivered again, but not from the cold. She'd just figured out what made her so uncomfortable when she'd locked eyes with Jerry. He looked kind of like the guy in that photo, the man with the beady eyes.

She forced the thought from her mind and inhaled the fresh air. The squall had moved on, but it was still overcast and gray and it looked like it might still be raining down at the beach.

"Funny how it can quit as quickly as it starts." Greg had come up behind her. She turned and smiled. That Beatles tie was so stupid looking. "You need a ride someplace?"

"No, I can call someone."

"It's no trouble, really."

"Okay then," she said. How dangerous could a guy with a Beatles tie be?

"I'll go tell my assistant." He turned and pushed the door open. He had a stiff-backed walk, as if he'd been in the military.

She followed him back into the store and waited while he talked to an older woman who was working the express lane. She looked like she'd spent the better part of her sixty-odd years behind a cash register. Sara met her eyes. She wasn't smiling. Did it bother her that she was only the assistant manager? Women still had such a long way to go.

"Okay," he said. "It's set." And again she was following him. This time to the parking lot. He'd parked in back so the customers could have the close-up spots, she supposed. He reached into the front pocket of his slacks and came out with a set of keys as he approached a Mazda Miata with a soft top. "Not a real British sports car, but a pretty good imitation." He opened the passenger door for her. A gentleman.

"Nice." She got in the car.

"Was it insured?" he asked as he was turning the

key.

"Yeah, but we'd never get a fraction of what we've put into it."

"You never do." He backed out of the space. "Which way?"

"Left toward the beach."

He put the car in gear and started toward the driveway. "Uh oh, problem." An older woman was standing next to a vintage Ford, staring in the window. A shopping cart full of groceries was next to her. He pulled the Miata up alongside her. "Can I help?"

Sara sighed. He hadn't been coming on to her at all. He was just a good Samaritan.

"I locked my keys in the car." The old woman stomped her foot. "I'm getting to be so forgetful." She was thin and wiry with gray hair. She didn't look like the kind of woman that would ever use one of those blue rinses.

"I know you." Sara got out of the Miata. "I never forget a car. Nineteen fifty-six Ford." It was almost the same color as her Healey.

"Yes, you stopped and gave me a lift when I ran out of gas on the 405. You took me to that Texaco. Then you gave me a ride back to the car."

"Yeah," Sara said. "That was a couple of years ago, you had this big dog with a slurpy tongue. Dottie, you're Dottie, I don't remember your last name."

"I remember yours. You're Sara Hackett. The race car driver."

"Not many people know that."

"Not many people stop to help an old lady on the freeway either. Two cops passed me by before you came along."

"You told me. You were pretty mad." Sara ran her hand along the Ford's roof. "She still run as good now as you told me then?"

"Like she just came off the showroom floor." The way she said it, Sara could tell Dottie was proud of the car.

"Do you have a spare key at home?" Greg asked.

"Yes. My husband's set." She turned to face them as lightning lit up the dark sky in the background. Dottie's eyes were the same color as the gray sky and they seemed to sparkle like that lightning flash. She had a quick smile and Sara thought she'd be a woman easy to like.

"We'll give you a lift and bring you back," Greg said.

"I feel stupid," Dottie said. "I should pay more attention to what I'm doing."

"I'll put your bags in the trunk." Greg opened it and Sara helped him load the groceries. Then he pushed the cart back to the front of the store.

"He can't help it," Sara said. "He's the store manager."

"It's awfully nice of you to help me out again," Dottie said.

"The thanks all go to him this time. He's giving me a lift too. My car was stolen."

"Not that Austin Healy?"

"That's the one."

"Oh, you poor thing," Dottie said.

"So how come you drive such an old car?" Sara said. She didn't want to think about the Healy anymore.

"We bought her new, Willie and me. Right after

we got married. It's the only car we ever owned. Then about twenty-five years ago she turned from being just a car into a hobby. Finding parts hasn't always been easy. More than once I think she's saved our marriage."

"How so?" Sara was intrigued.

"Part hunting turned into kind of a sport. We loved it. Nobody else would understand. We needed each other to do it right, to enjoy it."

"I understand," Sara said. It used to be like that for her and Clay, back when being married was more fun than it was now.

"Okay, we're ready." Greg was back. "You'll have to scrunch together in that seat. Sorry."

"I'll sit in the middle," Sara said. She got in and Dottie climbed in after her. It was a tight fit. Her leg was up against the stick and she felt his hand brush against it when he put the small sports car in gear.

"Where to, Dottie?" he asked.

"Toward the beach."

"And the rain," Greg said. He made a left as Jerry's unmarked came tearing into the parking lot. Why? What would take them away from a robbery in progress? Maybe the black-and-whites got there first. Maybe they caught the guy. Maybe he got away. But whatever, why come back, unless they wanted to give her a lift home?

She almost told Greg to stop, but she caught herself. Something told her Jerry hadn't returned just to give her a lift and she didn't want to deal with it right now. She couldn't get that well stocked refrigerator out of her mind. Clay didn't shop. He didn't, and he wouldn't, no matter how much money he had. Somebody else had done that shopping for him.

A few minutes and a couple of miles closer to the beach and they were in the rain. "Turn right on Pacific Coast Highway and right again on Main Street. It's the quickest way," Dottie said.

Sara studied the upper middle class homes as Dottie directed them. They were well set back from the street with manicured lawns, kept perfect by an army of gardeners. Giant eucalyptus trees offered shade from the sun on those days when it was needed, but now, in this funereal light, they looked spooky.

Dottie steered them to a parking space in front of an older home about two blocks from the police station where Clay worked. The yard looked freshly mowed, but no professional gardeners touched this woman's lawn. Apparently Dottie took care of her house by herself, Sara thought. In most neighborhoods in Southern California her lawn would be considered neat and tidy, but here it looked kind of shabby.

"You can pull up in the driveway and park under the carport." Sara looked up and down the street. Sure enough, Dottie's was the only home with a carport. She wondered how well the old woman got along with her neighbors.

"Do you want us to bring in the groceries?" Greg asked.

"That would be so nice," Dottie said, and they each carried a couple of bags to the front porch. Dottie set hers down and reached under the doormat. She came up with a key and opened the door.

"Isn't your husband home?" Sara asked.

"No, I lost him ten years ago next week."

"But I thought you said he had an extra set of

keys."

"I said my husband's keys were at home. I didn't say he was alive."

Creepy, Sara thought as Dottie shoved the groceries inside the front door. Then Dottie went into the house and came back with a set of keys and an umbrella. She was a little ditsy.

"I don't live far from here. Can you drop me before you go back?" Sara said. "I'm in kind of a hurry." Try as she might, she couldn't get that refrigerator or that unmarked out of her mind. There was something weird about the way Jerry came back.

"Remember, you can call me if you need anything," Greg said as he pulled up in front of her house.

"Me too. You can call me, too," Dottie said. "I really owe you now."

"I'll remember that," Sara said. She got out of the car and dashed through the rain to the front porch. Under cover of the porch roof she turned and waved. Dottie waved back, then they drove off.

Music was coming from inside the house. John Lennon singing *Imagine*. Odd. It wasn't Bob Dylan and it wasn't loud enough to wake the dead. Clay usually listened to early Dylan when he was alone, loud.

She stood on the porch and watched the rain for a few seconds. She didn't see the Jeep. That meant it was in the garage. He would have seen the Healey gone. He knew she was home. Did he know it was stolen? Did Jerry call and tell him? He'd be upset about it. Who wouldn't be? She wasn't looking forward to facing him.

She fished in her purse for the key, then realized

she didn't need it. She checked the door. It wasn't locked. He never locked the door when he was home. He wasn't afraid of anything. She opened it and went in.

The music was louder now. John Lennon had been right. Life was better without boundaries. Without churches, schools or government. She let his music and his lyrics ripple through her.

She was a Beatles fan and she especially liked John Lennon, because when she heard his songs it was as if he was singing to her alone, as if he'd seen into her soul. He'd put into words what she could only feel.

She heard sound from in the kitchen, then the smell carried her away. He was cooking beef. The smell was heavenly. She was surprised that she hadn't noticed it earlier. Then she smelled the garlic. Whatever it was, it was going to be good. He could be a great cook when he wanted to be.

Jerry must have called him and told him she was back early. That's why he was playing John Lennon and not Dylan. It was for her. Clay was making dinner for her even though she'd been stupid enough to let the car get stolen. She'd been worried over nothing. Clay was so unpredictable.

A bell rang out from the kitchen. The oven timer. She barely heard it above the music. Was he baking? Or maybe he was broiling the beef. That must be it. Maybe sirloin steaks. But then what was the garlic smell?

The song stopped. He must have shut it off with the remote. She heard talking. Sara caught her breath, then realized it was the portable TV next to the microwave. Clay was a news junkie, it had been the only way to get him to eat breakfast with her.

She kicked her shoes off in the living room and padded on through the dining room and on into the kitchen. Then she saw her. She was blonde. Gobs of hair flowed over her shoulders. She was barefoot and she wore some kind of shift thing that barely covered her ass.

"What are you doing here?" Sara said.

The girl-woman spun around. She was pregnant.

CHAPTER SIX

"LET HIM GO!" Paige yelled. She felt her head go hot as quick anger flashed through her. He had Peter from behind, those skinny hands wrapped around his arms. Rice glared at her and that fat head made her madder. "I said, let him go." The sky had gone dark and Rice's pasty white face looked ghostly against the black cloud background. Evil.

The van was almost on them, slowing down. She saw the man through the front windows clear as if she was watching him on television. His head looked small sitting on that big neck. Tiny ears, like one of those dogs that had them clipped off. Big fat nose, squashed against his face. Those beady black eyes locked onto her and for a second she thought he was going to run her over.

Time was moving funny like when she was getting ready to take the plane off with her dad. Her mind was moving on fast forward while the rest of the world plodded along in slow motion. Instantly she realized what was happening. They were going to kidnap them. These were the guys her father had been warning them about ever since she could remember. It wasn't just a made up thing to scare them into being good. It was real.

"Run, Paige! Get the cops!" Peter jerked back and forth, trying to get away. It looked as if Rice was hurting him the way he was trying to hold him still. The man was crazy, Paige saw it in his eyes. One second he was as friendly as could be. Now he was snarling. He was holding on to Peter like a maniac, his fingers digging into Peter's arms. He was hurting him. Now Paige knew it for sure. "Go, Paige!" he yelled. "Get away!"

How could she leave him? He was her brother. She wanted to help. She wanted to run. She could do neither. She was stuck as if her feet were cemented in.

"Let me go!" Peter screamed. He kicked out at Rice, catching him in the shins with his heels. Rice let go with his left hand and slapped Peter in the head. "Paige!" He was still struggling. Rice hit him again, the sound of the slap stinging her as surely as if she'd been slapped herself.

Rice grabbed Peter's arm again and started dragging him backwards so he couldn't kick at him anymore. For an instant Paige thought he was beaten as Rice pulled him back, his feet leaving two trails in the dirt. Then he started kicking out again. He squirmed and Rice let go of one of his arms to hit him again.

"Paige, run!"

The guy in the van slammed on the brakes and the black truck skidded to a stop, sand and pebbles flying from its back tires. In less than seconds he'd be out of it. No time to think. Rice hit Peter. Paige saw and it shocked her into action.

"Run!" Peter screamed again.

Paige attacked. "Let him go!" she wailed.

"No, Paige!" Peter squirmed aside to avoid her charge. She brought her arm above her head, whipping it around like she was letting go of an underhanded softball pitch, but she kept her fist closed, connecting with Rice's crotch as she flew by.

"Fucking bitch." Rice doubled over, but he kept his one handed grip on Peter.

"Let him go." Paige jumped onto his back. The Bulldog Man was getting out of the van. Paige sunk her teeth into the back of Rice's neck.

"Motherfuck!" Rice cried, but he let go of Peter.

"Run!" Peter said as he jumped clear of Rice. Bulldog was out of the van now.

"Where?" Paige jumped off Rice's back. They were halfway between Huntington and Bolsa Chica. The cliff wall to the north, sand and the sea to the south. Nothing east or west but a mile of dirt road in either direction. Except for some surfers out trying to catch a wave the area was deserted.

"The sea!" Peter yelled.

"Don't run." Rice slapped her face with an open palm. She staggered back. He grabbed out for her, but she avoided his lunge and ran toward the sea.

Then the sky opened up.

Paige struggled for air as her sandals slapped the sand. She was running into the wind and it was stealing her breath away. Rain pelted her as she tore across the beach. All she could do was keep charging toward the water and hope she made it before they caught her.

She asked her body for a burst of speed, but her right foot slammed into a bottle or a rock and she went rolling onto her side. She struggled to her feet and came up running. The sea was visible, despite the rain, and she longed for it. She slipped again in the wet sand and flew forward, hands in front of herself. Again she pushed herself up and shot out for the sea.

Please, God, she prayed as she forced herself on. Her lungs were screaming for air and she had no more. Her heart was pumping, like a locomotive gone crazy, demanding oxygen. Her legs burned like they'd been stabbed with a branding iron. Every muscle in her body said, *slow down*, but the chill charging up her back said, *run faster*.

And she ran faster, because she heard it behind her, racing across the sand. They were chasing them with the van. She hoped Peter made it. She wanted to stop and check, but there was no stopping now. She kept running, grabbing air with lungs and loose fists as she pumped her arms. The dark rumbling sound of the van was getting louder as she ran toward the water. Her head hurt where Rice had slapped her. Her ears were ringing. The water was so far away. The sand seemed to be grabbing at her sandals, slowing her down. She stumbled, but didn't trip. Rain was pounding down, but it didn't cover the sound of the van as it roared over the sand. It was coming after her.

She risked a look over her shoulder. It was behind her, closing up the distance between them like she was standing still. Its lights came on, twin eyes cutting into her like swords. She tried to look away, but couldn't. She was trapped in the van's bright lights. She stumbled and went down. She looked away from the van as she pulled herself to her feet. Somehow Peter had gotten ahead of her. He fell, but was up and running in an instant. The fall hadn't slowed him down a bit. She looked back. The van was almost on her. She started after Peter, toward the water, but the van flew by, so close, throwing sand in her face. She turned away and started back toward the road. It was hopeless now and she knew it.

It was stupid to go back that way, but she wanted to lead them away from Peter. He was a great swimmer. If he made it to the water they'd never get him.

She heard the van chewing up the sand as it spun around. Then it stopped. Why? She stopped too. Peter was halfway to the water. He was so close, but had so far to go. She was thinking more clearly than she'd ever thought before. They couldn't decide who to go after, her or Peter. She had to help them make up their minds and fast. She started backing slowly away from the black monster, never taking her eyes off of it.

"Come after me. Please come after me," she whispered as she took another slow step. Water was drizzling down her face. Her hair was soaked and felt heavy. She was cold.

The van came to life charging toward her. They'd taken the bait. They must have figured that Peter would be easy. Pretty dumb. That Rice man had seen him surf. Did he think Peter was going to stand at the water's edge like some kind of idiot?

She whirled and ran toward that dirt road. This time the van slowed as it came alongside her and Rice jumped out. He tackled her like she was a football player running with the ball. She squirmed in the wet sand, but he was too powerful. She bit him on the neck and he screamed, but by now the Bulldog Man was out of the van. He pulled Rice off of her, then lifted her like she weighed no more than her feather pillows.

"Stop the fighting," he said. His voice was rock hard like his body and somehow she knew she shouldn't resist.

She turned her head, squinting through the rain. Peter was at the water now. She sighed and went limp. He was safe. There was nothing these men could do about it. The big man tossed her through the sliding door, then jumped in after her as Rice jumped behind the wheel. In no time the van was eating sand as they charged to the sea.

"You'll never get him," she said.

"She's right," Bulldog said. "Let's get out of here."

"No. We have to get them both."

"We blew it," Bulldog said. "We hang around and we're gonna get caught. It's still light."

"Fuck!" Rice cursed, but he turned and started toward the road. Then he turned left toward Bolsa Chica.

"You made it easy for us to get you so your little brother could get away, didn't you?" Bulldog said.

She didn't answer.

"That's nice. You love him. I just hope your father loves you as much." Then the Bulldog Man covered her eyes with a dark blindfold. She hated the dark. She always slept with a light on. She brought a hand up to pull it off, but he grabbed it and pulled it behind her back. She screamed when she felt him tie her hands. He must have been a rope expert, because she was tied tight in no time.

"Quiet or I'll have to gag you, too. If I do that it could be hard for you to breathe. Do you understand?"

"Yes," she said.

"You gonna stay quiet?"

"Yes."

* * *

Nick Nesbitt couldn't believe it. He'd been anchoring the local news on KYTV for six weeks now and there hadn't been one major story he could call his own. His ratings were sinking fast and at this rate they'd be in the toilet before the end of the month and he'd be on the street looking for a job.

He had to do something quick. He was a newsman, dammit. He didn't belong out here in this cheap rain gear. Shit, if Fat Eddie hadn't always carried it in the van he'd be out here getting drenched and all because some birdbrain producer had a kid who had seen these stupid goddamned murals.

"That's a pretty good one, Nick," Connie Jakome said. She'd been an unpaid intern at the station before he was made anchor. She was devoted to him when others doubted his ability and he'd rewarded her with a paying job, but not before he fell in love with her. But she wanted more. She wanted to be on camera and that just wasn't on. He was afraid she'd be good. She had that fire. He'd be damned if he was going to train his replacement, no matter how much he loved her.

He looked at the mural. It was a cartoon caricature of a Paris street scene. The Eiffel Tower was in the background left. It must be winter, because a tree dominated the center of the mural. It was white, branches without leaves. To the right of the tree was a Metro sign. The foreground was stuffed with people. An old woman sitting on a bench, knitting. A gendarme standing next to an outdoor cafe, men and women milling about. Colors, bright and vivid, were intertwined with pastels. The artist had a flare. Nesbitt hated to admit it, but he liked it. So be it, this was the one.

He'd immortalize it on a four o'clock news show that wasn't even his own. He hated kissing ass like this, but he had to do whatever the suits wanted until he was in solid. So when they asked him if he'd do it, he agreed, even though he didn't want anything to do with the story. To make matters worse, they'd probably show it again during his own broadcast at six and again at eleven. Maybe even tomorrow morning.

And he'd be standing right next to it, rain dripping from his face. And in this stupid yellow rain gear. For a second he thought about taking it off, but that would look even dumber, standing in front of a winter scene in soaking clothes. Shit, who cared about wall art? There was a world out there that counted. Murders, rapes, political scandals. Stuff viewers wanted to know about. Nobody gave a rat's ass about any stupid murals painted on the side of a cliff that nobody was ever going to see.

He looked over at Fat Eddie behind the camera. "You ready?"

"Yeah, boss."

"Okay, time check." He didn't need it. He knew how close he was. He was a pro.

"We're live in twenty," Connie said. The camera lit up, bathing the mural in light. He moved into place next to it. Alright, I'm counting down," she said. "Ten, nine, eight—"

"Help!" the voice pierced through the rain. A mournful wail that sent the hairs on the back of his neck standing on end.

He put a hand up to shield his eyes from the light as he tried to see beyond Eddie.

"Help!" There was such urgency in that voice. Nick shivered with the pain in it.

"Get it, Eddie!" he said. Eddie spun around seeking out the voice with the lights.

"Nick, you sure?" Connie said.

"Find it, Eddie!"

"Looking, boss."

"Three, two, one," Connie said.

"This is Nick Nesbitt live from Huntington Beach where we have an emergency in progress." He knew he wasn't on camera as Eddie probed through the rain. He knew he was putting his career on the line. If it paid off he was in solid. No more puff pieces. If not, they'd toss him out on his ass and nobody would touch him. He'd be lucky if he could get a job pumping gas in Modesto.

"Help!" Once again the voice tore through the rain, but this time it was going out live. Over a million people were hearing it. Nick could imagine them staring at their screens as the camera panned back and forth through the rain, seeking.

"Got him, boss," Eddie said. It was probably the first time his voice had gone out over the air. Very unprofessional, but Nick didn't care. The drama was thick. They had to be going nuts back at the station. "It's a kid." Eddie again. Nick saw him as he chugged toward them, wet, panting. It was the Radoslaw boy. Cyril Radoslaw's boy. His gamble had paid off, big.

"This way, son," Nick said. He didn't have to fake the concern. One look at the boy was enough to tear your heart out. How many people were glued to their sets? A once in a lifetime story.

"My dad is Cyril Radoslaw, call him quick. They kidnapped my sister." The boy was panting. Spitting the words between breaths, but they were clear enough.

"Who? Where?" Nick said.

The boy looked around, blinking his eyes against the lights. He saw Connie and went to her, falling into her arms. Eddie stayed on him. Nick felt like screaming.

"They had a black van. There was two of them. Just now." He pointed. "They took off toward Bolsa Chica. You've got to get the police."

"We will, we will," Connie said. She wasn't miked, but Nick was close enough. The world was hearing. And they were seeing her kind and caring face. She looked like a Madonna.

"How long ago?" Nick said.

"Less than five minutes." The boy was still breathing hard, but not crying. And that God damned camera was still pointing at Connie and the kid. Nothing for it. He stepped into the spot and moved next to them. Connie was soaked, her blonde hair hanging around her face. The kid was catching his breath. He looked like one of those war ravaged kids from the Middle East or some God damned place.

"Did you hear that?" he said into the camera. "Cyril Radoslaw's daughter has just been kidnapped in Huntington Beach. They were last seen heading toward Bolsa Chica in a black van." He turned away from the camera, toward the boy. "Did you see what kind of van? Did you get the license?"

"Didn't get the license. It was a Ford. Not so new. The big kind. An Econoline."

"How many men? Did you see them? Can you describe them?"

"Two," the boy said. "One was a big man. Mean, with short hair. The other said his name was Rice. He was skinny."

"That's enough," Connie said. "No more, Eddie."

Nick stepped away from Connie and the boy. Eddie followed him with the camera. Connie looked pretty good with that boy. Heart strings were being tugged out in TV land and by contrast he stood alongside them in the stupid yellow rain suit with the stupid hat. He whipped the hat off.

"I hope the police are watching," he said. "To recap, Paige Radoslaw has just been kidnapped in Huntington Beach by two men in a black van. The kidnappers were last seen heading toward Bolsa Chica Beach. Be on the lookout for this van. If you see it call the police." He sighed. "We all hope that Cyril gets his daughter back safe and sound before the night is over. This is Nick Nesbitt live in Huntington Beach." Eddie killed the lights.

Larry Waylen, his producer back at the station screamed through his ear piece. "Get the camera back on that kid. Stay with this, Nick."

"Can't," Nick said. He was getting his bearings now. He saw a story in progress and he went after it. But no way was he going to abuse this kid. Anybody else, maybe, but this was Cyril Radoslaw's boy.

"Don't do this to us, Nick," the voice in his ear raged.

"Got no choice. He's a minor. The police are gonna be pissed as it is."

"Fuck them. This is hot."

"Larry, you got the story of the century. Live. Right now we're the good guys. Everybody's gonna love us. We keep the camera on the kid and we're gonna look like the money grubbing whores we really are. Just tell the world that we are going to see the boy safely back to his parents and that we're going to assist the police and the family in any way possible and for Godsakes don't over use that tape. Once a broadcast is enough. Let's not Rodney King this thing to death. Believe me, it'll look a whole lot better if we take the high road on this one. You know, integrity. A little of that never hurt anyone."

"Maybe you're right," Larry Waylen murmured through the ear piece. "But you are going to take the boy to his parents. You'll be right there if they want to go on camera. Right?"

"Oh, yeah."

"Cyril Radoslaw's daughter," Larry said. "How stupid."

"Stupid," Nick said. "They better hope the police find them first."

CHAPTER
SEVEN

"YOU'RE SARA?" the pregnant woman said. Sara gasped and stepped back. She was young. Lisa's age, maybe less. Dishwater blonde hair worn in a ponytail, like a fresh and smiling teenager. Like Debbie Reynolds or Sandra Dee from one of those '50s movies that Clay collected and watched all the time. Tammy or Gidget, something like that.

She had a freshly scrubbed Midwestern look. A kid straight from Kansas. A policeman's wife. Sara discounted the thought as quickly as it had come. The way she'd said, "You're Sara," chilled her and told her this young woman didn't belong to any cop friend of

Clay's. She belonged to Clay. It was written all over her innocent face. The hurt of discovery. The shame. And something else. Relief?

"How long?" Sara said.

"Six months."

"His child?"

"Yeah."

"Tough on me." Sara wanted to scream. To strike out at the girl. But she looked so fragile. Frightened now. And lost. A child that needed her mother.

"Tough on me too," the girl said.

"Pardon me if I don't feel sorry for you." Sara's first thought was that it wasn't Clay's child, but the girl didn't look like the kind of person that slept around. If she said the child was Clay's, it probably was, impossible as it was to believe.

"I didn't know he was married. He never said. And none of his friends said either. Then I got pregnant. The night I was gonna tell him the wonderful news, he tells me he's married. I went away, but now I'm back. He's gonna ask you for a divorce."

"And you two are gonna live happily ever after. That sucks." Sara went to the breakfast table, pulled out a chair and sat. That cinched it. It was Clay's child. The girl was an innocent. Sara bet she'd never lied in her life. "I need a drink."

"What?" the girl asked.

"Gin and tonic." Sara was amazed at how calm she was, as if she was one of two women acting on a stage. She knew the woman she was playing should be hurt, angry, but Sara wasn't feeling anything. She was just numb.

"I'll get it."

"You know where it is? Stupid question. Of course you know where it is. You've been living here. In my house. That's why there's food in the fridge."

The girl opened the cabinet next to the refrigerator and pulled out a bottle of Gordon's. She opened the fridge and took out the tonic. Then she filled two glasses with ice from the freezer.

"You shouldn't drink, the baby."

"I've been good. A small one won't hurt." She brought the drinks to the table and set one down in front of Sara. She set the other in the place across from her and started to sit, but stopped herself. "I'll get the TV. Then we can talk."

"Do I want to?" Sara said.

"We need to." The girl started for the television. Then stopped.

"This is Nick Nesbitt live from Huntington Beach where we have an emergency in progress." His voice sounded squeaky over the tiny speaker.

"It's the Asshole Nesbitt," the girl said. Sara wasn't quite sure where the newscaster picked up that name, but everybody called him that.

"Help." The cry pierced her. She looked at the small television. The picture was jumping around. It was the beach. It was raining. Then the camera found him. A boy. Long hair. One of the surfer kids. Maybe someone drowned.

"Got him, boss." Another voice from the television as the camera zoomed in. The boy put a hand up to block away the light. "It's a kid." That same voice. Probably the cameraman.

"My dad is Cyril Radoslaw, call him quick. They kidnapped my sister." The boy was breathing heavily, as if he'd run a long way and was trying to catch his breath. Was this really happening right now? Cyril's daughter kidnapped? Only a few blocks from her home?

"Who? Where?" Nesbitt's voice from off camera as the boy looked back and forth, like a hurt animal. His hand was still up. He was trying to blink away the light. The camera followed him as he went to a woman. He fell into her arms.

He pulled away from her. "They had a black van. There was two of them. Just now." He pointed off into the distance. "They took off toward Bolsa Chica. You've got to get the police."

"We will, we will," the woman said. Like the boy, she was drenched. Sara saw the anguish on her face. The woman seemed to be absorbing the boy's terror.

"How long ago?" Nesbitt's voice, still off camera.

"Less than five minutes." The camera went in for a close-up of the boy. He looked like he was fighting tears. Sara had never met the kids. They'd been out both times Clay had taken her over to the Radoslaw' home in Newport Beach for dinner.

The boy was catching his breath as Nick Nesbitt stepped into view. He was wearing the kind of raincoat and hat her mother used to make her wear to school on rainy days when she was a little girl. On her it had always looked cute. On him it looked stupid, especially next to the woman and boy, wet with rain and tragedy.

"Did you hear that?" Nesbitt said. He seemed to be looking her straight in the eyes and Sara was captivated by him, despite his stupid rain hat. "Cyril Radoslaw's daughter has just been kidnapped in Huntington Beach. They were last seen heading toward Bolsa Chica in a black van." Nesbitt faced toward the boy. "Did you see what kind of van? Did you get the license?"

"Didn't get the license. It was a Ford. Not so new. The big kind. An Econoline."

"How many men? Did you see them? Can you describe them?"

"Two," the boy said. "One was a big man. Mean, with short hair. The other said his name was Rice. He was skinny."

"That's enough," the woman said. "No more, Eddie."

Nesbitt moved away from the woman and the boy. The camera followed him. He pulled that hat off. "I hope the police are watching," he said. "To recap, Paige Radoslaw has just been kidnapped in Huntington Beach by two men in a black van. The kidnappers were last seen heading toward Bolsa Chica Beach. Be on the lookout for this van. If you see it call the police." He sighed. "We all hope that Cyril gets his daughter back safe and sound before the night is over. This is Nick Nesbitt live in Huntington Beach."

The picture cut to a plastic looking man in the studio and the girl turned the television off.

"I don't believe it," Sara said. "How can something like this happen in broad daylight?"

"It's the times we live in," the girl said.

"They're such nice people, the Radoslaws."

"Pretty scary," the girl came back to the table and sat. "Clay told me Mr. Radoslaw would keep a twenty-four hour guard on his kids if he could, but Clay keeps telling the man that it's his software he's got to protect, not his kids. Clay thinks the kids gotta be free to have fun and grow up without security guards following them wherever they go. I guess he was wrong."

"It looks like it." Sara sighed. Obviously this girl knew about Clay's new job with Cyril Radoslaw. She bit down on her lip. This couldn't be happening. It was a nightmare. She picked her drink up. She wanted to slug it down, wash all this away. But she put it back on the table. Drinking wouldn't solve anything.

"I'm really sorry about all this," the girl said. "You can't know how sorry."

"What's your name?" Sara wanted to know and she didn't want to know.

"Carole. With an E." Did she really not know he was married? Could Clay really have done that?

"Carole with an E, can you imagine how depressed I feel right now? I know other people have problems worse than mine, but I can't help how I feel. It's like I have the weight of the world on my shoulders and nobody cares. I want to lash out. To scream, to cry. Maybe I even want to hit you." Carole looked startled. "Oh, relax, I'd never do that, besides, you're pregnant."

"That's a relief," Carole said.

"For you," Sara said, "but I feel like I'm at the bottom of a slimy pit and up is too far to think about. Do you know what that feels like? Can you know?"

"Oh, yeah, I know. But my pit's a lot worse. Deeper. More slimy. Darker."

"What do you know about anything?"

"I know Clay's a low life rat. I know if I wasn't Catholic I'd have aborted this baby. I know I never should've told him. I know I've got just enough money of my own left to buy a ticket back to Iowa. I know my dad's gonna make me eat crow, just like he's done to my mother for the last thirty years. And I know I've gotta go back and take it, because bad as it is, the alternative is so much worse. Oh, I know a lot of things." There was a fire in her eyes that hadn't been there before.

"Alternative?"

"Your husband. He wants to divorce you and marry me. And I was gonna do it, even though I know it's wrong, because I wanted my baby to have a father. It was all set. He was gonna tell you the second you got back. It was gonna be a quicky Vegas divorce then a quicky Vegas wedding. But the last couple of days I've been thinking maybe no father at all might be better than Clay."

"You don't love him?"

"I did, but now I think I'm afraid of him. When I found out I was pregnant I went away. I didn't want to lose him, but I didn't want to be responsible for breaking up a marriage. Stupid me, I went to a priest. He told me the father has a right to know. I never should have listened, because that's all Clay talks about, how he's going to be a father."

"It would be a big deal for him. He has a low sperm count. It's hard for him to father a child, but not impossible."

"You know, he never even cared when I left. He could have found me if he wanted. My boss from my old job knew where I was. I was never more than a young piece of ass to him. And all his friends knew it. They're all low lifes. Just like him."

"What do you mean, his friends knew?"

"We've been over to Jerry and Janet's a bunch of times since we started dating. Way before I was pregnant. They never said a thing. He took me to the Marine Corps Birthday Ball for his reserve unit. Lots of guys winked at him, but I just thought it was because he had a good looking date, not because he was married. He took me to the cop picnic just before I left town, same thing, winks, but I didn't get it."

"I don't believe it. Janet didn't say anything?"

"Nope. In fact she was real friendly."

"This is the most humiliating thing I've ever heard. I can never face these people again."

"How do you think I feel? He made fools of us both." Carole turned toward the door. "Sounds like his Jeep driving up."

The engine died in the driveway. Sara tingled with apprehension. Clay didn't expect her for another week. How would he react? Then she remembered the arguments they'd been having and how close they'd come to being violent and all of a sudden she didn't want to be there anymore.

The sound of the door startled her. Carole's eyes went wide.

"I'm back." Clay's voice resonated throughout the house.

"We've missed you," Sara said.

"You're early." He came into the kitchen shaking his head. He looked from Carole to Sara. "So what do we do now?" He smiled that boyish grin. He was a big man with wide shoulders, thick arms and thin waist. That combined with his dark wavy hair and Irish good looks made him irresistible to most any woman.

"That's it?" Sara surprised herself by not screaming. She didn't have it in her. She felt like she did after a hard day's racing. Used and spent. Sleep was all she wanted now. Things would sort themselves out in the morning.

"Well I guess she told you about the baby. I can't

abandon it, can I? What kind of father would I be?" His clear green eyes penetrated her. She had to fight to keep from squirming.

"What about Kelly?" Fear rattled through her. She'd lose her now. She bit onto her lower lip again to stop it from quivering. It was a damned good thing Kelly was gone. This would destroy her. First her parents killed, now this.

"Come on, Sara, her grandmother was probably going to win anyway. She's got all that money."

"She's my brother's child. Rick and Jenny said in their will they wanted me to raise her."

"And that doesn't mean squat when it comes to the kind of lawyers Estelle has. They'd twist you around so much you wouldn't know up from right, left from down. Estelle's getting the kid. Sorry."

"I'm not exactly poor and I've got a lawyer," Sara said.

"Yeah, you're well off and could probably put up a good fight, but let's face it, you're nowhere near Estelle's league. She's gonna win. Kelly's gonna go live in Hawaii."

"Clay, I think you should probably take Carole and go." She wanted to scream, but she fought it back.

"Me? Go? That's not fair, Carole's pregnant. We can decide who gets what later, but for now I think I should be the one that stays in the house."

"You've got to be kidding," Sara said.

"I know the house was yours before we got married. I know you paid for it. But I've been contributing to this marriage for the last three years, you know. I've paid the taxes and the upkeep. I bought the new carpets and paid for the pool. It's my house, too."

"No, Clay, it's not. The deed is in joint tenancy. Me and Lisa. We bought it together as an investment with the money our parents left us way before I ever met you. She was kind enough to move out so that we could live here. She's been paying rent in that apartment for the last three years when she didn't have to. But forgetting all that, you can't really think you can dump me for a younger woman and take my house, too. You can't think that, can you? Because if that's what you're thinking, you can forget it. There's not a judge in California that would give it to you."

"But the money I've put into it?" His face was turning red. Surely he couldn't really believe what he was saying, could he? He was a police officer. He had to know better.

"I can't believe we're talking about this. You're trying to take my house. This sucks, Clay. It really sucks. So you paid a few taxes and bought some rugs. You've paid no rent for the last three years. Take a second and think about what you're saying."

"Okay, maybe you're right. But you still can't throw Carole out. She's pregnant."

"Get a hotel, then find an apartment, buy her a house, live on the streets, I don't care. I just want to go to bed and forget this horrible day."

"What about the pool?"

"Give it a rest, Clay."

A scowl crossed his face. He clenched his fists. For a second it actually looked like he might hit her.

"Clay, we should go," Carole said, diffusing the situation.

He focused his glare on Carole. Gone was the boyish man she once loved. There was something else there. Sara was starting to get afraid. "You don't belong here anymore, Clay. You've got to go."

"Just like that? It's over?" He said it like he'd done nothing wrong.

"Isn't that what you were going to tell me when I got back?"

"Yeah, maybe." His face softened.

"Do you want me to leave while you pack your things?" Sara said. She didn't want to leave. He might follow her to the garage and see the Austin Healey was gone. Now wasn't the time to tell him it had been stolen. Let Jerry tell him later. She didn't want to get him angry again. The last thing she wanted was a scene.

"No. It'll only take me a few minutes." He started up the stairs.

"Thanks for not making it too rough," Carole said.

"I didn't do it for you."

"I know, but thanks anyway."

They spent the next ten minutes in silence while Clay moved about upstairs, probably throwing things into a suitcase. Sara sagged into her chair. She felt like the life was draining out of her.

"I'm sorry," Carole said as Clay came down the stairs.

"Okay, Babe, ready to go." He used to call her that. Now he had a new babe.

Sara stood with Carole and walked them to the door. It was all very civilized. She stood in the doorway as if she was seeing off friends who had come to visit. The rain had stopped. She watched till the Jeep turned the corner. Then she closed the door. It occurred to her that she hadn't mentioned the

Radoslaw kidnapping. Clay probably didn't even know about it yet. Well he'd find out about it soon enough.

She sighed. She had to run or she'd flop back on the sofa and sink into a well of depression. She was a runner. It's what she did when it all got to be too much. It was how she coped. She forced herself upstairs. She shrugged out of her clothes in a haze and slipped on her sweats.

She stumbled down the stairs and out the door. It was getting dark. She started off at a jog, limbering up mind and body. Clay was gone to her, but maybe Kelly didn't have to be. She could call Estelle and work something out. Maybe it wouldn't be so bad after all.

If she had to, she'd move to Hawaii. Maybe Lisa was right. Estelle just wanted what was best for her granddaughter. Sara could live in Hawaii. Maybe sell the house. She could buy another with Lisa. They could keep racing, base themselves out of Honolulu instead of Huntington Beach. Lisa would love it. Kelly too, because now there would be no reason for a tug of war between Sara and her grandmother.

She started running faster, crossing Pacific Coast Highway at Main Street. Then she was on the sand, jogging down the bike trail. When she got to the fork she took the bottom one, the very trail that Paige Radoslaw had been kidnapped from earlier. She shivered with the thought despite the sweat pouring off her body.

At Bolsa Chica she turned and poured on the speed as she headed back toward Huntington Beach. She sprinted across PCH at Main and kept up the pace till she was two blocks from home. Her heart was pounding and she was sucking air as she jogged in place, winding down. She walked the last block.

After a shower she thought about crawling under the covers naked, but then she thought of Clay and Carole and what they'd been doing in her bed. She put her Levi's and tee shirt back on and went downstairs. She flopped on the sofa in the living room and was asleep in seconds.

She woke about three hours later in a cold sweat. She sat up. Never could she remember being so thirsty. The depression had worn her out, both physically as well as mentally. She was exhausted. She pushed herself up from the couch and went to the kitchen for water. She didn't bother with a glass, she just turned the faucet on and lowered her head under it and drank.

She was hungry too, but she didn't know for what. She checked the fridge and settled on an apple when the phone rang. She picked it up.

"Hello."

"Help me." The voice sounded hurt and lost. It was Carole.

CHAPTER EIGHT

PAIGE BOUNCED AROUND as the van bumped over the beach sand. Every thud a painful jolt. She was on her back, hands between herself and the metal floor. The rope dug into her wrists. She couldn't see, but she knew there was stuff in the back of the van with her. Smelly stuff. Something banged into her.

She bit back a scream. The man said they'd hurt her if she screamed. She was tossed onto her side as the van turned. They must be on the dirt road. It seemed like they'd turned left, so they were going toward Bolsa Chica. It was hot in the van. Sweat ran under her arms. She had to go to the bathroom, but she was afraid to say anything.

"How long you think before the kid gets the description of the van out?" She recognized Rice's voice. He didn't sound friendly anymore. She bet he didn't work for her dad at all. It was all probably a big lie. She'd been so stupid. 'Stay away from strangers,' her dad had always said and she did the direct opposite. Not just today, but all the time. She didn't feel so smart now, didn't think her dad was so paranoid now.

"Lifeguards and cops around the beach all the time. Pretty quick." The big man's voice was harsh, raspy like he was talking from the bottom of his throat. It scared her.

A big thud and she was thrown onto her stomach as they rounded a corner. She gasped as she slammed into something and the wind was knocked out of her. She gagged, doubled up and fought for tiny breaths. They were going fast and didn't even notice her when she got her breath back and tried to roll away from whatever it was that had smacked into her.

"Red light," the big man rasped. The van stopped.

"Help!" she screamed as loudly as she could. "Help me!"

"Go," the big man said.

"I'm doing it," Rice said and the van started moving again.

"Shut up," the big man shouted. Paige quieted. His voice was a knife. "That was your one time to fuck with me. Do it again and I'll break your neck. I mean it."

There was quiet in the van. She knew he was waiting for an answer. "I won't do it again. I promise."

"You better not. Just keep quiet back there."

"Yes, sir."

"Better," he said.

Paige rolled onto her side. There was something squishy next to her. And the back of the van smelled funny. Cleaning stuff. Soap and disinfectant. She scooted downwards a little bit so that her bound hands were next to the squishy thing. It was a mop. There were rags too. Dirty rags. Yucky stuff in them. The van turned again. Something bumped into her head. A bucket?

She felt woozy. Something funny was going on in her stomach.

"You better stop," she said. "I'm gonna throw up."

"You better not," Rice said, "because if you do you're gonna be sloshing around in it."

"And we'll be smelling it. Slow down. I'm gonna go back and help her."

"What do we care? We're changing cars," Rice said.

"I don't want vomit all over the girl, alright?"

She heard him climb back. She remembered what he looked like. How could she forget? She pictured those dark eyes. A shudder rippled through her. Her stomach muscles clenched out of control. Puke was coming up. She felt his big hand pull her from the floor. He held her head as the vomit spewed out. She gagged, coughed. More vomit. She couldn't breathe. She gagged again, then sucked in quick breaths when she could get them. He pounded her back. She belched. More vomit. Dry heaves. It seemed like forever before she could breathe again.

"Finished?" he rasped.

"Yeah."

He dropped her on her side, away from the vomit. "Don't think I'm a nice guy because I didn't let you puke yourself to death. I'm not."

Paige believed him.

* * *

Just look at the big fuck, Rice thought, that cozy little piece of ass in his arms and he probably didn't even grab a feel. He was so into his body he was asexual. Nothing but muscles and mean and a dick the size of a pea. If it was him, he'd be squeezing them fine titties. Yes, sir. They'd be soft. He could hardly wait. He was getting stiff. She'd be heaven. Tight too. Tight without going in the back door. A thrilling shiver passed between his shoulders. He was so tired of men.

"So, Guthrie, how'd she feel? Soft and tender or ripe and ready?"

"Cop car, two back." Guthrie was looking out the side mirror.

Rice looked in the rearview. Sitting high, he got a clear look at the law. They seemed to be deep in some kind of argument. Main Street in Seal Beach was coming up. He moved into the left turn lane and the cop car passed without a second look from the men inside.

"So when you guys gonna call my dad?" the girl said. She sounded real scared.

"What makes you think we're gonna?" Rice said.

"You kidnapped me. Didn't you do it for ransom? Like in that movie."

"Maybe, maybe not," Rice said.

"Tell her what she wants to know, Rice. She'll be

a lot less trouble when she knows how quick this thing will be over."

"Yeah, we did it for ransom," Rice called out. "But it was supposed to be secret. Now that the cops know, it's a whole new ball game."

"Maybe they don't know." God, she had a sweet voice. Kind of squeaky. Yeah, she was scared.

"They know. That hot shit surfer brother of yours went screaming right to them. Guaran-fucking-teed." Sweat was dribbling between his legs. He was still hard, his balls hurt.

He eased the van out into the intersection and made his left just as the light changed. He drove toward the beach a ways, then made a U. He went into his first coughing jag of the day just as they were pulling back up to PCH. Sweat ringed his forehead. It was the AIDS. Had to be.

"You don't sound so good," Guthrie said.

"I'm fine." He was lying. He couldn't let Guthrie know how sick he was. In this world you never let anyone know your weakness. Not if you wanted to stay alive.

* * *

The van stopped. "We're changing cars," Guthrie said. "What I'm gonna do is take off your blindfold. You can sit in the back seat, and as long as you stay good, that's where you stay, but if you get out of line, you ride in the trunk."

She heard them get out. The sliding door opened. He scooped her up with his big hand. "Going to set you down." She touched ground with her feet. She stood. His hand was on her face, then the blindfold was off and she was staring into those eyes.

"You don't want to give us any trouble."

"No trouble," she said. She was crying, she couldn't help it.

"This way." It was the other one, Rice. He was holding open the driver's door to a white two door car.

"Go," Guthrie said.

She looked over at Rice holding the door open and for some reason now she was more afraid of him than she was of Guthrie. He leered at her and she knew that look, knew what he wanted. Her dad better come up with that ransom money real quick or she was gonna be in real trouble.

"Come on, we ain't got all day," Rice said, eyes slitting. Guthrie pushed her and she started toward the car. For a second she thought about running. She knew where she was. That long road between Westminster and Seventh, the one that went to Long Beach State. Studebaker Road.

"Hurry up."

She took a step forward. A car was coming. She turned toward the sound of it.

"I wouldn't." Guthrie was right behind her. She felt his hot breath on her neck. Smelled it. Garlic. Bad.

She picked up her pace, in a hurry to get in the car now. She didn't want his hands on her again.

She lowered her head to get in as Rice grabbed her ass. She felt him slide his hand between her legs and squeeze. She jumped in, landing on her side. Rice laughed. Then they got in. She squirmed around so she could sit up. Rice gunned the car and they shot away from the curb.

The sky was crimson with reds and pinks behind

them as Rice turned onto the San Diego Freeway on ramp.

"Saw you cop a feel," Guthrie said. "Save it for later. Business first."

"Who put you in charge?" Rice said.

"No one's in charge. I just don't want her cunt getting in the way. There's a lot of money at stake."

"So I fuck her some. You really care?" Paige heard the urgency in Rice's voice. He wanted to do it bad.

"You keep away from her till we know the deal. You stay away from me, too."

"You can't get AIDS from touching. Don't you know anything?" Rice said.

Oh no, Paige thought, AIDS.

"Just stay away," Guthrie said. "Once the money's taken care of you can have the girl, not until. We might need pictures of her in good shape."

"I won't hurt her face."

"We'll see," Guthrie said and Paige shivered.

"Look, you guys want the money, call my dad." She shook with every word. It wasn't her voice. She wasn't in control. She was so scared. "I'll tell him I'm okay and he'll pay right up." She had to get them to like her or she was in real trouble. That cop had said to cooperate and that's just what she was gonna do. Don't give them any reason to hurt her. Daddy would pay the money and she'd be home before she knew it. Then he'd come after these men and there'd be no place they could hide. Her father was thorough. She might only be fifteen, but she'd heard the stories.

Rice floored it and they shot onto the freeway, heading north. The day was dying fast, but there was enough light left for her to see his face through the rearview mirror. She should have shouted for help when she saw that car go by. Guthrie was crazy, but Rice was crazier. And he wanted to do things to her. She saw it in his eyes. And he had AIDS. She was in trouble.

Guthrie turned around to face her. "It's a long drive. You be quiet and I'll keep him off you. You don't and you're his. You wouldn't want that. You can still have a nice life, just be good." He looked bad with his snake eyes. She shuddered, because he looked good compared to Rice. "Sit back, go to sleep. It'll be over soon and you'll be back, safe and sound with Mommy and Daddy."

She settled back, but she couldn't sleep. She couldn't even close her eyes. There was a new smell, acrid, like bitter tasting coffee. She wondered what it was. Then she knew. Fear.

She turned with her back toward the window. Her hands were still tied behind her back, but she was able to push the switch to lower it. The window started to come down. Maybe she could stick her head out and scream. Someone would see and maybe call the cops on a cellphone.

"Don't," Guthrie said. How'd he know? He hadn't even turned around.

"Just wanted a little air. It smells in here."

"Put it back up."

"Okay, sorry." She pushed the switch the other way and brought it back up.

"You going to be okay?" Guthrie was talking to Rice, who was sweating worse than she was. And shaking a little too. He coughed again.

"I can hold my end up. Don't you worry none." He was spitting the words. How could she have been so fooled? His fat head was shaking. The sweat made the hair around his bald top glisten. Oily, sweaty, dirty.

He reached a hand back and scratched his neck, pulling his collar down. There was a big red sore there. Puss. She shivered like she'd been dipped in an ice bath. It was the same kind of sore that her friend Meagan's older brother had on his forehead and arms. And he died. AIDS. Rice wasn't lying, he did have AIDS. That cop was wrong. She should have shouted when she had the chance. She would if she got another one.

She still had to go to the bathroom. Worse. "I gotta go."

"What?" Guthrie said.

"I gotta go." Maybe they'd pull over and she could make a run for it. She was pretty fast. Fastest girl in her high school. If she ran off the road where the car couldn't go, she could probably out run them. Rice was dead dog sick and Guthrie was a big man. He couldn't be too fast.

"I'm not stopping now," Rice said. "You'll have to hold it for awhile."

"I gotta go pretty bad."

"Can't be helped," Guthrie said.

"You can go when we get to the Grapevine," Rice said. He eased the car across two lanes of traffic to the fast lane. The rush hour traffic was finished. It was close to dark now. Headlights were starting to come on.

"That's miles away. I can't hold it that long."

"You're gonna have to."

"We can't stop now," Guthrie said. "Someone might see if we pulled into a gas station." That was exactly what she wanted, but he knew that.

"You could pull over to the side of the road."

"That's fucking crazy." Rice was on edge. "You'll hold it." He was talking quiet, but the way he said it, it seemed like he was screaming.

"Try to think about something else," Guthrie said. "It won't be so long, you'll see."

But it was long. It seemed like forever. They were driving through the night. She wondered which way they'd go. They passed the Harbor Freeway "Hey, it's quicker to go over that way."

"How do you know where we're going?" Rice said.

"You said you were going to the Grapevine. The San Diego Freeway takes longer. It's always crowded on Friday nights."

"How do you know?"

"My parents take us up into Westwood all the time."

"Tough shit."

"She might be right," Guthrie said.

"Too late, we're not going back."

"But I gotta go. You're gonna get caught in that Westwood traffic and we'll be hours."

"So, wet your pants."

"But I don't wanna."

"We can't risk a station," Guthrie said.

"Pull over to the side. You can hold my hand, but you gotta look the other way."

"What if a cop stops?" Rice's voice changed. She hoped it wasn't because she said he could hold her hand.

"Fat chance," she said. She wished she could see his eyes in the mirror so she could maybe get an idea about what he was thinking, but it was dark now.

"Okay, I'll pull over. But you gotta be quick," Rice said.

"The way I gotta go, I'll be quick."

He flipped the turn indicator on and changed across four lanes of highway. In seconds he was slowing down on the shoulder. Thunder roared as he stopped the car. She looked for lightning, then realized it was a jumbo jet landing at LAX. Rice eased the car to a stop, then put it in park. Guthrie started to get out.

"I'll do it." Rice was out of the car in a flash, holding the seat up for her. Stupid. She should be getting out on the passenger side so no one could see. He must want to hold her hand while she peed awful bad. What kind of pervert was he? "Okay, let's be fast about it." He grabbed her arm and jerked her out. His hand was sweaty. Clammy like a dead fish.

She pulled him around to the side of the car. "You gotta untie my hands." He fumbled with the knots. She was gonna have to drop her shorts. He was gonna love that. "Hurry." He finished and pulled the rope from her wrists. "We gotta get off the road a little bit." She pulled him into the bushes that grew alongside the freeway.

"Okay, this is good. Let's get this over with," he said.

"You're supposed to look the other way."

"Give me a fucking break. Take the pants down and do it."

"You lied," she said. Cars were flying by, headlights slicing through the night, but none of them were pointed her way.

"You wanna take a leak or not? Not's fine with

me. We can go back right now."

She looked at the car. Not too far away. Guthrie was watching. She looked at the oncoming headlights. No safety there. She grabbed the button of her shorts with her free hand like she was going to undo it, then she kneed him in the nuts, hard.

"Cunt!" he screamed, but he didn't let go.

She hit him in the head as he bent over. He roared in pain as Guthrie was opening his door. She chopped at his arm and he let go. Guthrie must be out of the car by now. She didn't know for sure, because she didn't look. She just ran.

She plowed through the bushes and slid into a ditch that ran alongside the freeway. It was only about four feet deep, but she was in the bottom of the vee of it and it was muddy and wet. And the mud seemed to be grabbing onto her sandals, sucking them into the cold earth. After a few lunging steps they were torn from her feet, but she didn't stop. Someone was coming behind her. For a second she thought about pulling herself out of the ditch and charging toward the freeway, but the cars would never stop in time. They'd splatter her all over the road.

She kept going. The ditch seemed to be getting deeper. Up to her shoulders. Muddy and bushy walls on both sides. It seemed like she'd gone a long way, but she was in shape. She was the fastest girl in school. She could go forever. No way could they catch her. She sucked air, thoughts running wild. Images flew before her sight, real and imagined.

The ditch was getting shallower. She couldn't hear anyone behind her. She must have out run them. Now the ditch was only up to her knees. She jumped out of it and ran away from the cars. She crashed through more bushes and smashed into a chain link fence. She bit back a scream and sank to the ground. She lay in the mud along the base of the fence. She was covered in bushes. She took shallow breaths. Quiet from even God's ears.

The freeway sounded like a rushing river. No other sounds. She was covered in darkness. Safe. She'd stay till morning if she had to. They'd never find her now. She kept herself stone still, ears soaking up the night. No sound other than that river of cars. Then she heard it. A car moving slowly by on the shoulder. It stopped. Moved on. Stopped again. Moved on and was gone.

She'd done it. She sighed. Not so smart, Mister Kidnappers. Not so smart at all. Wait till she told Peter. She wanted to sit up. She really had to pee now. But instinct held her fast. A bug crawled up her arm. She ignored it. She waited a few more minutes that seemed like forever.

No sound.

Nothing.

Her bladder was bursting. She had to go. Bad. Now. She pushed herself into a sitting position. So slow, careful not to make even the smallest sound. She sat and listened some more.

Still no sound other than the cars moving through the night. Then the roar of another airplane coming in overhead. It chilled her. She sat immobile, feeling the thunder of the jet engines as the giant sound shook through her. After a minute or so it was quiet again. She was sure she was alone. Positive.

She reached up, linking her fingers with the chain link. She pulled herself to her feet. She stood close to the fence, breasts touching it. She'd never gone to the bathroom outside before, never gone without a toilet. She unbuttoned her shorts and lowered them.

She looked around. Moving her head slowly back and forth. No one there. She held onto the fence and squatted. In an instant she was urinating. A strong stream that seemed to send shock waves of sound shooting through the night.

A big hand clamped over her left arm. "You should have stayed low and quiet." It was Guthrie. He slapped her with his fat hand and the world went dark.

CHAPTER
NINE

SARA HIT THE GARAGE DOOR OPENER on the visor and started the Montero. In seconds she was on Pacific Coast Highway heading north. The sky was clear now. She rolled down her window and inhaled the sea air.

In Seal Beach she hung a left on Main Street and drove into Old Town. Newly discovered, Old Town was making a comeback. The street was alive. People were milling about on the sidewalks outside the popular seafood restaurants, talking, smiling, waiting for their tables. The ice cream store was packed. The bars overflowing. Some folks were just walking the street. A wonderful place, Sara thought as she drove toward the beach. She parked in front of the Italian restaurant at the end of the block. She honked and Carole came out the door.

The pizza was the first thing Sara noticed. The second was the swollen eye with the fresh cut under it. It was dark out, but not so dark that she couldn't see that it was bruised and black.

"Thought you might be hungry." Carole jumped in the passenger side.

"I haven't eaten." Sara remembered her own black eye, but somehow she didn't think what she was seeing now was an accident.

"Let's get out of here."

"He did that to you?"

Carole put her hand up to the swollen eye. "Yeah, really popped me a good one. Let's just go, okay?" She reached over the seat and set the pizza in the back. It smelled delicious. Sara hadn't realized how hungry she was.

She put the car in gear and soon they were heading south on PCH. "You wanna give me a piece of that pizza and tell me about it?"

Carole stretched over the back seat. Sara glanced over. Her shift rode above her belly. She was real pregnant. No denying that. What kind of man hits a pregnant woman? Answer—no kind of man she wanted anything to do with. And she'd been married to him for three years.

The aroma hit her fresh when Carole got the box open. She handed Sara a piece and she bit into it, holding the wheel with her left hand, eating with her right. Traffic was flowing smoothly.

"Now, what happened?" Sara said.

"I told him I wanted to break things off and he went nuts. Screaming, throwing things. I thought he was going to kill me. He might have, but raging as he was, he had to know everyone in the motel could hear. Plus, he registered in his real name. No way could he have done it and gotten away with it. Cop or not, he'd be fried."

"Gassed."

"Huh?"

"We gas them in California."

"Oh, yeah."

"But not so much anymore." She glanced over at Carole. She had the pizza in her lap and was opening the box again.

"I like to think they'd gas a man that killed a pregnant woman." Carole took a slice out of the box and bit into it. She chewed, swallowed. "You want me to go on or not?"

"Yeah, sorry. I won't stop you again." The girl was perceptive.

"He lost it because I told him I didn't want to be with him anymore. He said he'd kill me first. He was a madman. It was like he has a Mr. Hyde inside. He grit his teeth so hard his face went white. It was unbelievable. You should have seen the way he was shaking. Then he hit me. 'No one steals my child,' he said."

"Jesus."

"I know I took your husband and probably ruined your life, but everyone else I know is a friend of Clay's. They'd tell him. I'm gambling you won't."

"I won't," Sara said.

"Where are you taking me?"

"Back to my place."

"No! When he comes back and finds me gone it's the first place he'll look. Maybe he already knows. It took you over fifteen minutes to get to the restaurant. He could have come back to the motel and already be on his way to your place."

"You're wrong. He'd never dream I'd help you."

"I don't know anyone else. Not really."

"And you don't know me. You'll be safe."

"Bullshit. You don't know him. He's not the same man you were married to. This kid's a big thing with him. It's making him crazy. There's no way I'm gonna be safe at your house. Not a chance. He'll get me."

"People just don't drag people away any more. There's laws, cops."

"Yeah, cops. Tell me about it." She was really scared. And that cut above her eye was real. That bastard.

"Even if he comes by the house, he won't get in. I'll swear you're not there."

"He won't believe you."

"Oh yeah he will. I'll scream my bloody head off. I'll tell him I hope you're dead. That my house is the last place on the planet you'd ever be. That if I saw a ten ton truck bearing down on you I wouldn't lift a finger to help. I'll have the whole neighborhood out listening to me screech like a banshee."

"You can do that?"

"We've been fighting a lot lately. It won't be anything new."

"Isn't there any place else?"

"A motel."

"No, the police can check the motels."

"I don't know anywhere else. My sister's

apartment maybe."

"Does he know about it?"

"Yeah but—"

"He'll find me. He knows you'll help. He'll check everywhere. Do you have a gun?"

"Sure." Sara didn't tell her that her gun was back in Long Beach, on *Wave Dancer*, safely hidden behind a galley cabinet.

"Then we'll go to your house. But you have to promise me he won't get in. You'll keep him out, even if you have to use the gun."

"You are really overreacting." Sara felt an icy ripple on the nape of her neck. Oh yeah, the girl was scared.

"I don't care. Promise me if he comes, you'll keep him away from me, no matter what."

"Alright, I promise. But it won't happen. No way. You'll see."

Sara punched the button on the garage door opener when she was halfway down the block. The door had barely clanged into place when she punched it again as she was in the driveway. It was going down even as she slid the Montero under it.

"Okay. We're here." Sara got out of the car. "You okay?" Carole was trembling, like she was going to cry.

Then she started. "I'm so sorry about all this." Tears rolled off her cheeks. She buried her head in her hands.

"Come on, Carole. Get out of the car."

"I can't."

"It's going to be okay." Sara went around to the passenger door and opened it. "Come on, I'll make you some hot chocolate and we'll talk this out."

"My mother used to make me that." Carole looked up and kind of smiled.

"Mine too. Come on." Sara held out her hand. Carole took it and she led her into the house. Carole flopped down on the sofa.

The phone rang.

"Don't answer. It's him."

"That's not possible. No way could he know." Sara picked it up. "Hello."

"Bring her back!"

"Clay?" Sara saw Carole's eyes go wide.

"You took her."

"What are you talking about?"

"Carole. She's gone."

"Good."

"She called you. I checked with the motel. Their switchboard logs all calls."

"You're crazy. Why on earth would I want to help your bimbo?" She didn't know if Clay was lying or not. He was a great poker player.

"I'm coming over. If she isn't there you'll be sorry." He was talking in a loud whisper. It didn't sound like him at all and it didn't sound like he was bluffing.

"Clay—"

"She better be there." He hung up.

"He's coming over. He knows." Sara put the phone down. She couldn't believe it. He'd threatened her.

"We have to go." Carole was wringing her hands, thumbs at war.

"I'll call the police."

"No! You're in denial and it's going to get us hurt. Clay told me you're some kind of racing champion. He talks about you like you're some kind of superwoman. You have to get us out of here, because now he's after you, too. And believe me, he's not normal. There's something real wrong with him."

"I can't believe that."

"Look at this." Carole jumped from the sofa and was in her face with a finger pointed at her eye. "I'm telling you I thought he was going to kill me. I don't have the strength to fight him alone. I can't even run by myself. Help me. Please, if not for me, for my baby."

"Alright, there may be someone. Someplace he'd never find you." Dottie, Sara thought, Clay didn't know about her, so no matter what police services he used the girl would be safe. "Let's go." She started for the garage, Carole on her heels.

"Old car," Carole said five minutes later as Sara parked behind Dottie's Ford and shut the engine off.

"Beautiful car," Sara said.

"Yeah, it is," Carole said.

Dottie was standing in the open doorway as they came up the porch steps. She'd heard Sara's car pull into the driveway. She was wearing faded Levi jeans and a faded Levi work shirt, with a purse slung over her shoulder. "I didn't expect to see you again. At least so soon."

"We're in trouble," Sara said.

"Come in and tell me all about it," Dottie said.

They followed the older woman into her living room. A light beige wall to wall carpet softly glowed under the light reflected toward it from two Tiffany lamps hanging in opposite corners of the living room. Dottie sat at one end of a yellow and green, tropical print sofa. Sara sat in one of the matching wing chairs facing the sofa and Carole sat in the other. There was a modern glass topped coffee table between the chairs and sofa and Sara noticed the latest edition of *Time* and *Newsweek* on it. Dottie liked to stay informed.

"So what's this all about?" Dottie asked. The telling took less than five minutes and when Sara was finished Dottie said, "You're welcome to stay as long as you want. You're under the general's protection now."

"The general?" Sara said.

"Sherman." Dottie called. The massive German Shepherd Sara remembered from when Dottie ran out of gas trotted into the living room. "Sit." It sat. "Nobody messes with me." She pulled a thirty-eight police special out of her purse. "Nobody."

"I guess not," Sara said.

"But that doesn't mean you can hide out forever. Sooner or later you have to face him."

"Not me," Carole said. "I'm going back to Iowa."

"Are you sure that's best for the baby?" Sara said. "The way you talked about your father, I'd think you might want to raise the child somewhere else."

"I've got a girlfriend in Atlanta. She'd put me up for a while, till I got a job, but I don't have enough money to pay my way till I get on my feet."

"I'll give you the money." Sara couldn't believe what she was saying. She hardly knew the girl, but she was pregnant, desperate and Clay was responsible. Sara sighed. Somehow that made her responsible.

"I'll pay it back," Carole said.

"That won't be necessary. Just take good care of the baby, that'll be payment enough." Maybe it wasn't her child, but Sara couldn't help it, she didn't want it raised by the kind of man Carole said her father was.

"I don't know what to say." A tear trickled down her cheek. Sara could tell she was trying not to cry.

"And you can stay here till we get you on a plane," Dottie said.

"What about you?" Carole asked. "You have a home here. You can't run away as easily as me."

"I don't have any intention of running away. I can handle Clay."

"Did he ever hit you?" Dottie whispered. The room went quiet, the only sound the big dog's breathing. Dottie reached down and scratched behind his ears. If a dog could smile, Sara would swear the dog was doing it. It seemed happy, but she'd hate to be on the wrong side of its anger.

"Never," Sara said, "but we've had some pretty loud arguments lately. And my sister said she's seen him so mad she thought he might do it. But he never has. If he did, he'd never hit anyone else again."

"That's what I mean. Men who do that sort of thing know when they can get away with it," Dottie said.

"Not always," Sara said. "Remember the Bobbit woman?"

"Yeah." Dottie laughed. "A blow for women everywhere, or should I say a slice."

"I've been pretty blind," Sara said, "and I'm not talking about the fact that my husband had an affair for so long that I didn't know about. He's been abusing me too, only I never saw it because he'd been doing it with his mouth. He'd get on my case and I'd jump right on his, without realizing what was going on. Maybe it's his nature and I never saw it, or maybe he's just angry because the doctors said he couldn't have kids, but whatever, it doesn't make any difference, it's abuse and I'm probably just as guilty as he is."

"What do you mean?" Dottie said.

"It takes two to argue, my tongue was just as violent as his."

"But who started the arguments?" Carole said.

"Exactly," Dottie said. "Who started them?"

"Clay," Sara said. "Always Clay."

"So you were just fighting back," Dottie said. "It's not the same."

"It takes two," Sara stood up.

"Where are you going?" Carole said.

"Home."

"That's stupid," Carole said.

"I'm not gonna let him run me out of my own house. Besides, you're the one hiding, not me."

"He'll make you tell where I am."

"At least spend the night here," Dottie said.

"Maybe," Sara said, "but I have to get some things, and I didn't lock the house. No way am I leaving it unlocked all night long."

"Okay, if you have to go, then I'm going with you." Dottie picked up her purse from the coffee table where she'd laid it. "I'll leave Sherman to look after Carole and I'll look after you." She patted the purse.

Sara shook her head. "I'm not afraid of him."

"You should be," Carole said.

"Even if I was, there's no way I'd let him run me out of my home."

"I still think I should go with you," Dottie said.

"I can handle this by myself."

"You're sure?"

"Absolutely."

"Alright," Dottie said, "then we'll do dinner first. I was just about to make myself something, company is always welcome."

"I had a couple slices of pizza," Sara said.

"Not enough. Besides, half-an-hour won't make any difference and it'll give your husband some time to cool off. What could it hurt? Come on, let's go out to the kitchen and see what we can rustle up."

On her way home, she thought about Clay, about Carole and about her life. Surprisingly, she was looking forward to moving. Hawaii would be nice. The house was paid for. She didn't need top dollar. She could take a little less and sell quick. Then she'd get a place with Lisa in Honolulu. Paradise.

She turned onto her street and saw the orange glow. "My house!" She parked at the curb and jumped out of the car.

"I just got home and saw it burning." It was Spider. He had a garden hose hooked up to her neighbor's faucet and was spraying the house.

"My stuff." She ran to the porch and opened the door. Smoke billowed out. She got a quick look at her living room. It had been trashed. Furniture overturned. End table drawers opened and emptied.

"Come on, Sara." Spider had given the hose over to a neighbor. Sirens sounded in the distance. "You can't do anything except get hurt." Heat radiated from the house. Flames licked through the living room. She saw the sofa burst into flame, felt Spider's hand on her arm. He pulled her away.

"I'm sorry," Spider said. There were tears in his eyes.

"It's not your fault." She fought tears herself. She

wanted to stay. Everything she owned was in there. Her life was in there. She couldn't bear to think about it. She could never replace what the flames had taken, were taking. Every instinct said stay and help fight the fire, but something told her Clay did this, and that same something told he'd be back. She had to go.

"I bet I could've stopped it if I got here quicker."

"No. Someone did this on purpose. Tell the cops it looked like a madman tore the place up first. They'll want to know." She went to her car.

"Where you going?"

"I don't know."

She couldn't prove it was Clay, but who else could it have been? Carole was right. He was crazy. She took Main to the Pacific Coast Highway, driving without thinking. Then she remembered that gun in Dottie's purse. Dottie wasn't the only one who had a thirty-eight and knew how to use it. She turned right on PCH, heading north, toward Long Beach, toward the marina.

Sara kept her gun on *Wave Dancer* because two or three times a year she cruised in Baja, either with Clay or Lisa, and she didn't like the thought of sailing down there unprotected.

She parked in the marina parking lot and jogged down the dock to *Wave Dancer*. Usually the gentle rocking of the boat in its slip soothed her, but tonight she took no notice. She unlocked the hatch and in seconds she had the cabinet open and the false back off.

"Shit," she muttered. The gun wasn't there.

She checked the brass ship's clock. Eight-ten. So much had happened in so short a time and it wasn't over yet, she still had to get Carole on a plane before the night was through. She locked the boat, then made her way to the car. Clay had taken her gun. Why? In the car, she checked the dashboard clock again. For some reason time seemed to be running out.

She racked her brain as she drove south on PCH. Clay had threatened her, burned the house and taken her gun. None of it made any sense. None at all. Then, back in Huntington Beach a new thought terrified her. If Clay wanted to find Carole, all he had to do was follow her. She looked in the rearview. She didn't see anything, but she knew he was back there. He knew how to follow someone without being seen, especially at night. He was a cop.

She picked up her car phone and punched four-one-one and asked for the number for the Lucky's Supermarket on Beach Boulevard. In less than a minute she had Greg on the line.

"This is Sara, I'm afraid I'm gonna need some more of your help."

"Whatever I can do."

"I'm in trouble."

"How can I help?"

"You got a back door to that supermarket?"

"By the freight dock."

"I'm less then ten minutes away. I have a crazy man behind me. Can you have your car by that door ready to go? I'll come in the front. He'll either come in after me, or wait till I come out. Either way, if we leave in your car we'll lose him."

"Call the cops."

"He is the cops. It's my husband."

"I'll be ready. Park in the handicapped spot by the entrance."

"Thanks." He wasn't flirting now. This was serious. She was glad he wasn't the kind of man who'd turn and run at the first sign of danger.

"Good luck." He hung up.

She turned onto Beach with an eye on the rearview. A car turned behind her, headlights close together like a Jeep. Clay. She shifted down into fourth, then third. Her Montero could leave him in the dust, and as good a driver as he was, she was better. She stopped herself. That was the last thing she wanted. Four wheel drives running amok on Beach Boulevard. She'd spend the night in jail and Clay would go drinking with the boys. Better to stick with the plan. She put in the clutch to shift back up into fourth when she saw those headlights start to close the distance between them.

The phone rang. It was him. It had to be. She picked it up. "What do you want?"

"Sara?"

"Estelle?"

"I've been trying to call you all day." The headlights were chewing up the distance between them. She held the phone between her ear and shoulder and downshifted into second.

"I can't talk now, Estelle," Sara said. Clay was getting closer. What was he up to?

"Something terrible has happened."

"Gotta go. I'll call you back." Sara hung up as she stomped on the accelerator. Her souped up Montero was faster than that Jeep. Lots.

The phone rang again. Sara eyed the gauges, building speed. Forty-five hundred RPM. She shifted up into third. Her way was blocked. She jerked the wheel to the right, shooting between the lanes and two cars, maybe an inch to spare on both sides, maybe less. The phone was still ringing. There was an intersection coming up. She grabbed a look in the mirror. He was falling back, but he was chasing. No way could he keep up. The phone was still ringing.

The light went yellow. A row of cars between her and the intersection. All showing brake lights. She grabbed a look at the tach. Five thousand RPM. The engine was screaming. She speed shifted into fourth, still riding the center line. The space between the cars was close, maybe too close. She should slow down. It's what he wanted. She threw a hand up and pulled on the shoulder harness. Lightning quick. Both hands on the wheel now. She silenced the phone with the horn, blaring a warning into the night.

"Fuck," she yelled. The light went red as she scraped between the two cars. Metal against metal thunder-shivered sound through the car. Both side mirrors popped off. Sparks flew. Then she was in the intersection, cars coming at her from both directions. She downshifted back into third without taking her foot off the clutch. The accelerator was pinned to the floor. The engine roared, but the car picked up speed.

Tires screeched as cars braked to avoid hitting her. "Yes," she screamed as she flew through the intersection. No way could he catch her now. The phone was still ringing. She eased off the gas and picked it up.

"Pull over." It was Clay.

"Fuck you." She hung up. Now their relationship was defined. No living with the son of a bitch now.

Red lights blinking. A siren wailing. Cops. It was on the other side of the street. They flew by each other as the black-and-white screamed into a U turn.

Traffic was starting to pull over. This was bad. Running from Clay was one thing. Cops was something else. No one got away from cops in hot pursuit. Only in the movies. She looked in the mirror. More red lights back there. Two cruisers in hot pursuit. Lucky's only two blocks ahead.

Another black-and-white coming toward her on the other side of the street. What was this? Why so much firepower? For her? Incredible. She hung a right and turned off the headlights as she fishtailed across three lanes. The cop car flew by, caught unaware. The one behind would be on her in an instant. She roared down the street, praying that no kids were out playing.

Corner coming up. She grabbed a quick look in the mirror as she squealed through a left turn. No cops. Next corner. Another screaming left. Please, God, no kids. Beach coming back up. Would they be waiting for her? Had she faked them out? They had to see she'd turned off the lights. She could have parked, turned left, right or gone straight. Would they even think she'd come back to Beach? How could they? They couldn't know she had a plan.

Tach redlining, going seventy down a residential street in third. Headlights dark. Crazy. Beach coming fast. Shit, cop car. Someone figured she might circle the block. Maybe just lucky. Too fast to downshift. She stomped on the brakes. Tires screeched. Downshift to third, back on the accelerator. No way could she outrun the cruiser.

The cop car was in the slow lane. She didn't think they'd spotted her. She powered into a sliding right, slamming into the side of the cruiser, sending it careening into the oncoming traffic. Another yellow light. She flew through it. Lucky's up ahead. Another sliding right and she was laying rubber all over the sidewalk as she roared into the parking lot.

A woman and two kids with a shopping cart. She pulled the wheel left, clipping the rear of several cars as she scooted between a rank of parked cars and the young family. She imagined the woman screaming, but the hailstorm of destruction she was creating in the parking lot cut off all other sound.

Another shopper pushing a cart. Sara punched the horn. A man jumped back as she plowed into his shopping cart. Groceries flying. People screaming. The handicapped spot so close. She stood on the brakes and the car screeched to a stop.

Sirens wailing.

So close.

She was out the door in a flash. Running toward the store. The homeless man from before was blocking her path.

"Hey, lady, stop!"

She slammed into him. He staggered back, holding on to her arm. She whirled and smashed him in the nose. Blood covered his face. "Let go!" He did.

She was in the store.

Greg was there.

Sirens louder.

"This way." He started running toward the back. She followed.

Seconds later she leaned back in the passenger seat as he slowly drove through the parking lot. There was a cruiser by the front door. Lights blinking, telling the world there was trouble here. The homeless man was down, a cop bent over him. Two other black-and-whites turned in the lot. Sirens and lights. Then Clay's jeep.

"What did you do?" Greg asked.

"Damned if I know," Sara said.

CHAPTER TEN

PAIGE WOKE TO PAIN in her arms. She was lying on her back, arms underneath her body. It was dark. It was hot. She was moving and she smelled gasoline. She tried to scream through her dry mouth, but she couldn't move her jaw, and the sound she managed to get out couldn't be heard above the constant rumbling noise of rolling tires on pavement. Something was over her mouth, preventing her from calling for help, and her hands were tied behind her back again.

She was in the trunk.

She wanted to kick out against the lid, but

Guthrie had hit her. He might do it again. There was
no telling what he would do. But she was afraid not to
kick out against her metal coffin, because what if no
one ever came and she was left in the hot trunk to
die? No, that wouldn't happen. Guthrie would come.
And when he came, something bad would happen.
Paige was sure of that.

She felt the car go into a sharp right turn.
Something fell and hit her on the head and she
smelled the gas smell up close. From the bang the
thing made as it ricocheted off her forehead, she
guessed it was a gas can. She tried not to gag on the
fumes. It wouldn't be good to cough with her mouth
taped shut.

The car made a sharp turn in the other direction,
rolling her onto her side, and something dug into her
shoulder. She didn't know what it was, it only hurt for
a second, but it was sharp. She was afraid if she rolled
onto it again, it would cut her.

One of the rear tires picked up a rock as the car
rounded the corner, a steady click, click, click that
shot through her.

Something moved down by her legs. It kind of
squeaked. She wasn't alone. It sounded like a rat. She
tried to lash out at it with her right foot and
discovered that her feet were bound. It moved again.
It had to be a rat. A fat ugly rat. A hungry rat.

The car swerved and the sharp thing dug into her
side. Every time the car turned, she was going to roll
over the sharp thing, and it would cut her, and she
would bleed, and the rat would smell the blood, and it
would eat her blood, and it wouldn't be enough to
make it full, so it would eat her till she was dead.

The car turned again. One of the rear wheels

must have gone over a curb, because Paige felt the shock as the tire slammed down onto the pavement. The gas can bounced again, making a loud ringing noise that scared the rat into screeching. It wiggled against her and she rolled over the sharp thing in a effort to get away from it.

She wanted to use her legs to push away from the sharp thing, but she was more afraid of the rat and she was having a hard time breathing. She lay still, catching her breath, scared. She felt it wiggle next to her leg again. It was big, not a rat. Something bigger. Something scarier. She bent her legs, tucking her knees into her stomach, trying to pull away from it.

She listened to the steady clicking of that rock and her ears told her the car was slowing. It must be a red light. And for a flash of a second a flash of red anger zapped up her spine, chasing away the fear. She lashed out with her legs, kicking the rat thing, hard.

It screamed, a muffled cry that didn't sound the way the rats in the movies did. She didn't wait to puzzle it out. She rolled onto her back and raised her legs like her mother when she did her leg lifts, then she brought them down hard onto the rat thing again.

And it cried out again. Not a rat. She listened and started crying herself as the light turned green and the car started to pick up speed. It was a person. She could tell now because of the way it was crying. They had somebody else in the trunk. They'd taken somebody else, too.

Peter. No. Too small.

A little kid. Probably as scared as she was—and she'd kicked it. Twice. Paige wanted to get even with that mean man who had scared her so much and tricked her into kicking a little kid.

The car turned again in a wide arc and she slid toward the sharp thing. Then it hit her. Maybe it was sharp enough to cut the rope that was binding her hands behind her back.

She used her feet to push herself against the bottom of the trunk, moving the sharp thing from her upper to her lower back. Then she was able to reach it with her hands. A small triumph. She felt the sharp thing and knew what it was. It was one of those things that you used to jack up the car when you had a flat tire. A tire iron, that's what her dad called it.

She turned it and tried to work the sharp, pointed end against the rope, but it wouldn't cut it. Her heart picked up speed. She began breathing fast, through her nose. She tried to stop her frightened tears and she started sniffling as her nose filled with snot. She tried harder to cut the rope as panic rose. She couldn't breathe. She tried to suck air through the tape covering her mouth. She swallowed snot. She got light-headed. She saw stars, gagged and passed out.

She tried not to breathe so hard as she came slowly awake. The snot in her nose had dried and hardened, leaving dust-filled boogers behind. She wanted to pick them out more than anything, but her aching arms were still bound. She lay quiet and listened.

Click clack, click clack, click clack, the clicking rock had acquired a clacking cousin, or maybe it had been there all along and she just hadn't been able to hear it. She could hear it just fine now, though. Her ears were wide awake, like they had never been awake before, and her nose was sharp, too. She smelled the gas can, and an old dirty oil smell, and a cigarette smell, and they were all mixed with the smell of her own sweat.

She had to keep from crying. If she cried her nose would make more snot. She would pass out again and maybe not wake up this time.

She searched behind her back for the tire iron. It wasn't there. She felt along the floor of the trunk, somehow it must have moved. Then she felt it. The solid steel seemed to be calling to her and she answered with aching fingers, grabbing it in a tight fist.

But again, the pointed end couldn't cut through the rope. She pushed the tire iron aside, and felt around the trunk the best she could with her hands tied behind her back. She squirmed around, felt the gas can, no help there. A plastic bottle. Oil? She started breathing fast again and had to bite her tongue to force herself to slow down. Could she slick up her wrists and slip out of the rope?

She moved the bottle between her hands and took the top off. It was oil. Slick and gooey. She leaned sideways and poured it over one wrist, then she turned and did the other. She folded her left hand. The rope was tight, but her hand slid out, easy as taking off a bracelet. Her hands tingled when the blood rushed to them. She'd done it.

She started to remove the tape from her mouth when she sensed the car slowing down. If they were stopping for gas, she could scream and maybe somebody would save her. But what if they weren't stopping for gas? What if they were stopping because they were wherever they wanted to take her? If she screamed then, Guthrie would probably hit her again.

The car stopped. She left the gag on and rolled onto her back to conceal the fact that she'd freed her hands as the back of her tee shirt soaked up the oil. She closed her eyes and pretended sleep. She heard the door open, then close. She heard footsteps walking on gravel. They were coming toward the trunk. She prayed they wouldn't notice the open oil can. She tried to stop her jaw from quivering and her knees from shaking.

A loud explosion roared through the trunk and she clenched her teeth against a muffled scream as it was followed by another, louder. Her ears rang for a third time as the man beating on the lid said in a purely evil voice, "Are you alive in there?"

She squeezed her eyes tight.

"Fee fi fo fum, I smell the blood of a spoiled little brat."

Oh, God, please make him go away. Please, please make him go away. But Paige knew Guthrie was going to open the trunk and he was going to hurt her a lot. She wondered if he would kill her in the trunk or if he was going to take her out.

She remembered the way Rice grabbed her. Was Guthrie going to let him rape her first? Then kill her? She shuddered. She wanted the men to go away, but when she heard the horrible sound of the key sliding and clicking into the lock, she bit into her lower lip, because she knew for sure they weren't going away.

The key turned. The trunk opened. She clenched her fists against the fear, and kept her eyes closed. She hoped she could fool him.

"Know what I have in my hand?"

Paige didn't want to know.

"So shiny, so sharp, so right for what I want to do," Guthrie said.

Paige braced herself and felt a pin pricking

sensation below her chin.

"Open your eyes or I'll shove it into your brain."

Paige refused, still pretending sleep.

"I'm not kidding."

Paige felt something break her skin and she felt a gooey wet tickling as small droplets of blood dripped down over both sides of her neck.

"Open them."

Paige opened her eyes wide.

"That's better. You see we can get along, you and me."

It was dark outside, but there was enough light from the moon for her to see into Guthrie's black, beady eyes and she saw nothing there. He had a big knife in his hand, a Bowie knife. Her eyes must have held a question, because he jerked the tape off her mouth. The ripping sound was worse than the stinging pain.

"What?" he said.

"Nothing," Paige said.

"Don't make me mad. I get nasty when I get mad."

"Are you going to kill me?"

"Everybody dies."

Paige stared into the vast nothing that was his eyes. He was crazy.

"Going to tape your mouth."

"I won't make any noise."

"Not when I'm finished." He threw the knife out into the night, then raised her by the neck and started winding the tape around her head, covering her mouth, cheeks, chin, ears, the back of her neck and with the last wrap her nose. Paige saw it coming and sucked in a deep breath through her nostrils before

Guthrie closed off her air and slammed the trunk down.

Her hands were going to her face even before the trunk slammed shut and the light was gone. Her oily fingers met her cheeks below the eyes and she slid them down along her nose, digging them under the tape. She tugged it down, pulling with all her strength. Her lungs were bursting with the need to breathe and the tape didn't want to give.

She inched her fingers down further under it and jerked out, pulling the tape from her nose. Then she pulled down again and the mummy wrapping slid over her nose and she filled her lungs with air. After a few breaths, she tried to dig her fingers under the several layers that covered her mouth. It was duct tape, very tough. She couldn't do it. She pulled her fingers out and started working the tape down, pawing at it over and over, until it slid down over her upper lip. She took in several breaths of the foul air. No air had ever tasted so sweet.

Now, able to breathe, she felt around her head and found the place where the tape ended and began to peel it off. The first four layers peeled off without difficulty, but the last layer hurt as it pulled hair from her head, but she had been through too much to be put off by a little pain. She ripped it off with the same speed a doctor uses to remove a bandage, quickly done and quickly over with.

"I'm sorry kid, I thought you were a rat."

The kid mumbled.

"Just a minute," Paige said. "Let me get untied, then I'll get you free."

She rolled onto her side and bent her body at the waist, stretching her arms and grasping the rope that bound her feet. She tried to untie it, but the knots were too tight. She tried to wiggle her feet out of the rope, but she couldn't get it over her heels. She thought about the oil, but she didn't think that would work on her feet.

"That Guthrie sure knows how to tie a rope," she said. "But there's gotta be a way to get it undone. Don't worry, we're gonna get out of here."

The kid mumbled again.

Paige began a thorough search of the trunk. She felt the tire jack bolted onto the center of the spare tire above her head. She ran her hands over and behind the tire and found what could only be battery cables.

She pulled them from behind the tire and grasped one of the ends in her hands. She opened and closed the clamp. She ran her fingers along the sharp teeth of its jaws and had an idea.

"Battery cables," she said. "Maybe I can use them like a saw." She grabbed one end of the cable in each hand and twisted, working it back and forth like she would a metal coat hanger she was trying to break in half. The bottom and top of the jaws separated a little further from each other with each twist, till she managed to twist it enough that the jaws came apart. Again she ran her fingers along the teeth and thought they would be sharp enough to saw through the rope.

"It's not gonna work," she said after several attempts at sawing on it and making no progress. "I'm gonna have to find something else."

She found the battery cables behind the spare tire, maybe there was something else there, too. She shimmied back over to the spare and reached over it. Nothing. She ran her hands into the well under the front part of the tire. Nothing. She searched the rear area and bingo, wedged between the tire and the well, she found a flashlight.

She pulled the light to her breast like a mother would a baby. She was almost afraid to turn it on for fear it wouldn't light. She counted to ten, then flicked it on. She sighed as the beam of light illuminated the cramped space. Then she saw the little girl.

She was tied up, like Paige had been. Hands behind her back. Feet bound. Grey duct tape over her mouth. Eyes wide in terror.

"It's okay," Paige said, heart going out to the child. Then she realized the kid couldn't see her. She was shining the light in her eyes. She put the light on her own face so the kid could see her. "We're gonna get out of here, I promise."

She pointed the light back at the kid in time to see her nod. She scooted around and pulled the tape off the kid's mouth. And sighed as the kid started sucking in air.

"Okay, I'm gonna untie your hands." She did. "Now your feet." For some reason she was able to untie the rope around the kid's feet, but not her own. She played the light around the trunk and saw a bright red tool box tucked up snug against the spare.

She pulled it away from the tire and opened it. She removed the top tray and its assorted nails and screws, then she rummaged through the tools—wrenches, screw drivers, a tape measure and a hammer—not quite sure what she was looking for. Then she found it, a metal gray utility knife.

She took it out of the box. She caressed the smooth metal tool with her thumb, then used that same thumb to flick out the razor sharp blade.

Boy, if Guthrie came back now he'd be in for it. One slash and no more beady eyes. A second slash and no more throat. Then common sense took over and she began to think. If Guthrie came back, she would be the one in deep trouble.

She slashed through the rope that bound her legs, wincing as blood started free flowing to her feet. She lay still through the pain and tingling, waiting for normal feeling to return.

She played the light over the top of the trunk, then directed the beam to the lock. There was no way she could open the lid, but she had to give it a try. She felt around the lock, hoping that maybe there was a cable or something she could pull on to open it. There wasn't.

"Are we gonna get outta here?" the kid said.

"We're gonna try," Paige said.

"I saw what that man did. He tried to kill you."

"Yeah, he did." Cold waves rippled through the hot sweat tingling her skin.

"We could use that hammer and pound on the lid. Maybe somebody might hear," the kid said.

"Maybe the wrong somebody," Paige said.

"Oh, yeah, didn't think." The kid was scared, but she wasn't cracking up.

Moving the beam, she checked out the spare tire, the tire iron, the jack, oily rags, the battery cables, and lastly she pointed the beam on the back of the back seat.

She put her finger to her lips and they listened.

She couldn't tell if they were in the car, but she heard a scraping sound, like someone was dragging a metal pipe back and forth across a concrete floor. It chilled her, because she couldn't figure out what it was. She tried to think. How long had it been since Guthrie had slammed the trunk shut? Five minutes, ten, maybe fifteen? When he came back, would he check to see if she was dead?

But if they were up front, sleeping or maybe reading, and she tried to get out of the trunk by kicking her way through the back seat, she would be in just as much trouble as if they found her alive.

She had to make a decision.

"We should go for it," the kid said.

"Yeah," Paige said.

She squirmed around so that she was laying on her back, feet facing the back seat, head facing the back of the car. She pushed against the seat. It gave a little. She saw hope and pushed harder. The seat wanted to give way, but something was holding it in place.

She drew her legs back by bending her knees to her chest and kicked. Pain racked her feet as they hit metal and she felt no give, only resistance. She wormed her way around to study the situation. From the top right end of the seat to the bottom left end was a metal brace and from the top left to the bottom right was its opposite twin. The pair of braces formed a large metal X. When she'd pushed and felt the seat give she'd been pushing on the seat. When she kicked and met resistance, she'd hit the braces. Even if she was able to push the seat out, she wouldn't be able to squeeze between the supporting bands.

The metal X blocked her way, so it would have to go.

She pulled the tool box to her and took out the hammer. She worked the claw end between the body of the car and the top part of the brace that started on the right side of the seat, and, using the end of the hammer as a lever, she pulled up and out. To her amazement the metal brace sprang free.

"That's good," the kid said as Paige pulled the metal strip away.

She squirmed around and kicked out against the seat. It gave with a popping sound. If they were up front, now was the time they'd come, but they didn't.

There was room for them to squeeze through and Paige wanted out fast as possible. It was time to escape.

She thrust her head through the opening. It was going to be a tight fit. Tight but possible. Arms first, she squeezed through, scraping breasts and back through her tee shirt. Once the top half of her body was through, her waist, legs and feet followed easily.

Out of the trunk, she helped the kid out. Paige climbed over into the front seat and opened the door.

"Come on, out of the car."

The kid scrambled out.

It was cold. They were in the desert. Stars rained light from a clear sky.

"What's your name?" the kid asked.

"Paige, Paige Radoslaw. You?"

"Kelly Hackett."

"Well, Kelly, I think we better get outta here."

CHAPTER ELEVEN

"WHAT'S IT ALL ABOUT?" Greg asked. He wasn't wearing his jacket, but he still had on that tie. His hands trembled on the wheel. She had no right to involve him, but she had nowhere else to go.

"My husband's low sperm count." Sara turned back toward the store for a last look at the lot full of cop cars and blinking lights. She sighed as it faded behind them. She faced him. The Miata seemed to glide through the night, purring like a big cat. Not the low rumble of her Healey, but she sensed speed. The Miata could get up and go.

"You wanna tell me about it?" He shifted up into

fourth as the traffic sped up. The excitement at the Lucky's Supermarket was nothing more than a brief interruption from the talk shows, songs or conversations going on in the many cars cruising on Beach Boulevard.

"Basically, my husband's been shooting blanks. He got a girl on the side and, against all odds, she got pregnant. So now that he's gonna be a dad he wants to divorce me and marry her, but she doesn't want him. He beat her and she called me for help. Somehow he found out and came after me. When it looked like I was gonna get away he called in his cop buddies. How they got so many after me so fast is anybody's guess."

"Cops stick together."

"Don't I know it. But that reaction is absurd. There were five black-and-whites back there at your store." She pushed the button to lower the window. Electronic windows. She didn't have that in her Healey.

"Your husband must be pretty popular." He signaled and moved into the fast lane. The car still smelled new.

"He is, but that was a complete abuse of police power. Cops go to jail for that kind of stuff. Nobody's that popular."

"It seems crazy." There was a red light coming up. He downshifted into third, then second. The Miata rumbled. Well, maybe a little like her Healey.

"Tell me about it." She didn't tell him about her house burning down. He was a nice guy and he'd gone to a lot of trouble for her, taken a big risk. But if she told him just how crazy Clay really had become, he'd freak. Anybody would. "But I think after the girl is safely out of town, he'll cool down. It might take a few days. He's gonna take a lot of ribbing from his friends. He won't like that."

"Will you be okay?"

"Should be." But she wondered if she'd ever be okay again.

"Someone could have gotten hurt back there. It looks like you scraped up a lot of cars in the parking lot."

"I'm sorry about that. My insurance will cover it. And if they don't, I will."

"Won't be too much trouble finding out the damages. I'm sure the police are taking names."

"I'm sure they are," Sara said. Then, " I hate to press, but I don't have a car and I'm gonna need one more favor."

"Ask."

"I think the girl my husband knocked up is gonna need a ride to the airport tonight."

"Sure, I'll take her." He sounded disappointed.

"Such a nice man. So eager to help," Dottie said as Greg drove away with Carole. She still had that purse slung over her shoulder. She was a real Wyatt Earp. Nobody messed with her. Sara believed it.

"Yeah." Sara was distracted by the television as they came back into the living room. They were replaying the Nick Nesbitt kidnap tape. The sound was off, but Sara didn't need it, she felt Peter Radoslaw's plea for help as if the sound were booming through mega speakers.

"So what now?"

"He burned down my house." Sara pulled her eyes away from the TV and turned her attention back to her host.

"What?" Dottie's hand went to the purse.

"Burned it up. All my stuff. He chased me down Beach Boulevard. Lots of cop buddies joined in. I barely got away. He's one crazy guy and I don't mean that in a funny kind of way."

"What are you gonna do?" Dottie sat on the sofa, hand still clutching her purse.

"I don't know. I can't figure out why they'd chase me all over hell and gone. I probably should have stopped. He couldn't have done anything to me in front of a zillion witnesses. Stupid. I really should have stopped."

"Why don't you call your husband and ask? He can't hurt you over the phone."

"Why don't I?" She picked up the phone and dialed.

"Robbery-Homicide." It was Jerry.

"What are you doing answering the phone?" Sara asked.

"I just happened to be here."

"Yeah, right. What's going on, Jerry. Clay burns down my house. An army of black-and-whites chases me down Beach Boulevard. You answer the phone on the first ring. Something stinks here."

"Right now it's looking like you burned it down. That's the assumption everybody's going on."

"You know me, Jerry. Is that something I'd do?"

"Everybody saw you drive away from the fire."

"That doesn't mean I started it. And another thing, who marshaled the troops so quick? It's just a fire. Since when do you guys do high speed chases for fires?" She took a deep breath to keep from getting angry. "You know if you wanted to talk to me about it, you could have called me on the car phone and I'd have come right in." She sighed. There was quiet for a few seconds on the other end of the line. She heard him breathing.

"I shouldn't do this, it could mean my job, but I've been pretty shitty to you behind your back."

"You mean about Carole. I know all about it."

"At first it seemed harmless. You know Clay's always been kinda like a little kid. When he showed up with her everyone figured it was just a passing thing. No one wanted to tell you. Who knew she'd get pregnant?" He paused. "They got the fire under control right after you left. They saved a lot of your house. Most of your stuff's okay."

"That's great."

"But they found Cyril Radoslaw in your bed. Dead."

"What?"

"Shot in the heart. A pack of condoms in his pocket. Your gun by the body."

"I gotta go."

"No, stay there. I'll be right over."

She hung up.

"What?" Dottie said.

"They found Cyril Radoslaw dead in my house. They think I killed him. They're on their way here right now."

"How? You didn't tell them where we were."

"It's like that caller ID thing. I forgot all about it. When you call the cops they get your name and address up on the screen. We're outta time."

"Not," Dottie said. Then, "Sherman, come." She started toward the door. "Come on, Sara. Let's go."

"Wait," Sara said, stunned, staring at the

television. It was that girl, the one in the photos. The photos she'd gotten by mistake. Her stomach tumbled as she rushed to the set and turned up the sound.

The pictured segued back to Nick Nesbitt. "Right now the whole state is praying for the safe return of Paige Radoslaw to her parents."

"Oh, shit," Sara said.

"Come on." Dottie said.

"Okay."

"We gotta hurry." Dottie went out with nothing but her purse and her dog. She took nothing from the house. She didn't look back.

"Gonna lock the door?" Sara said as Dottie was getting in the car.

"Forget the house. The clock's ticking." She started the car and reached over to open the passenger door. The dog jumped in. "Hurry."

Sara jumped in too.

Dottie backed the car out of the driveway. Slowly. She drove the car four houses down, turned into a driveway and killed the engine.

"What are you doing?"

"Doesn't look like anyone's home. Look!" Two police cruisers slid around the corner, sirens off.

"This is stupid." Sara ducked as a third black-and-white screamed around the corner, followed by Clay's jeep.

"Can't outrun them so we have to out think them. We're hiding."

"Here?"

"Exactly. We're hiding in plain sight. It's our only chance."

Sara poked her head up and looked out the window. The black-and-whites were blocking the street on both sides of Dottie's house. Clay had driven his Jeep right up onto her lawn. Why wasn't he a suspect? He lived at that house too. At least he did right up till a few hours ago. Cops, they stuck together.

"Stay down." Dottie started the car.

"What are you doing now?" Sara looked up at the older woman. Her hair was down, touching her shoulders. She was smiling. Sara couldn't see them in this light, but she imagined her gray eyes glistening.

"Backing down the driveway." Dottie favored Sara with a quick look. Then she craned her neck around and looked out the back window as the car moved out of the driveway. She honked and waved at the cops. None of them waved back. Sherman barked. In the street, she backed almost up to one of their cars before putting it in first and driving away. "How long before they get a make on the kind of car I drive?"

"I'd guess pretty quick." Sara was still scrunched down.

Sherman barked again.

Dottie laughed.

"You think that was fun?" Sara said.

"Kind of, but I don't think they're likely to forget this car. They're gonna feel stupid. Probably be mad, too."

"I'll bet." Sara sighed as they turned the corner. She sat up, thinking she was in the clear. A car passed them going the other way. An unmarked. It was Jerry. Driving alone. They locked eyes for an instant, then he looked the other way. "Clay's partner."

"Did he see you?"

"Yeah, but I don't think he'll tell. Not right away. He kind of warned me that we should get away.

We're gonna have to get rid of this car. Then we need a place to stay. And I have a phone call I have to make and it scares the hell out of me."

"Tell me."

"Earlier today I took a bunch of film in to get developed. Twenty rolls. Eighteen of them were mine. Two I scooped up at the house when I got back. A couple hours later I picked them up. Half of them. The other half weren't ready yet. I got a roll of someone else's by mistake. Pictures of a pretty young girl. All taken with a telephoto lens. It was that girl on the television, Paige Radoslaw."

Dottie turned right on Pacific Coast Highway. The sea on the left shimmered in the moonlight. A surfer moondogged a wave. Traffic was still heavy. Friday night. Date night.

"I don't think I got that film back by mistake. I think it was Clay's."

"Oh, no."

"Yeah, and I'm terrified that it gets worse. I'm the legal guardian for my brother's little girl, Kelly. He and his wife were killed in an auto accident almost a year ago. My sister-in-law's mother, Estelle, is fighting me for her. She's very wealthy. We're supposed to go to court soon for the judge's final decision. Estelle called me just before the car chase. She said she'd been trying to get me all day. She had terrible news, but I hung up before she could tell me."

"Why?"

"I was kind of pressed. Clay was coming up behind me. Other cops. I barely got away. I said I'd call her back. I think I'd better. Real quick. I'm worried."

"Where's your niece now?"

"She's supposed to be with Clay's mother, at Disneyworld in Florida."

"Supposed to be?" Dottie turned right on Goldenwest.

"Yeah, supposed to be." Sara felt like crying as Dottie turned into a gas station and pulled up to a phone booth.

It was one of those places where the attendant sits in a small brick room behind a locked door and bullet proof glass. He slides a tray out, you put your money on it and he turns on the pump. The gas station bordered on a large park. Giant elms and eucalyptus trees swayed in the evening breeze. Moonlight glowing through them gave off a graveyard atmosphere. Ghostly.

Sara got out of the car. The phone booth was at the back of the station. A breeze sprang up, whispering through the trees. She could see the back of the strongbox the attendant was imprisoned in. He couldn't see her. A car went by on Goldenwest, white headlights turned into red taillights. She couldn't tell if it was a police car or not.

She picked up the phone. She'd called the number often enough, she knew it by heart. She called collect.

"Estelle Arthur." She'd answered on the first ring. Unusual for Estelle. She was a busy woman and hated the telephone. It was a job for the maid.

"It's me, Estelle."

"Oh, thank God. I'm at my wits end. I don't know what to do. I was just about to call the FBI."

"Don't do that, Estelle. That would be bad."

"You don't know what I'm talking about."

"I think maybe I do."

"How can you know? Have you talked to them?"

"Do they have Kelly?" Sara shook as graveyard shivers rippled through her, because she already knew the answer.

"Yes. I don't know what to do. They want money. A half million. Of course I'll pay, but I'm so scared. They want me to bring it to L.A. day after tomorrow. I'm afraid they'll hurt her even if I pay it. I want the cops."

"No!"

"Maybe it's the best thing. They know how to handle these things."

"It was Clay."

"What?"

"It was Clay. I'm sure he had help, but it was him. If you call the cops, he'll know and he'll hurt her."

"Oh, my God." Then, "How do I know you're—"

"Don't even think it, Estelle. Just listen for once. I know you're not so good at that, but please try, because you and I, and maybe one other woman friend I have are the only chance Kelly has." Sara looked over at Dottie in the Ford. She was listening to every word.

"Okay, I'll listen, but I'm not promising anything."

"When they call you again, tell them you have some demands of your own."

"What do you mean?"

"You have to hear Kelly on the phone. She has to tell you she's all right. If they don't do that, then you don't pay. Period."

"What if they won't let me?"

"Then she's already dead."

"Oh, God."

"Also, you tell them if they hurt the other girl you

won't pay. Even if they let you talk to Kelly, you don't pay. You have to hear them both. Talk to them both."

"What other girl?"

"They took another. She's fifteen and her father can't pay."

"Can't or won't," Estelle said, the hardness Sara was so used to creeping back into her voice.

"It's Cyril Radoslaw's daughter."

"My Lord, he can pay."

"They killed him. Somehow they got him to my house, then they put a bullet through his heart. My money's on Clay. Right now they think I did it."

"How do I know it isn't you?"

"You know, Estelle."

"You're right, I know you. You could never do something like that. But what if the other girl's already dead and Kelly isn't?"

"Let's hope she's not," Sara said.

"I feel sorry for her, but it's not my problem."

"Oh yes it is. Kelly's had a hard time adjusting to the fact that she lived through the accident and her parents didn't. How do you think she'd feel if we bought her out and let the other girl die? We don't take one without the other. I don't want it. Kelly wouldn't want it. And if you think about it, you won't want it either. All or nothing, Estelle. Be hard. Be firm."

"I don't need to think about it. I know when I'm wrong. You're right."

"Okay, you be hard. No bending. You tell them you'll pay, but they do it your way or no way."

"I'm used to that."

"And remember, whatever you do, don't let on that you know it's Clay."

"I'm not stupid."

"Sorry."

"Do you think we'll get her back?"

"We're gonna give it our best shot. I gotta go. Hang tough. I'll call you when I can. Oh and one other thing. If we succeed we don't need to fight anymore. I'll move to Hawaii. She needs us both."

"Good luck," Estelle said. Then she hung up.

Sara got back in the car.

"So it's you, me and the general against the kidnappers." Dottie started the car.

"Just us."

"Then we'll have to do." Dottie took a right out of the gas station.

"Where we going?" Sara asked.

"The airport. We'll stick my car in long term parking and rent something new before they kill our credit cards."

"But they'll just trace the car through the card."

"Oh I think we can fool them on that one."

An hour later Dottie was taking the plates off of a white Ford Taurus in the covered long term parking lot at John Wayne Airport. Once off, she put on the plates of the identical car she'd rented with her credit card.

"Thousands of these cars on the road. Any cop runs these plates, they're gonna say white Taurus. With luck the owner of this one will be out of town for a few days and even if he comes back before we're through with the car, chances are he won't notice till the cops have him up against the wall."

"Where did you learn how to be a crook?"

"Television."

"I was just thinking. Remember when I said I'd only picked up half of the photos. Well, I didn't see them all. The other half are still at the photo place. What if the other roll I picked up is with them? What if there's more of the kidnapper's pictures on it?"

"Maybe we should go get those photos," Dottie said.

"They don't open till 10:00. We need someplace to stay till then. Someplace the cops would never look."

"I know the perfect place," Dottie said.

"Where?"

"The LaMirada Drive In."

"We're going to a movie?"

"Not exactly."

About twenty minutes later Dottie exited the freeway. Not long after, she turned the car into a massive parking lot outside of a drive-in theater. The lot was empty, except for a long line of cars, vans and pickup trucks lined up at the entrance. Many of the cars had boxes and crates lashed to their roofs. Dottie pulled up to the end of the line and shut the engine off.

"Sellers waiting to get in and set up for the swap meet tomorrow."

"So early?" Sara said.

"It's first come, first serve. You want a good spot you line up the night before."

"I've been to the swap meet. Those people didn't look like they'd been up all night. They looked like regular businesses. People selling furniture, lamps, clothes, stuff like that."

"Those are the ones with the regular spots, mostly like you said, regular businesses. The owner brings some inventory out here on the weekends to sell for cash so he can cheat the IRS. Those kind of guys got all the reserved spots. Takes forever on a waiting list to get one of them. The rows in back are set aside for the guy that's cleaning out his garage and folks like these." She pointed to the cars in front.

"Folks like these."

"People that would rather wait in line all night than have their name on a list. Gypsies, pirates, bootleggers, thieves."

"All of them?"

"Not all, but a lot."

"How do you know this?"

"My son used to sell bootleg records out here. I helped. When he quit, I started coming out and selling my quilts. I never made any money at it, but these people became my friends. I just couldn't stop coming, especially after I lost my husband. We're safe for now." She opened the door and got out. "Come on, there's some people I haven't seen in a while."

Sara got out of the car. "Why'd you quit coming out?"

"I don't know. It just seemed to get harder as the years went by."

"Are you sure it's okay? Talking to these people, I mean."

"Should be. It's dark. Even if they put a picture of you on television, no one here will recognize you. Besides, these people got their own problems. They mind their own business and leave you to yours."

"Think one of your friends might have a cellphone we could use?"

"What for?"

"I'm gonna call the FBI. Estelle's right, we can't

do this on our own. Clay doesn't know I figured out about Kelly being taken along with the Radoslaw girl. So if he finds out I went to the feds, he'd have no reason to take it out on Kelly. And once I meet with them face to face, I can tell them about Clay."

"Are you sure?"

"It's the best way."

"There." Dottie pointed. "It's my friend Jake. He sells tools. Most obtained by five finger discount, I think." Dottie waved. "Hey, Jake."

He was a tall black man, leaning against a GMC van. He had a small phone to his ear. One of those that looked like a Star Trek communicator. He looked up when he heard Dottie's voice, said a few more words into the phone, then flicked it closed.

"My favorite lady." He had a voice like a well, deep and watery.

"My friend needs to make a phone call."

He handed over the phone. Sara flicked it open and walked away from them. She punched 411.

"Information."

"Ma'am this is a life and death situation. I need the emergency number for the FBI. Not one that will be answered by a tape recorder." Sara called the number the operator gave her.

"FBI." The voice was male, young. He sounded sleepy.

"My name is Sara Hackett. I need to talk to the SAC on the Radoslaw kidnapping."

"Yes ma'am. One second. I'm connecting you." Sara heard the phone ringing. They get a plus for efficiency, she thought.

"John Rule. How can I help you?"

"I'm Sara, John. I think we should talk."

"What do you know about Paige Radoslaw?"

"I know who took her."

"We think you did."

"Why, because Cyril Radoslaw wound up dead in my bed with a bullet in his heart?"

"You just told me two of the three things we're holding back from the press. Two things only the killer would know."

A plus for efficiency, Sara thought, but a minus for brains. "You can't think I had anything to do with it."

"You set up the kidnapping because you knew your lover was going to terminate the relationship. And you killed him when he came to your house to demand that you let his daughter go. Tell me where you are so we can end this. It'll go easier on you if you do."

"What was he going to do with the condoms? Fuck me one last time?" She hung up. She'd probably just told him the third thing they were holding back. She should have told that idiot that Jerry told her about Radoslaw, but she ran her mouth before putting her brain in gear.

She sucked her lower lip between her teeth, gently chewing on it. How did Radoslaw get to her house so quickly? And why would Clay kill him? That didn't make sense. How could Clay collect from a dead man? Maybe he already had, but Sara doubted it. No way would Clay have the man come to his home to pay the ransom. But maybe Radoslaw came on his own, after all Clay and Jerry were supposed to be advising him on security. Maybe once he got there he figured it out, or maybe he figured it out earlier, either way, he must have confronted Clay and Clay must have killed him. It was the only thing that made sense.

But why would anyone try two kidnappings at once? That was just stupid. Clay had always been so conservative. He always checked out a problem from every possible angle. Either he was crazier than she thought or she was missing something.

"Problem?" Dottie asked when Sara handed the phone back.

"They think I did it all."

CHAPTER TWELVE

"QUIET." PAIGE POINTED to an open window. The lights were on inside. Guthrie and Rice were sitting at a round table. Smoking. They were looking away from the window, watching a television. Paige doubted they could see out with all the lights on inside, but she didn't want to take a chance.

"We can hide in the back of that old pickup." Kelly pointed to an aging pickup truck. The tires looked bald.

"No, it's too close. We gotta get farther away. Come on, stay between the car and them." She pulled Kelly back behind the cover.

"What are we gonna do?" Kelly grabbed her arm, squeezing hard.

"The road's pretty far and we'd be out in the open if they come out," Paige whispered. "Let's go that way." She pointed to a giant horse's head, bobbing up and down as it sucked oil from the earth.

"Come on. Run." Paige pulled the child after herself as she sprinted barefoot over open ground toward the giant machine creaking in the night, making the same noise she'd heard from the trunk. It was a long thirty second run. The longest thirty seconds of her life. She pulled Kelly behind her as she slid in the dirt and crawled behind the bobbing horse.

They lay on their bellies and looked back at the house. From where they were they couldn't see the men through the window anymore, but no one had come outside. No one knew they were gone. Not yet.

"It's a giant Snoopy." Kelly kind of smiled as she looked up at the big machine. "What is it?"

"An oil well."

"It doesn't look like an oil well. It looks like a big horse dressed up like Snoopy."

"I know where we are," Paige said. She'd stopped here last summer with her parents and Peter. Her dad had just bought a new car and he wanted to drive it up to San Francisco. It was a fun trip, a fun vacation. They'd stopped at the famous Nelson Ranch Inn for steaks. It was her father's all time favorite restaurant and hotel. Just south of the turn off for the hotel was a huge oil field. All of the oil horses were decorated. Some were cartoon characters, others animals or giant insects. Right now they were hiding under a giant bobbing Snoopy.

"Where? Where are we?" Kelly asked.

"A long way from home."

"How we gonna get back?" She snuggled up closer to Paige.

They lay under the moonshadow of the giant cartoon dog with their eyes glued to the light coming out of that window. Paige felt the little girl shiver and she couldn't tell where Kelly's shivers stopped and hers started.

"See the giant bee? Let's go there," Paige said.

"But it's farther from the road."

"Come on." She pulled Kelly up and once again they were dashing through the night toward an oil well. "Safe," she said, sliding like she was coming in to second base to break up a double play.

"Yeah, safe," Kelly echoed.

"We can't stay here. No place to hide. The moon's too bright." Paige looked up at the giant horse's head. It was painted with yellow and black stripes with two antenna sticking up toward the starlit sky with balls on the ends of them.

"Which one, the giraffe or zebra?" Kelly asked.

"The giraffe is farther and it's got a building next to it. Let's go there," Paige said.

"We're gone." Kelly took off.

Paige caught her easily, but didn't pass. It was a long run and the cool sand felt good on her bare feet. When they got to the bobbing giraffe they found a chain link fence around it. There was a building next to the well. It was just inside the fence.

"We're a long way from the road now," Paige said.

"A long way."

"Yeah, a long way from that house, too."

"Long way from the house, too."

"But we can't stay," Paige said. "If we climb the fence to hide behind the giraffe we'll be sitting ducks."

"Yeah, sitting ducks," Kelly said.

Paige studied the fence and the building. "If I can climb to the top of that fence, I could pull myself up to the top of the building. Then maybe I could pull you up. We could hide there till morning."

"You wanna?" Kelly said.

"They'd never ever think we climbed up there."

"Okay." Kelly looked up at the roof. "It's high. Sure you can pull me up?"

"I can try." Paige went to the fence. She missed her shoes as she stuck a foot in the chain link. It hurt. She grabbed toward the top of it and pulled herself up. The fence was about six feet high, another three to the top of the building.

"It's hard to balance without my shoes." She held her hands next to the building and worked herself up till she was standing. The roof was shoulder high. She bent her legs and pushed up. She pulled herself up onto the roof without any trouble. "Okay, now you."

"Coming. Like climbing the fence at school."

"What grade you in?" Paige asked.

"Third. I'm only seven, but I'm smart. I skipped first."

"Wow, skipped first grade. I didn't know you could."

"You can." Kelly scrabbled up the fence. Standing on the top of it, the top of her head was even with the roof.

"Give me your hands."

Kelly held them up. Paige got on her knees, took Kelly's arms in a Viking grip and pulled her up onto the roof. "They'll never find us up here," Kelly said.

"Only problem is that it doesn't look like a lot of people come around here."

"They gotta come to check on the animals."

"You mean the wells?" Paige said.

"Yeah."

"But do they come every day?"

"I hope," Kelly said.

"Me too."

Again they were on their bellies. They scooted to the edge of the roof. They could see the house off in the distance. It looked small from where they were, not dangerous at all, but Paige knew better. Guthrie, the man with the beady eyes that looked right through you, was inside there. And he'd tried to kill her.

It was going to be a long night.

"How long were you in the trunk?" Paige asked.

"You were there first," Kelly said. "They had me tied up in some house by the airport. It was real close to the runway. I know 'cuz I kept hearing planes landing. It sounded like they were coming right down on top of me. They were gone for a long time today. When they got back Guthrie picked me up and dropped me next to you in the trunk. For the longest time I thought you were dead. I couldn't hear you breathing 'cuz of the noise the car was making. Then you kicked me. Boy that hurt."

"Sorry."

"It's okay. I know you didn't mean it."

"We were in there for about five hours. No joke, we could've died."

"You almost did. Guthrie tried to kill you. I saw."

"Yeah. It doesn't make any sense. Kidnappers are

supposed to hold you for ransom." They were quiet for a few seconds, then Paige asked, "How did they catch you?"

"I just got back from a vacation with my uncle's mom. I wasn't home fifteen minutes when Rice walks right in the front door and grabs me from in front of the television. I screamed, but it didn't do any good, 'cuz my Uncle Clay was at the store getting ice cream. They took me to that house and tied me up. They only untied me so I could go to the bathroom."

"Did they feed you?"

"McDonald's. That wasn't so bad. I like Mickey D's. But I was never worried. Next week my aunt comes back from Australia. She woulda got me free."

"Your aunt?"

"She's a race car driver. She can do anything. Soon's she's back, these guys are in real trouble."

"But how could she find you?"

"She'd figure it out. She loves me. 'Course now she doesn't have to, 'cuz we escaped."

"We're not out of the woods yet."

"Pretty close."

Paige looked across the cold, dry ground to the ghostly light caused by the flickering television. Were they ever going to come out to the car and check on them? Maybe they should have gone for the road. They could have been there by now.

*　*　*

On the television, Rambo and the colonel were facing off the whole Russian Army. Guthrie had his face glued to the screen like he was a priest and it was the altar. Rice couldn't believe it. God sure short-changed the big man when he passed out the brains.

Rice got up and went to the kitchen. He opened a cabinet next to the refrigerator and took out a pack of beef jerky. There was a forty-five automatic on the shelf above it, next to the coffee. Guthrie had guns all over the house. A real Rambo. The dumb fuck.

"You want a beer?" Rice closed the cabinet and opened the fridge.

"Yeah." Guthrie never talked when he could grunt.

The dog barked. Rice looked down at the mutt. Why a guy like Guthrie would have such a stupid animal was beyond him. The man was so big. The toy poodle so small. Ugly fucking thing. Fluffy white with a shampooed poodle cut and a pink collar. Rice wanted to step on it.

The phone rang.

It rang again.

"You wanna get that?" Guthrie called out from the living room. Of course Guthrie couldn't answer it. He was splayed out in front of the idiot box, worshiping.

"You're closer." Rice opened the refrigerator and pulled out two Red Stripes. Jamaican beer. Nigger beer. He almost couldn't drink it. But when you're thirsty, you're thirsty, nigger beer or no.

"This is my favorite part." Fuck, the whole God damn movie was his favorite part. Rambo, a real idiot. No wonder Guthrie got off on him. Probably whacked his pud to him.

Rice took a pull on his beer, handed the other one to Guthrie, then picked up the phone. "Yeah."

"Gimme Guthrie." It was Jerry.

"Can't talk now. Rambo's on."

"You're kidding?"

"Hey, he's your brother."

"You talking about me?" Guthrie turned from the set.

"No," Rice said and Guthrie turned back to Rambo.

"Maybe using him was a mistake," Jerry said.

"Yeah, well it'll work out."

"We got a new problem. We need both girls alive and in good shape. No marks, no bruises."

"I thought with all the TV, we were gonna dump the older one."

"The old lady says she'll pay, but she has her own demands."

"Fuck her. Tell her we'll kill the kid."

"I did."

"What'd she say?"

"Her way or the highway."

"Tough old broad. What's she want?"

"Both kids."

"How'd she know we had the other one?"

"How do I know? She knows. She's not going to the cops. But she says two or none. If we can't cough up Paige Radoslaw, she says she doesn't want her own grandkid."

"What'd you say?"

"I told her the price was double. Two kids, twice as much. Sounded fair to me."

"Fuck. Me too."

"Sounded fair to her, too. She's paying one million cash money. That's two hundred and fifty for each of us. We're almost home. I'll be up tomorrow for the phone call."

"What phone call?"

"She wants to hear their sweet voices. She don't

hear them, she don't pay. I'll come up with my cellular, just in case she gets cute. They can't trace that."

"Then what?"

"Sunday morning we make the exchange at LAX."

"Now you're kidding."

"No, you just make sure those brats are clean and presentable."

"How we gonna do it?"

"You take the kids to the walkover bridge from the United terminal to the third floor parking area across the street. She's at one end with the cash in a briefcase. I'm behind her. She sees you and the kids on the other side, she hands me the case. I check it. If it's okay, I nod and you fade into the woodwork."

"If it's not?"

"Kill the kids."

"Fuck. How do I get away?"

"You don't. It's what you wanted, remember? A chance to go out in style. If we make it, you spend the rest of your days in the sun. If not, you die in a prison hospital. That's the deal. But I wouldn't worry about it. She's gonna pay."

"She better."

"I'll call tomorrow." The line went dead.

"We gotta get the kids out of the car." Rice put the phone down and picked a leather jacket off the back of the chair he'd been sitting in. He slipped it on over his dirty tee shirt.

"What for?"

"Because your brother said so, that's what for."

Guthrie pushed his chair back and stood, muscles rippling through his tight tank top. "I killed the big one." He said it with a flat voice, like he didn't care.

"What?"

"You said we weren't gonna need her anymore."

"No, I said I didn't think we were gonna need her anymore. I was wrong. We need her."

"Then it's your fault." Guthrie grabbed the keys from the table and started for the door.

Rice followed him out to the car. He stood back as the big man opened the trunk.

"They're gone," Guthrie said.

Rice stared into the empty trunk. "Don't look like you killed her too good."

* * *

"They know we're gone now," Kelly said.

"Yeah, they do." Paige shivered in the cold. She kept her eyes on the two men as they opened the trunk. The shock of discovery over, they appeared to be arguing. What were they going to do now?

"Looks like it might rain," Kelly said. "That'll make it harder for them to find us."

"Rain, how can you tell?"

"Rain clouds coming in from over there." She pointed. "Dark ones. See how you can't see any stars out that way. It's 'cuz the clouds are blocking them out."

"How do you know this?"

"My aunt Sara's got a sailboat. She takes me out on it all the time. She's teaching me weather, and a lot of other stuff."

"Your aunt the race car driver?"

"Yeah, the one that's gonna make those men wish they were dead."

"What's your uncle do?"

"He's a cop."

"Then he should be the one rescuing us."

"Should, but he doesn't love me. He pretends, to make Sara happy, but I know. I don't think he'd miss me much if I was gone. Your parents love you?"

"I guess. Sometimes my dad acts like we belong to him. You know, like we're only his children and not our own selves."

"So then you must have a brother or a sister?"

"Yeah, a younger brother, Peter. They almost got him, too. But he got away. Look! They're going back inside."

"What do you think they're gonna do?"

"Don't know. They're coming out. Can you see what he's got?"

"No."

Paige watched as they got in the car. "Duck." Bright light flashed from the passenger window. "It's a searchlight."

"Can they see us up here?" Kelly said.

"I don't think so. Not if we keep flat."

Paige picked her head up and peered out at the car. Rice gunned the engine like he was a kid at a stoplight ready to race. It sounded like a lion roaring into the night. Kelly snuggled up tight against her as Guthrie played the light over the dark ground.

"I bet he wants to kill you again," Kelly said. "Then he's gonna kill me."

"Not if they can't find us."

"And they won't find us up here. Will they?"

"No. We're safe here."

Rice floored the car. The engine screamed as the tires spun, throwing dirt and rocks aside as the car shot out toward the road. The searchlight was so much brighter than the headlights. If they'd gone that way they would have been caught for sure. There was no way to hide from that light. It turned the dark in front of it into day.

"They're going away." Kelly snuggled even closer. She was shivering. Paige put an arm around her. "They're going, right? They're not coming back, are they?"

"I don't know." Paige felt every tiny quiver as the little girl shook. "I don't think they're gonna give up real easy."

The car was at the road now. It stopped. Guthrie got out. He checked both ways with the light. Then he ran it over the ground.

"What's he doing?" Kelly said.

"I don't know?"

"Tracks. He looking for our tracks."

"No. You have to be an Indian or something to be able to do that?"

"You think?" Kelly said.

"Yeah, absolutely."

"I hope my aunt gets here before they find us," Kelly said.

"They won't find us."

Guthrie got back in the car. Paige heard the door slam even from where she was, because he'd slammed it hard. He was mad.

"Look at the sky," Kelly said. Paige looked up. "If we were at sea I'd say a squall was coming soon." Half the sky was covered with the slow moving clouds. "If it rains all our tracks will be washed away. Then even the best Indian in the world wouldn't be able to find us."

"You know a lot for a kid," Paige said.

"That's why I skipped first grade."

"Oh, yeah."

The car started moving again. Coming back. Kelly snuggled close to Paige again. It was getting louder as it got closer and once more Paige thought of a lion. A lion coming to gobble up the giant giraffe they were hiding next to.

"Oh no! They're gonna check the animals," Kelly said. The car slowed at Snoopy, that searchlight making it glow in the dark as Rice drove the car around it. Then they took off toward the bobbing bee and it was lit up for a few seconds as they checked it out. "They're gonna come here next."

"Stay down," Paige warned. But they went to the zebra instead. Paige watched as they lit up the oil well. The bobbing zebra seemed to be grinning at her. The car stopped for a few seconds. Guthrie got out. Paige saw a small shed by the pumping well. It might be possible to hide there, so Guthrie was checking it out. He was being thorough. He got back in the car.

"Now they're coming here. We gotta be real quiet."

"Quiet," Kelly whispered back.

"We gotta move back to the middle." Paige tugged on Kelly's arm and they scooted away from the edge. She trembled as the car approached, real loud now. Louder than the squeaking well. Louder than her thumping heart. They were in the center of the roof now. She rolled over onto her back. Kelly did too. Over half the stars were gone, and the clouds were moving toward the moon. The air smelled fresh and crisp. Paige felt an electric kind of dry tingle in the air.

The car skidded to a stop below. Paige imagined

them right next to the building. She didn't dare poke her head over the edge to look. She didn't dare breathe. She heard a door open. Another. She bit her lower lip. Kelly grasped her hand and squeezed. She squeezed back.

"Fuck." It was Rice. He sounded mad.

"I don't know how they done it." Guthrie was mad too. It didn't take a brain to figure it out. "Jerry and Clay are gonna be so pissed." Kelly super-squeezed her hand. She winced, almost crying out. She squeezed back and Kelly eased off some of the pressure.

"I gotta pee," Rice said.

"You always gotta pee."

Paige heard the zipper sound, then the splashing sound. He was probably peeing right next to where they'd been standing a little while ago. The splashing stopped. She heard the zipper sound again.

"I don't wanna be here tomorrow if we don't get them back," Rice said.

"Jerry will kill me," Guthrie said and Kelly tightened her grip again.

"I got friends in Mexico," Rice said.

Guthrie grunted. A door slammed. Then the other. The car charged away. Paige rolled back onto her stomach and crawled sniper style over to the edge. They were headed back toward the road.

"They're going."

"Yeah, to Mexico," Kelly said.

"He didn't say that exactly."

"Yeah. They're outta here. We made it, got away from the kidnappers, but we're not safe yet. Not by a long shot."

"What do you mean?" Paige asked.

"Guthrie said that Jerry and Clay are gonna be mad."

"Yeah, he said they're gonna be pissed."

"I'm not allowed to swear," Kelly said.

"Okay, mad."

"Yeah, mad. It's scary 'cuz I know who they are. Remember I said, my Uncle Clay's a cop. His partner's name is Jerry," Kelly said.

"And Jerry and Clay are the names of the two cops my dad hired when he fired the security company that was supposed to be guarding us. I should have thought about it when you said your uncle's name was Clay."

"We gotta get outta here," Kelly said. "They're cops and they're smart, not like those two stupids. When they get up here and start looking, they won't give up. They'll find us."

Paige saw the taillights off in the distance. Then they turned and were gone. "It looks like they got on the highway."

"We gotta split."

"Okay. I'll go down first." Paige scooted over to where the fence was, turned around and hung her legs over the side. "I can't find it." She lowered herself a little more. "Got it." Her bare foot was on the top of the fence. She helped Kelly down. Then she eased herself to the ground. It was cold to her feet.

"It's a long way to the road and you don't have any shoes. Want me to go and come back with help?"

"No."

"Good, 'cuz I really didn't want to go by myself anyway. It's a desperation moon."

"What?"

"When the clouds cover it all up except for only a

little hole for it to desperately peek through, it's called a desperation moon. My dad told me that."

Paige looked up. "That's nice. I like it."

Kelly squeezed her hand. "It reminds me of him."

"Let's get started." They walked. It seemed like forever to Paige before they got to the interstate, but it was probably only ten or fifteen minutes. There was a drainage ditch between them and the highway and a chain link fence on the other side of the ditch.

"I don't wanna go down there," Kelly said.

Paige looked down into the dark ditch. "Me either."

"Can you walk any more?"

"Sure." Her feet hurt, but not that much. She saw where the kidnapper's taillights disappeared. That must be the overpass by Nelson Ranch. It was a long way, but she'd walk awful far to keep from going down in that ditch. "Let's go."

About a half hour later they were approaching the overpass. There was a motel on their side of the highway, a giant truck stop gas station and a small store with a deli Paige remembered. All of a sudden she was hungry. "You got any money?"

"No." Kelly said. "I did, eleven bucks, but Guthrie took it away from me."

"The Nelson Ranch is across the highway. My dad stays there a lot. They'll help us." She led Kelly to the overpass. They stopped in the center for a second and looked at the cars below. They looked south. Taillights traveling to Los Angeles. Headlights going to San Francisco. She took Kelly's hand. "Come on."

There was a drainage ditch on this side of the interstate, too. Paige imagined trolls and monsters down there. She craved the warmth of the hotel.

"Guthrie. Look!" Rice shouted.

"Oh no," Kelly said. "It's them."

CHAPTER THIRTEEN

"DOTTIE, YOU WANNA STEP into my parlor for a minute? Bring your friend." The speaker was a coffee-with-a lot-of-cream colored woman. She was leaning out the passenger window of the camper parked in front of Jake's van.

"Hi, Jane. It's been awhile." Dottie turned toward the woman.

"Better get in the truck," Jane said.

"When my girl talks, better jump." Jake opened the back door of the camper. Dottie climbed in. Sara followed.

"Make yourselves comfortable," Jane said. "I've

just been watching television."

"Nice," Sara said. The camper was one of those that went over the cab. The bed was up there. It looked comfortable. Jane was sitting at a table, sort of like a salon table in a sailboat or a booth in a restaurant.

"So you got tired of sleeping in the van?" Dottie sat on the bench seat against the wall and scooted in next to Jane.

"Yeah, I finally put my foot down and told Jake if he didn't buy me a camper or a small RV, I wouldn't come out anymore. It got old sleeping on top of those hard tools in that cold van. Besides, we got lots of tools now, so we can take two spaces."

Sara sat on a sofa type affair opposite the table. She wondered if it was called a settee in a camper like it was in a boat. Jake came in after her and closed the door. The inside was cozy. She smelled bacon. The twelve volt overhead light was bright enough so she could see everything, but not bright enough to read by.

"What's up, honey?" Jake sat next to Sara as he looked at his wife across the table.

"I just finished recording this. I was gonna call Jake in to see it and who do I see out there, but the devil and her sidekick themselves." She picked up a remote and pushed the power button. A television mounted high and to the right of the back door came on.

"This is Nick Nesbitt with the latest on the Radoslaw kidnapping and murder." It was a headshot of the newscaster in the studio. He was wearing his famous blue blazer and he looked smug with his shock of white hair, like one of those right wing evangelists who hide behind the bible.

"Earlier this evening we had the exclusive live coverage of the Paige Radoslaw kidnapping." The picture cut away to what Sara remembered earlier. The cameraman groping in the rain, looking for the voice crying out for help. After the replay of the Peter Radoslaw piece they cut back to the studio and Nesbitt.

"This reporter has learned that the police now have a suspect in the Radoslaw murder."

"My God," Sara said. The camera cut to her house in Huntington Beach. Jerry said that most of it had been saved, but it looked like a burnt out hulk to her. Not a shadow of what it once was.

"Earlier tonight Cyril Radoslaw was found murdered in this house. The killer started the fire in an attempt to destroy the evidence, but fast work by neighbors and the Huntington Beach Fire Department saved most of it. The body was discovered in a back bedroom, untouched by the fire."

"My house," Sara said.

"This woman, race car driver, Sara Hackett," Sara's picture came up on the screen, it was her passport photo, "wife of Huntington Beach Police Officer, Clay Tredway, is the number one suspect in both the kidnapping and the murder. This reporter has learned that Cyril Radoslaw was in the habit of slipping away from his security to carry on his many love affairs. The police are operating under the assumption that Radoslaw tried to break off the relationship and Miss Hackett engineered the kidnapping of his children in retaliation."

"How can they think that?" Sara said.

"There's more," Jane said.

"When Radoslaw came to Hackett's home to confront her, she killed him, set the house on fire and fled. Dozens of witnesses saw her leave the scene of the crime."

"They also saw me drive up and discover the house already on fire," Sara said.

"Miss Hackett is believed to be at large with this woman," Dottie's picture covered the screen, "Dorothy O'Brien. They are driving a vintage 1956 two door Ford sedan. Both women have handguns registered in their names. They are believed to be armed and dangerous. Should you see these women do not try and apprehend. Call 911."

Jane hit the power button and the screen went dark.

"We fooled 'em with the car," Dottie said.

"Yeah." Sara inhaled the bacon smell. She was hungry.

"Hey, Dottie, I thought I was a criminal, but I don't come close to your league," Jake said. "Murder, kidnapping. They are gonna throw away the key."

"How could they dare say I was having an affair?" Sara said. "They shouldn't be allowed to say that. There should be laws."

"Ain't no laws when it comes to the press disrespecting a person's privacy. It's news. You're famous now. You got no rights. I'm assuming you didn't do it, or you wouldn't be here with this nice old lady."

"Who you calling old?" Dottie cut him with a look.

"Sorry." Jake smiled. "So you two young ladies are in a mess of trouble and you come to the swap meet to hide out. Pretty slick. Cops never gonna look here, but what about tomorrow?"

"I wanna know about the kidnapping. What about the girl?" Jane asked.

"More than one girl," Sara said. And she told them all about it. Everything from when she found the pictures that didn't belong to her until when they narrowly escaped from the police at Dottie's.

"So what do you think is on that other roll of pictures?" Jake said.

"I don't even know if the other roll is with the second batch of photos. I never got to see all the first batch. But it's the only lead I can think of to get Kelly back. It's so frustrating, because I can't do anything about it till tomorrow at 10:00. And now, with my picture in front of the whole world, it'll take a miracle for me to get the photos out of there."

"Someone else could pick them up for you." Jane leaned forward, elbows on the table as she stared into Sara's eyes. She reminded Sara of a big cat, sleek and ready to strike.

"My name's on the receipt. It's a pretty famous name right now? If the owner saw it, he might call the cops. Spider wouldn't, though."

"Spider? Spider who?" Jake said.

"He's the kid that works at the photo store. He lives on my block. He's a good kid. My friend." She stopped for a second. Then, "Hey, I just thought of something. He was there, at my house, trying to put out the fire when I drove up. He knows I couldn't have started it."

"Sure you could've," Jake said. "You could've started it. Left, then come back after it got going so the neighbors would see you drive up. That's probably the assumption the police are going on."

"Spider wouldn't think that. If he could, he'd hand over the pictures and not tell anyone."

"If that's the case," Jake said, "then he and you, and now us, are the only people that know about them."

"Yeah. I should get them before anyone finds out. I could call him. Maybe he's got a key. Maybe I could get them tonight."

"Doesn't the mall close?" Jake said.

"The stores do, but not the mall. At least not till the last movie lets out. They've got security guards. I've seen them. They keep you out of the mall after the movies empty out. You know, they direct you to the closest exit."

"So even if your friend Spider has a key, we couldn't get the photos till 10:00 tomorrow," Dottie said.

"Maybe if we created a diversion," Sara said.

"Now you're talking my kind of ball game."

"Jake, you shouldn't get involved."

"Come on, Jane. It's a friend of Dottie's. Besides, the cops are messing with her. I hate that. You know I hate that."

"You just hate the cops."

"Yeah, that too." He smiled, teeth gleaming. "I admit it. I don't like the cops. Never met one wasn't a pushy son of a bitch." He turned to Sara, "You get that key from your friend Spider and we'll get those pictures for you."

"You can break in there and get them?"

"No, you're gonna do that. I'm gonna create the diversion."

"Oh, Lord," Jane said. "Not that."

Jake handed Sara his cellphone. "Call your friend

Spider."

Sara punched the numbers. He answered on the first ring. "Spider, it's Sara, can you talk?"

"I'll take it in my room." She heard him shout out, "It's Carlie. I'm gonna go upstairs and talk." A few seconds later he was back on the line. "I'm here."

"So that's your girl? Carlie Wilson?"

"Yeah, neat, huh?"

"Pretty neat," Sara said. "Lisa's gonna be broken hearted."

"Kinda shitty, the trouble you're in."

"Yeah. You can help."

"Anything. Say it."

"The guys that took that girl, Paige Radoslaw. They got Kelly, too."

"Oh, shit."

"Yeah. It's real bad and it gets worse. Clay was in on it."

"Double shit."

"Remember those pictures? I think there might be a clue on them. Maybe. I hope. I need them."

"I got a key, but we got a new owner and he's real paranoid. He put in one of those alarms last week. You know the kind that screams so loud it wants to bust your eardrums. He doesn't know about my key or he woulda wanted it back."

"I need that key."

"Meet me at the mall. I'll be in the pizza place. They stay open till midnight. I'll sneak out. Take me maybe twenty minutes to get there."

"Are you gonna get in trouble?"

"Sure. See ya." He hung up.

"Time?" Sara handed the phone back to Jake.

"Ten forty-five."

"We gotta hurry."

"We can do this." Jake stood.

"Just come back to me, baby," Jane said.

"Hey, I'm dark as oil and twice as slick. Ain't no one gonna catch me, 'cept maybe ol' General Sherman."

"He loves you." Dottie scooted out from the booth. Jake was at the door.

"Yeah, last time you were out here he damn near licked me to death. You tell him to keep his tongue in his mouth." He stopped, looked at Dottie. "And I ain't riding in the back seat with him. I'm driving. Gimme the keys." Sara handed them over.

He slid behind the wheel. Dottie got in back with the dog and Sara rode shotgun. He drove the car like one used to driving fast on the street. He pulled into a convenience store parking lot. "Get three bottles of something. Quart or liter size. Glass bottles."

"Me?" Sara said. "What about my picture on television?"

"Ain't nobody gonna recognize you from that photo. 'Sides, ain't no television in that store, so no way would that idiot kid behind the counter know you."

"You come in here a lot?"

"On occasion. It'll be okay, don't worry, I'll be right here, with the motor running."

Sara got out of the car. She didn't ask why he wanted glass bottles. She kind of knew. In the store, she caught a distorted look at herself in the high circular mirror that was supposed to foil shoplifters. She frowned. Her long hair, fine and usually flowing, was stringy and damp. She needed a shower. And she had bags under her eyes. She needed rest. She hadn't had either in over twenty-four hours.

Still looking in the mirror, she raised an arm and smelled herself. "Yuck." The kid behind the counter laughed. Any other time she'd have been embarrassed.

She turned away from the mirror and walked over to the cooler. She passed a rack of bakery goods on the way and picked up three packages of cinnamon rolls packed in cellophane. She was hungry. She had to get something in a quart bottle. Milk would do, plus milk and rolls would kill the grinding in her stomach.

No milk in glass. Only plastic. OJ too, plastic only. Nothing in glass in the cooler. Didn't they use it anymore? She looked away from the cooler. There was a wine rack on the other side of the store. At least they didn't use plastic for everything. Not yet.

Still holding the cinnamon rolls, she made her way across the store. She picked up a bottle of California white zin and was reaching for another when she realized they wouldn't work. They were corked and she didn't have a cork screw. She could buy one, but a screw top would be easier. She put the zin back and picked up three bottles of something much cheaper. A so-called fruity red with a screw top. Wino wine.

She grabbed another quick look at herself in the overhead mirror on the way to the register and froze. Two cops were coming through the door. One black, one white. Shit. She was toast. No. Keep cool. She edged back, turned away from the mirror and started down an aisle. She had to get rid of the wine. A woman with three bottles of screw top garbage was sure to draw their interest. Especially the way she looked, all tired and haggard.

She hid the wine and rolls behind a box of Wheaties.

"Pack of Marlboros," the white one said. Good, they just stopped for cigarettes. Maybe they'd leave quick.

"Sure thing," the kid behind the register said. He had a squeaky voice, high like a girl's. It grated on her like chalk screeching across a blackboard. She tore her eyes away from the front counter and stared at the Wheaties box.

"I gotta get some bread, promised the wife," the black one said. He had a voice like a tuba. "Where is it?" She imagined the kid pointing. Her hands were shaking. Bread, where was the bread? Shit. Behind her. She picked up a box of some kind of chocolate cereal and pretended to read the package. She couldn't think of anything else to do.

The cop came up the aisle. He stopped right next to her. She felt him sigh as he bent over and picked up a loaf of bread. Then she felt his breath on the back of her neck as he looked over her shoulder. This was it. The ball game. She was going to jail.

"Won't find no fiber in that one. Just sugar and cardboard."

"No, guess not." She laughed, hoping it didn't sound forced.

"Got kids, huh?" he said.

"Yeah, they won't eat anything else."

"I make mine eat the stuff with fiber in it. It's for their own good. Let 'em slide early and you pay later. Besides, I like knowing they're not eating all that junk."

"Maybe you're right," Sara said. She sounded

hollow to herself, like she was talking from in a tunnel. She hoped he didn't notice. She put the chocolate cereal back and reached for the Cheerios. She started to pick it up.

"That's just as bad. Try this." He plucked a box of some high fiber crap from the shelf and handed it to her.

"Thanks." She was quaking inside. She'd almost uncovered the wine.

"All part of the job, community service." He looked her right in the eyes. Couldn't he see the fear there? He tipped his fingers to his hat, like a movie salute, then took his high fiber brown bread to the counter. Apparently he didn't watch television. He paid and they left.

She took a second to get herself together and realized that she'd been more afraid than she had to be. All the time he'd been standing there, she'd been seeing Clay. She felt the sweat dripping under her arms. Clay had turned her into an abused woman and somehow she'd failed to notice. Her love had been freely offered, but he'd taken her self respect, too. Would she ever get it back?

She moved the Wheaties, picked up the wine, but left the rolls. She made for the register. The clerk gave her a look she didn't like when she paid. She couldn't blame him. "It's cold out tonight," she said, giving him his money's worth.

"Yeah, cold." He handed her the change. She couldn't wait to get outside. She pushed through the door, waved to Jake and Dottie, turned and went to the side of the store, where she unscrewed the tops and emptied the wine out onto the parking lot.

"You ain't so dumb," Jake said when she got back

to the car.

"Figured you didn't want to do it at the gas station."

"Cops scare you?"

"No," she lied. "I've got a high pressure job."

"You really a race car driver?" Jake pulled out of the parking lot.

"Really am. Me and my sister. We race in the roughest places in the world. Off road racing."

"So you got what it takes?"

"I like to think so."

"Well, we're gonna find out tonight." Jake pulled into a Texaco on the other side of the street.

Sara listened while Jake told the attendant that he'd picked up the two ladies down the road. They'd run out of gas, " 'cuz women never checked their gauges." Sara bit her tongue and kept silent as Jake paid for the can and the gas.

"That boy, Spider," Jake said as he pulled out of the station, "he's taking a big risk for you, why would he do that?"

"We're friends."

"That's it?"

"I don't have many friends. I can count 'em on my fingers, but the ones I have are real. A couple old. A couple young. My sister. Dottie. Now, maybe you, we'll see. When a friend asks for help, you help. No choice, because a friend wouldn't ask unless she really needed. Spider will be there for me, because he knows I'd be there for him."

"So how much do you trust him?"

"Did you hear me ask him if he believed in me?"

"No."

"Did you hear me tell him I was innocent?"

"No."

"That's how much I trust him. All the way. And that's how much he believes in me."

"You're a complicated person."

"Not so complicated. Simple really. I love my niece. I'm terrified for her and Paige Radoslaw. I want more than anything for them to be free. I'd give anything. My life."

He turned onto the freeway, flooring it as they went up the ramp and they settled into silence as the Taurus chewed up the miles.

"Stay," Dottie said as they approached the pizza parlor. Sherman sat. "He loves this place," she said. "Pepperoni's his favorite. I hope they haven't closed the kitchen yet."

Jake held the door and the women entered. Sara wondered how often they changed the sawdust on the floor. It looked dirty. Spider was sitting in the booth farthest from the door, his back against the wall. A regular gunfighter.

"I was getting worried you wouldn't make it in time. Last movie is over at 12:05. Fifteen minutes. Then they lock the mall."

"Darn, Sherman doesn't get his pizza, he'll be so disappointed," Dottie said.

"Okay, I'm gone." Jake dangled the car keys. "Give me five minutes to do what I have to. Let's hope the alarms are loud. I'll be back here at midnight straight up, engine running. That gives you five minutes. Enough time?" He was looking at Spider.

Spider nodded.

Sara looked at the Pepsi clock on the wall. The second hand seemed to take forever as it wound around it.

A waitress came over to the table. "Sorry, we're closing."

"We're leaving in just a minute. We're waiting for someone."

"From the movie?" the waitress said.

"Yeah," Sara lied.

"Just didn't want you to think you could eat."

"No problem," Sara said, but she was talking to the woman's back. The exchange took less than half a minute. Three to go.

"We should go stand by the entrance," Dottie said. "Just in case it starts a little early."

"Gonna start a fire?" Spider was no dummy.

"Yeah," Sara said.

"Cool."

Dottie led the way out of the restaurant. "No pizza today, Sherman." Sara caught the dog's eyes reflected from an overhead streetlight and was sure she saw disappointed there. "Come," Dottie said. The dog snapped to her heel as they walked to the mall entrance.

"Should be pretty quick now," Sara said. A bell started ringing in the distance, then an alarm.

"Let's do it." Spider banged through the doors, Sara running behind.

A couple of teenagers came out of the theater early. She saw the backs of two security guards as they charged down the mall, headed for the far side. Spider sprinted past the theaters and hung a right past the pet store. He was fast, but Sara stayed with him.

"Okay, we gotta be quick. The pictures are behind the counter." Roll down bars blocked the entrance to the photo store. There were no doors. No glass. He dropped to his knees and inserted a key into a lock by the floor.

"Hurry."

"Sometimes I gotta fiddle with it."

Sara was jumping. He was taking forever. The alarm was way over on the other side of the mall, but she could hear it good. She looked back the way they'd come. No one there. They had this part of the mall to themselves. But not for long. Pretty quick people were gonna be running all over the place.

"Hurry."

"Maybe he changed the lock."

"Shit."

"Got it." He turned the key and stood up. "Almost there." He grabbed the roll up bars and pulled them up about three feet. Immediately a siren wailed. Louder than any police car she'd ever heard. Louder than the Rolling Stones at the Anaheim Convention Center. Louder than God.

He dropped to the floor, slid under the bars and dashed behind the cash register.

"Got 'em!" He had a yellow bag in his hand. He ran toward the bars. For a second she thought he was going to run into them, but he dropped like he was sliding into home and slid under.

"Hey, you!" Sara turned. It was a security guard and he had a gun out. "Hands up or I shoot!" He was young. Mid twenties. A cop wannabe. Sara believed him.

Something roared from behind the guard. He turned as Sherman flew through the air like a wraith. The gun went off, the bullet going wild as the giant dog barreled into him. The guard hit the floor. Hard. His gun went flying.

"Good dog!" Dottie screamed. Sara charged after

Dottie and Spider. The great dog stood above the guard, giving Sara time to make her escape. "Sherman, come!" Dottie yelled when Sara was at the corner by the pet store. The dog released the guard and sped through the mall toward his mistress.

"What's going on?" Someone said. The theater was emptying out now. The mall was filling with kids curious about all the alarms going off.

Spider burst into the crowd, Sara, Dottie and Sherman in his wake. He punched through the exit doors, holding them open for the women and the dog. The white Ford Taurus was waiting in the parking lot right outside the doors, engine running, both passenger and back door open. Sara jumped into the back seat, Sherman piled in after her. Dottie slammed the back door shut, hopped in the shotgun seat and pulled the door closed after herself.

"Here you go!" Spider tossed the photos in the window and flashed Sara the thumbs up sign as Jake gunned the accelerator. The rear tires smoked, caught and they raced out of the parking lot.

CHAPTER FOURTEEN

"RUN!" PAIGE GRABBED KELLY'S HAND and started back toward the interstate. Guthrie was back there, coming like a train. She didn't want to get caught again. They'd come too far.

Late night travelers and truckers were tunneling through the night below the overpass. So close, but way too far away. The overpass meant capture. "This way!" She jerked Kelly along with her as she jumped into the ditch that ran alongside the interstate. It was like a dark tunnel. She didn't want to go in there, but it was a chance. Better than none.

"Over here." Guthrie's voice thundered through

the night, easily heard above the river of cars and trucks speeding by on the highway. "They're down there."

"Stop," Paige whispered. Kelly did. "Look." She pointed up. The clouds were moving fast now. They blacked out the bright moon. She put her mouth to Kelly's ear. "This is a pretty wide ditch. He could walk right by us and not see. We should stay still."

"Why?"

"They might think we're more up ahead than we are. If they go up there looking for us we can go back and get help at the hotel."

"I wanna run," Kelly whispered.

Lightning lit up the sky. Thunder cracked. For an instant Paige saw the stark terror in Kelly's eyes, then it went dark again. The girls dropped to the ground.

"He's coming," Kelly said. "I know it."

As if hearing her, Guthrie called out, "You can't hide forever." His voice was a deep throated sound, a cross between a raspy roar and a baby's cry that brought the fright rushing full force into Kelly's whisper.

"Come on, quick." She tugged on Paige's arm.

Paige hesitated. It made more sense to hide and be quiet. If she had stayed still back on the freeway before Guthrie hit her, they never would have found her and she wouldn't be here now. And if they'd stayed on top of that building, they wouldn't be here either. It seemed like every time she stopped hiding, she got in trouble. Besides, he couldn't see down here. He couldn't know they were here. There was nothing up ahead except cattle pens a good quarter mile away. The sensible thing to do was hide. He'd leave after a few minutes and they could try to get back to the hotel.

Lightning again. Thunder again. The heavens opened up. Sheeting rain pelted them, turning the dirt sides of the ditch into gooey mud. Almost instantly the girls were soaked. Paige pushed herself into a sitting position, straining her eyes, trying to see out in the dark.

No sign of Guthrie or Rice.

She scooped up a handful of thick mud. Didn't soldiers wipe it on their faces so the enemy couldn't see them at night? Camouflage. She rubbed it over her arms. "Come on," she whispered. "Cover yourself with the mud." Kelly grabbed a fist full of the stuff and started rubbing it over her white tee shirt. The kid didn't need to be told twice.

"I won't hurt you," Guthrie called out. Yeah sure. What a dumb thing to say. Did he think they were gonna give themselves up?

"Get the car. We'll use the light." It was Rice.

"Okay, we gotta get outta here," Paige said. She stood, pulling Kelly up with her. She bent to her ear. "Try to be quiet till we get a little ways away. They can't drive alongside the ditch forever. There's cattle pens up ahead. There will be people there."

As suddenly as it started the rain stopped. Paige looked up to a ceiling of black. There were no stars. It was so dark she couldn't see the clouds. She could barely make out Kelly's face and she was right next to her. She pulled Kelly along after herself as she moved down the ditch. Mud squished between her toes and the ditch seemed to be getting deeper the farther they went. Would they be able to crawl up out of it?

She looked back and saw the light. "Down." They dropped into the mud. "Don't look at it." The light played over them and moved on. "They're way back there. I don't think they can get the light any closer."

"Listen," Kelly said. "Someone's coming."

"Quick against the side, cover your face."

Kelly leaned against the vee of the ditch and Paige started scooping up mud and covering her with it. She worked fast and soon Kelly blended in with the muddy wall. Then she started putting it all over herself.

"Quiet," Kelly whispered. "He's getting closer."

Paige crossed her arms in front of herself and lay next to Kelly. She hoped they were sufficiently camouflaged. She took shallow breaths. Her heart was thumping. Kelly moved closer to her. She was so still, barely breathing.

"Paige? Kelly? You down here?" It was Guthrie. Rasping breaths like a dying train. Did he think they were gonna answer?

He was coming closer. Clomping through the mud. Paige put an arm around Kelly and pulled her in close. She was shivering. Paige flexed her arm and Kelly simmered down some. She felt Kelly's heart race. One minute she was hardly breathing, the next her heart was pounding out of control. Paige tightened her grip. "Shhh," she said into her ear. "Easy."

"I know you're down here." Guthrie was getting closer. His clomping footsteps splashed through her, speeding up her own heart. "It'll be better for you if you give up. Don't make me hunt you. Don't make me mad." Chills zapped up and down her spine. Kelly started shivering again.

"I mean it, give it up." He was so close now. Paige felt a drop of rain. Oh please, God, don't let it rain now. The rain would wash off their mud camouflage and Guthrie would see them. Another drop. The night was so cold. Guthrie was going to kill them for sure. But first Rice would rape her. She bit her lip to stifle a cry.

"Where are you?" He was right next to them. He stopped. Kelly stopped her shivering. Paige heard the big man's wheezing breath. Felt it. He sounding like an old man who smoked too much. How could that be? All those muscles. "You fucks, when I get you." He said this low, under his breath. He didn't know how close they were. He was blind in the night.

"Do you see them?" Rice called from above.

"No. They must be up ahead." Guthrie's voice radiated anger and it burned through Paige. "We'll get them." He was moving around. Agitated. He stepped on her foot. He was wearing heavy boots. Pain bolted up her leg. She bit harder into her lip, drawing blood, but she didn't scream out.

"I can't get the car up there. So we can't use the light." Rice was shouting from back by the overpass. "I'll stay here in case you miss them and they come back."

"I'll check ahead," Guthrie yelled, "then come back this way in case they faked me out."

"Go," Rice yelled.

"I'm going." The boot came off her foot. Paige silently sighed as Guthrie clomped down the ditch. They lay still, letting him get a good distance away.

* * *

"Fuck." Rice clenched his fists. This whole thing was turning to shit. Clay'd promised him easy money. Snatch the Radoslaw kids. Hold them for a couple of days and then the old man was supposed to pay up, handing the money over to his security people to pay the kidnappers, without ever figuring out that he was handing it over to the kidnappers themselves. That was dumb enough, but then to go and kidnap his own niece because he had to have his girlfriend in his wife's house. Stupid.

And what was the big deal about the girlfriend being pregnant? It was making Clay nuts. How come he couldn't just get rid of it? What an asshole.

And what an asshole thing they were doing. 'Two kidnappings, two ransoms, two perfect crimes,' that's what Clay had said. And that Jerry went along with him.

Dumb fucks. Ain't no such thing as a perfect crime. Not now, never has been. Prison's full of guys that learned that. And those dumb fucks were supposed to know that, too. They're cops, after all. They'd be lucky to get away with one, he'd argued after Clay told him he wanted him to snatch the niece, but no way would he listen. Dumb fuck, they shoulda done the niece from the get go and forgot about the other two. You don't fuck with a man like Radoslaw.

But Radoslaw was dead now and he had the girl. Fuck it was gonna be a one-of-a-kind night. As soon as that asexual idiot was asleep, he'd planned on going out to the trunk and doing that young thing right there on the ground.

Fat chance now. Rice rubbed his balls. They ached. He stroked his cock. He was ready. If Guthrie got them back he was gonna do her first thing. God the tits. They stood up firm. She didn't need no bra. He tingled all over. His legs went weak. He rubbed his balls again. Couldn't stroke it, though. Couldn't cream his pants. Not here. Guthrie wouldn't understand.

He looked down into the ditch. Nothing. He thought about using the spotlight again, but rejected the idea. Not good to draw attention. Would they get away from Guthrie? Dumb fuck, probably. Where would they go?" Back here? No. She must have heard. She'd be expecting him. She'd go on ahead. To the cattle pens? Probably not, but a road crossed the interstate up there, not too far past them. She could get help. Did she know about it? Maybe.

Then he'd be fucked. It wasn't the money now. Or the fear of going back to prison. He shook with desire. It was the girl. He had to fuck something like that before he died. He had to fuck her while he still could.

Rice laughed, almost a growl. Then he spun on his heels. Seconds later he pulled onto the interstate. Oh yeah, she'd go on ahead, but it wouldn't do her no good, because he'd be waiting. He popped the glove box and fetched out some Kleenex. He unzipped and pulled it out. Driving never slowed his hand down none.

* * *

Paige put her lips to Kelly's ear. "We have to climb out. Guthrie's gonna come back this way. He might find us the next time."

"How?"

"I'll push you up." Lightning flashed again. Thunder pounded again. Rain poured down again. The walls were slippery. Paige started to help Kelly up, but Kelly dug her hands into the muck and was able to get to the top unaided. Paige dug a bare foot into it and found purchase. She took another step up. Slipped, but grabbed into the dirt to keep from falling. In seconds she was out.

"Now what?" Kelly said.

"Maybe I can lift you over the fence." There was a chain link fence between them and the highway. Cars were flying by, spraying water from their tires. A big truck honked as it shifted into the fast lane to pass a slow moving car. Its headlights blurred as they cut through the black night and the sheeting rain. Paige felt like a bug under a faucet. Wind whipped through her hair. It was hard to breathe, harder to see.

"What about you?" Kelly grabbed her hand. "Are you gonna climb over, too?"

"I can't," Paige said. The fence had razor wire circled around the top. She might be able to lift Kelly over, but no way could she climb over herself. She'd be cut to ribbons.

"I don't wanna go by myself."

"You gotta. You can stop a car and get help."

"No! We have to stay together."

"We can't," Paige said. "If you stop a car they can get the police."

"You forgot, my Uncle Clay is the police," Kelly said. "They won't help us."

"These are different police. They'll help. Then they'll put your uncle in jail. Now come on. Rice is back there with the searchlight. If we don't hurry he'll turn it on and catch us before I can get you over."

"I still don't wanna."

"Come on, Kelly. It's the only way." Paige pushed her toward the fence.

"I'm not gonna leave you." Kelly grabbed onto

the fence and wouldn't let go.

"Stop it." Paige squeezed her arm. "Don't act so spoiled. It's our only chance and you're blowing it. I can get away by myself, but if I have to keep pulling you along we're gonna get caught. You don't want that, do you?" The rain was coming down harder now. It was like Paige and Kelly were alone in the world. Even the passing headlights were almost invisible.

"I'm not going. I'm staying with you." Kelly was shaking. Paige squeezed her arms tighter.

"Calm down and quit it. You're talking way too loud. We gotta hurry. He won't go up that ditch forever. Pretty soon he's gonna come back."

"I won't leave," Kelly screamed.

"Stupid," Paige said. She couldn't stay. Rice might have heard. She let go of Kelly's arm, took her by the hand and started off north, away from Rice back by the overpass.

"I'm sorry," Kelly wailed.

"Don't talk. Keep quiet," Paige said. She started jogging through the rain. Mud squished between her toes as she pulled Kelly behind her. Her feet were numb. She was cold and the child was a dead weight stuck to her right arm. She could run, but not with the kid attached. She could get away by herself. She knew she could. But no way could she leave Kelly.

She stooped low as she jogged through the rain. She hoped they were going faster than Guthrie below in the ditch. They had to move and she wanted to get ahead of him. She remembered the millions of cows up ahead. There had to be people there. People meant help.

Kelly pulled on her arm.

Paige stopped.

"You're hurting my arm. I can't keep up." The kid was crying. Or maybe it was just the rain washing down over her face.

"You gotta try." She started up again. She knew it had to be hard for the girl. Her legs were shorter than hers, but there was nothing she could do. It was run or get caught.

"Stop, Look!" Kelly jerked her arm, forcing her to stop again.

"What?"

"Look!" She pointed to a wooden plank that went across the ditch.

Paige strained her eyes forward, squinting through the rain. Nothing but the fence on one side and the ditch on the other as far as she could see. Behind the same. Eventually Guthrie would climb out of that ditch and he'd see them up here. The best thing would be to cross over. Would Guthrie see them from below? Not if he was ahead of them. But if they'd passed him, then he'd be back there, still coming. He couldn't help but see them cross overhead. She didn't know how far she had to go to the cows. She had to decide. She did.

"Okay. I'll go first." The ditch was about ten feet across, the board about a foot wide. She could do it. Could Kelly? Sure, she was a kid. Besides, it was their only chance. She held her hands out to her sides like a tightrope walker and started across. Slow steps. Her bare feet were slippery on the wet board. She felt the grain with her toes. Scary.

The board sagged in the center. She was too heavy. It was going to break. Her left foot slipped. Pain shot through it. Splinter. She dropped to her knees. The board sagged more.

"Move, move," Kelly yelled.

"Don't yell. They might hear." Paige's foot hurt. Was it bleeding? She started up, crawling. She should have gone across on her knees from the get go. She was so stupid. The other side closer now. She was at the end. She'd made it.

She sat in the mud and the rain and checked her foot. She felt the splinter, a toothpick size piece of wood sticking into the ball of her foot. Big pain. She pulled it out with a jerk. More pain.

She looked across the ditch. Kelly was halfway over. Crawling. Pretty smart. Smarter than her. Paige stood up, put weight on the damaged foot. It hurt, but she could walk. Run if she had to. She needed shoes. Kelly was across. She took her hand and helped her up. They weren't safe yet. But they were safer.

"That way." Kelly pointed away from the highway, the fence and the ditch. It looked like a farm. Small irrigation ditches that went on as far as she could see. They were growing something. She didn't remember anything like this between the cow pens and the hotel, but it had been a year since she'd been up here with her family.

"Okay, let's go." And once again she took Kelly's suggestion.

Paige didn't know what they were growing, but it was gooey under her feet. She saw a building ahead. Bleak and dark. The closer they got the more scary it looked. They stopped. The building loomed out of the flat fields, forbidding. Two stories of old time wooden ghost house.

Maybe there would be people. Maybe help. But in her heart she knew better. They should give the building a wide berth and keep going through the fields. She couldn't. She had to check. She pulled on Kelly's hand and they approached the house. When they got close she saw that it was boarded up.

She turned to go when she saw Guthrie lumbering toward them. Frankenstein out of the rainy black. He hadn't seen them yet. She pulled Kelly to the side of the building. It had an old fashioned wooden back porch. They huddled against the side of it, squatting on their knees. There was an opening into a crawl space under it. She didn't want to go in there. She peeked around the corner. Guthrie was getting closer. She put her mouth to Kelly's ear. "I'll go first."

The kid shook her head.

"I'm going under. If you don't want to, too bad. You can go with Guthrie." She hated talking to her like that, but this wasn't the time to be nice. The clouds parted overhead. Moonlight peeked through. It was still raining, but not as hard. She could see better, but so could Guthrie.

She bent down to look through the crawl hole. It was gloomy and hard to see, but enough cold moonlight filtered through the slats for her to see there was nothing in there. No wild dog, or coyote. No big deal. All they had to do was crawl in and they'd be safe.

She took a deep breath, crouched low and started in. It wasn't so bad. She crawled toward the center of the enclosed space, scooting on her belly.

It wasn't a bit like she'd thought. It was like she was in another world. She imagined that she was crawling into a pirate's cave after sunken treasure, but then she felt Kelly crawling in behind her and she was jerked back to the danger outside. She stopped and looked around. Kelly scooted up next to her.

Something squeaked. She looked toward the place where the sound had come from, off to her left, under the steps. It was dark there. She couldn't see anything. She was frightened, but she quickly calmed herself. Probably a cat hiding from the rain. She wasn't afraid of cats. She didn't want to think it could be anything else.

She moved forward.

She felt a drop of water on her arm, then one on her head. A little of the rain was seeping down, running through the slats. Once in the center, she turned around to face outward. Kelly squirmed closer.

Paige gasped.

There, between them and the crawl space, squatting just under the porch, framed in the gray half light coming in from the outside, was a giant rat, bigger than she'd ever thought they could grow. She turned to look behind herself. The other side of the porch was boarded up. The only way out was the way they'd come in.

"Go away, Mister Rat," Kelly whispered, but it didn't move.

Paige heard more squeaking, this time off to her right. She turned and looked. Just dark. Chills ran up her spine. The hair on the back of her neck tingled. Goosebumps shivered along her arms. They were trapped with the rats.

She scooped up a handful of dirt and threw it at the monster in front of her. It screeched and charged her. She covered her face with her arms as it flew over her head, thumped onto her back and ran down her legs on into the dark.

She hugged the damp ground. She heard rustling behind her. More of them. She fought the urge to run out into the night. She thought she felt one by her foot, but she used her logical mind to shake the feeling away. There was no way they would get so close. They were more afraid of her then she was of them.

But her emotional self disagreed and she stuck her thumb into her mouth to keep from screaming out. She felt the goosebumps. The dirt under her hands. The chills along her spine. They wouldn't hurt her. She had to stay calm.

Footsteps. Clomping loud. Guthrie. He clomped up the porch. A ripping sound. A bang. He was pulling the boards off the back door. Was he going to go in? Did he really think they'd go in there? Another board hit the floor above, then another. A thud. Again. Was he kicking the door in? It screeched when it opened. He went into the house.

Time to move. There would be someone at the cow pens ahead. There would be people. There would be light. She grabbed Kelly's hand and gave it a squeeze. It seemed like she'd been doing that forever. She took a deep breath. A rat squealed. Now that Kelly knew they were leaving there was no holding her back. She scooted past Paige, going like a slithering snake. In an instant she was at the crawl space.

Paige grabbed her foot. She didn't know why. Instinct. It was a miracle the child didn't scream out. Guthrie was back on the porch. He was going down the steps. Kelly scooted back and huddled next to Paige. He was coming around to the side. He was going to get them. He was going to let Rice rape her.

He stopped by the crawl hole. The girls saw his legs from below the knees. His muddy military boots. Paige flexed her foot, the one that he'd stepped on earlier. She could see out clearly. It was sprinkling lightly now. The moon was back.

A clicking sound. A lighter fluid smell followed by the smell of a smoking cigarette. Paige's heart was pounding. Kelly was shivering next to her. What was taking him so long? Please, God, don't let him look. He took a long drag and exhaled, the sound shooting through the night.

He must be shielded from the light rain by the roof's overhang. That's why he was standing there. A cigarette break before he started searching again. Why didn't he rest up on the porch? The steady sound of urine splashing. She smelled it. He had to pee, that's why. Paige squinted. She saw the stream between his legs. He was peeing right in front of the crawl hole. They were gonna have to crawl over it to get out. Yuck.

After awhile he finished his cigarette. Paige saw the glowing tip as he tossed it into the night. But he didn't leave. He just stood out there, breathing. Again Paige thought it funny that such a man with all those muscles should sound so out of shape. The lighter sound again. He was going to smoke another cigarette. The rain had stopped now. All was quiet save for Guthrie's rapid, raspy breathing. He inhaled the first drag, then clomped away.

"We gotta get outta here," Kelly said after a few minutes.

"No, we're gonna stay."

"No! There's rats here."

"Yeah, I know, but every time I stop hiding I get

found. I've learned my lesson. We're not leaving till morning. Then we know they'll be good and gone."

"I don't wanna stay here."

"Listen, If you woulda let me get you over that fence, we wouldn't be here, but you didn't, so now we are. I can't out run them with you, so we gotta hide. And this is a good spot. They already checked here."

"I'm sorry," Kelly said. "I didn't wanna go over that fence. I don't wanna be alone. Now the rats are gonna get us and it's my fault."

"No. They're scary, but they won't get us. We're gonna be okay. You'll see. Just be quiet. And don't go to sleep."

"Don't worry. I won't."

CHAPTER FIFTEEN

THEY BARRELED ONTO THE FREEWAY at seventy-five. "Someone coulda gotten the license number back there," Jake said. "Enough people were looking. It's possible."

"Even if they did, I don't think they'd put it together with us, at least not right away. We should be okay." Sara dug a pack of the pictures out of the bag and flipped through them. Race pictures. So were the next five packs. "Hold it," she said as she flipped through the sixth. She handed some of the pictures to Dottie in the front seat.

"I know this place," Dottie said. "These are oil

wells. They've hired artists to dress them up as a tourist attraction."

"I've never been there, but I know about it, because my husband and his partner go up there shooting all the time."

"Uh oh," Jake said.

"Jerry's brother is the watchman there. His name's Guthrie. Clay says he wasn't bright enough to be a real cop. The oil company's furnished him with a home and a car. He lives there. Nothing but oil wells and dirt. It's up somewhere toward San Francisco."

"About halfway," Dottie said.

"There was a photo of a man that kind of looked like Jerry in with all those of Paige Radoslaw," Sara said. "It must be his brother. It must be Guthrie."

"Looks like you gotta go up north," Jake said.

Looks like it," Sara said.

"Gonna go charging up there like the Lone Ranger?" Jake said.

"Yeah, I am. Kelly's my little girl now," Sara said. "My responsibility."

"I'd go with you, but I can't."

"You've done more than enough."

"No, you don't understand. I can't. I've only been out of the hospital a week. Triple by-pass. That's why I did the diversion, otherwise I'd have gone in and got the pictures myself. It don't take much for me to start a mean fire, but I just don't have what it takes right now to be any more use to you. I hate it, but it's the way it is."

"You're so young."

"I hate it that you're feeling sorry for me."

"I'm not," Sara said. "You were there for me. No one else would've done what you did. You burned up thousands of dollars worth of stuff and risked years in prison so I could get these photos. You're a real friend."

"I'm going with you, Sara," Dottie said. "Me and Sherman."

"I didn't doubt it for a second," Sara said.

"Is there anything else I can do?" Jake said. Sara heard the sadness in his voice as the car cut through the night and she did feel sorry for him.

"Yes, give me your phone number. If you don't hear from us by this time tomorrow, call the FBI. Tell them everything I told you. It might do some good."

"I can get you an army of help."

"No, I want to get on the road right away. We'll drop you at the swap meet, then we're outta Dodge."

The speedometer read forty when she entered the on ramp toward Los Angeles and sixty when they shot out onto the Santa Ana Freeway.

Sara let the needle climb to eighty, thought about passing the semi ahead, then decided against it. She didn't want to be stopped for speeding. She settled back to seventy-five and rode in the wake of the big truck.

"You get tired, let me know," Dottie said. "I can drive."

"I will," Sara said. "Why don't you try and get some sleep."

"Are you kidding? Sleep? I haven't felt this awake in fifty years."

"Yeah, I know what you mean."

"Almost out of gas," Sara said four hours later. She'd been following the same semi for the last two hundred miles.

"Were almost there," Dottie said.

"Almost isn't gonna make it. I'm gonna have to take the next ramp and get gas."

"There it is, slow down," Dottie said.

She tapped the brakes and slowed the car as she took the off ramp. She was sorry to lose the steadying comfort of the big truck that had been leading her through the night. She turned right at the top of the ramp and drove by an all night Mobil station. It was one of those places where you went inside, paid, then pumped your gas. Just like the one back in Huntington Beach. Nobody trusted anybody anymore.

There was one car at the pumps, a fifty-five Chevy hot rod, black lacquer paint with red and orange flames on the front fenders, and a young teenager pumping gas into it. Sara saw a girl in the car. It was almost morning. They'd been out all night someplace.

"Beautiful car." Sara pulled over and parked in the dark, fifty yards past the station.

"Gorgeous."

"I'll pull in when they leave. There's a better chance they'll recognize me, so you'll have to go in and pay, then pump the gas. I'll stay in the car."

Sara watched while the boy finished filling his tank. That car looked like it could fly. The boy replaced the pump when he finished. Damn kid had a swagger, even when he thought nobody was looking. He got back in the hot rod and started it. Sara heard the unmistakable rumble of a car that was more at home at a hundred on the highway than thirty in the city.

She envied the kid. Then she saw the red lights sitting on top of a black and white Jeep Cherokee in the rear view mirror. She shut the engine off.

"Now what?" Dottie asked.

"Step out of the car please," boomed an amplified voice from the police car.

Dottie opened her door and stepped out and was caught in the spotlight. Her silver hair caught the light rays giving her an angelic appearance.

Sara opened her door and hesitated as Sherman slunk down in the back seat. She had to think of something. Would a pair of small town cops be interested enough in big city crime to remember their faces from a news broadcast? She could only hope not as she slid out of the car.

She felt the spot moving from Dottie to where she stood. In another instant the light would rake over her and she'd know if she was in trouble. Would they ask for her license if they didn't recognize her? Would they recognize her name?

The light was about to hit her when the hot rod squealed out of the gas station, racing slicks smoking like a dragster's, the roaring engine cutting up the night. The car slid out of the driveway onto the access road laying a hundred foot strip of black rubber on the pavement as it careened toward the interstate and the spotlight stopped its arc.

The Cherokee screamed into life and bolted after the Chevy. In a flash of an instant both pursuer and pursued were out of sight, swallowed up by the interstate.

"Let's get out of here." Dottie jumped back into the car.

"We won't get very far without gas." She eased

herself back in the car and felt the sweat on her palms as she slid her hands over the wheel. It was a close call. If the youth in the hot rod Chevy had waited a second more before stomping on the gas, she would have been caught in the spot and she might have intrigued the police more than a spoiled teenager with a fast car.

She started the car and pulled up to the pumps. Dottie ran into the office, laid down two twenties, came out and pumped the gas. The Ford ate twenty-seven dollars and seventy-six cents worth of fuel. They left without going back for the change.

"Flashing red lights coming up the interstate," Dottie said.

"Cops figured it out." Sara turned right on a road running away from the interstate toward a small town. "They'll assume we're back on the highway."

"This car must be hot," Dottie said. "Someone must've got the license back at the mall."

"Or one of the cops recognized you. Thank God, not right away."

About a mile from the interstate the two lane road turned into the main street of a small town. Two blocks of small shops surrounded by a small residential community. The street was poorly lit, two out of three street lights out, and poorly kept, a third of the stores were vacant. Sara wondered if the town had ever seen better times. Was it a dream waiting to happen or a dream that died?

The street was empty. Doors were barred. Blinds were drawn over locked windows. A tumbleweed blew across the street in front of them.

They rolled past a used clothing store on the right, a pharmacy on the left, past a shoddy Chinese restaurant, a shoddier Mexican restaurant which blared the slogan in faded yellow paint, *La Comida Mas Fina*, and between it and a dry cleaners was a small dirt parking lot.

"Pull in there," Dottie said and Sara obeyed. "It won't be long before they're looking around here. We can't stay and we need a new car. We're gonna have to steal one."

"Great. It's like five in the morning." Sara shut the engine off. "But if we had a phone and a local phone book we could call around. Find someone who wasn't home. They might have a second car in the garage, keys in the kitchen, maybe by the refrigerator. What do you think?"

"That's the dumbest thing I ever heard," Dottie said.

"Pretty dumb." Sara laughed. "But short of breaking a window and hot wiring something, I can't think of anything else."

"So we're gonna add breaking and entering to our list of crimes?"

"We already did that," Sara said, "back at the mall, remember?"

"Oh yeah." Dottie looked up and down the deserted street. "We have two choices, the used clothing store or the dry cleaners. The other stores will have alarms. Me, I prefer the used clothing store. I've always liked old clothes."

"You've done this before?" Sara kidded.

"Scared?" Dottie said.

"A little. You?"

"Terrified." Sherman licked the back of her neck and she quivered. "Let's go."

They got out of the car and walked back half a

block to the used clothing store. They looked in the window, straining to see in through the dark, but all Sara could see was the reflection of the barren street with its ghostly shadows and it sent a tingle running through her.

"Let's go 'round back," Dottie whispered. They squeezed between the used clothing store and the Chinese restaurant. Sara didn't like being cramped between the two buildings. The weeds and loose dirt crunching under her shoes seemed awfully loud. Sherman growled low, further heightening Sara's apprehension.

"Look." Dottie pointed, once they were at the back entrance. "Alarm tape on the windows."

"Do you know how to get in without setting off the alarm?" Sara whispered.

"Of course not."

"Let's try the dry cleaners. Who'd steal somebody else's clothes in a town like this?" This time Sara led the way.

"No alarm." Sara pointed at the cleaner's back door. "And no bars on the windows." Centered in the top half of the back door was a screen-covered sliding window. The screen was weatherbeaten, rusty and worn. It came apart in her hands. She lifted the window, it wasn't locked. She reached in and unlocked the door from the inside. Not even a dead bolt. Just a simple lock that you might find on any house built in the fifties.

Sara opened the door and entered. "Come on," she whispered. Dottie followed her inside, closing and locking the door after herself.

The dark room started blinking on and off with a red glowing light. "Down," Dottie said as the police car pulled up and parked out front.

"It's that car from earlier." A not very friendly voice from outside said.

"Really think it's those two women?" An even less friendly voice answered.

"That's what they say. To bad we didn't cotton to it straight off."

"Well, we got 'em now. Where do you suppose they are?"

"Dunno."

"Think they're robbing the town?"

"Get serious J.D., If you stole all the money in every store on this street you might could buy a cup of coffee, if you was lucky. No, more 'an likely they're long gone. They traded cars. I don't know how, but that's what they did. Who woulda thunk it here?"

"What're we gonna do, Mike? Wait till they come back?"

"Didn't you hear? They ain't coming back. I'm gonna go call Malcolm down to the Mobil and have him tow that car outta here."

"We gonna strip it?"

"Damn straight."

At least they wouldn't be calling it in, Sara thought as she lay between Dottie and the dog. Ten minutes later they heard the sounds of a tow truck as it pulled into the parking lot next door. It hooked up to the rented Ford and towed it away. The police car followed, leaving them basking in the black night, huddled behind the counter, taking shallow breaths and wondering what to do next.

"This was not one of my brighter ideas," Sara said.

"We shoulda just traded plates again."

"That would've been far too simple. I'm going to look around."

Sara found a small office adjacent to a bathroom. Sherman brushed by her and started lapping water from the toilet bowl.

"Yuck," she said, but the dog continued to drink.

In the office she found a wooden desk, scratched and covered with papers, an electronic calculator, a matching chair and nothing else. She sat at the desk. The papers were last weeks receipts. Apparently the owner used the shoe box method of accounting, gather all the receipts, make a pile, throw them in a shoebox and figure it out later. The top two desk drawers filled the shoe box function.

She found a personal phone book in the bottom drawer. It appeared to list the names, addresses and phone numbers of the cleaner's patrons.

"Find anything?" Dottie asked.

"A phone book with his customers' names and addresses."

"Do you want to call or should I?" Dottie said.

"I'll do it." Sara flipped through the book, calling numbers at random. It took ten calls before she was blessed with no answer. "Here we go. Mike Mckinna. Thirteen Church Street. Great, look at this." She showed her the phone book. Under the address were the words, *Next to the Cemetery.*

"I was afraid that even if we found someone not at home, we wouldn't be able to find the house. But we should have no trouble finding a cemetery in a town this size."

"No," Dottie said. "No trouble at all."

"Let's go," Sara said.

Five minutes later they found it.

"The Lost Souls Cemetery." Sara read off the sign.

"Where's the house?"

"You don't have to whisper," Sara said in a quiet voice. "Nobody can hear us."

"What about them?" Dottie pointed into the cemetery.

Sara saw a white house on the far side of the cemetery. "That has to be it." She started walking down the street.

"Where are you going?" Dottie asked.

"Around the block. Church Street must dead end into the cemetery."

"Car coming." Dottie grabbed Sara by the arm and pulled her into the graveyard. They huddled behind a hedge while the car passed.

"It's the police." Sara was whispering again as the black-and-white Cherokee rolled on by without stopping.

"We'll cut across the cemetery." Dottie was holding onto Sherman's collar. "It's safer than the street." She led her through the sea of tombstones, toward the white house. The clouds let through enough light to cast opaque shadows from the gravestones, and they glistened from an earlier rain.

"I feel like the shadows are reaching out for me," Sara said.

"It's a little scary."

"I'm twenty-eight years old and I've never been in a cemetery before. I don't like it." She heard something, a scraping sound. She froze. "Did you hear it?"

"Must have been the wind blowing some of those across the grass." Dottie bent down and picked up a bunch of artificial flowers. She tossed them back on the grave. "Come on." She continued leading on through the graveyard.

At the side of the cemetery they found a brick fence between them and the house.

"Stay," Dottie said. Sherman sat. Then, "You want to give me a hoist? I'd do you, but I'm old."

Once over, they found themselves between the fence and the back of a two car garage. The fence was about three feet from the garage. They were in a dark area, perfect for one of those homeless beggars to hide in, or maybe an animal.

Sara felt as trapped as the dead neighbors next door in their coffins. Her heart was pounding. She felt like she was being drawn out of a long dark tunnel when Dottie led her away from the dark space.

"At least we don't have to worry about the neighbors calling the police," Dottie said.

"Look at that." Sara was looking at an Isuzu Trooper. Not new, but it looked road worthy. She'd driven Troopers before she shifted to Mitsubishi Monteros. They were good four wheel drives. Dependable. It was parked in front of the garage. She checked the doors. Locked.

"We gonna break in and hunt for the keys?" Dottie said.

"If we can. Why don't you knock and see if anybody's home?"

Dottie took the thirty-eight out of her purse and rapped on the back door.

"No answer." She tried the door. "Like the car, locked."

"That window is open," Sara said.

Dottie came off the porch and followed her

pointed finger. It was open, but only a crack. Sara wondered if they left it like that all the time or if they forgot to lock it.

"I'll get down on my hands and knees. You can stand on my shoulders." Dottie started for the window.

"You sure about this?"

"What, you think I'm too old to support you?" Dottie said as she got down on her knees.

"No, I didn't think that at all." Sara said and using Dottie as a stool, she opened the window, then pulled herself through it.

Inside, she found herself on the kitchen sink. She squeezed on in. She tried to turn once her buttocks were through, but she slipped and landed on the tile floor with a quiet crash that echoed through the quieter house. She pushed herself up and opened the back door. Then she went straight for the refrigerator.

She pulled open the door, bathing the kitchen in a murky light. "Tupperware," she said, taking out a plastic container and checking the contents. "Tuna casserole." She resealed the lid. "We'll take this with us for later."

"Close the fridge. I found a flashlight." Dottie closed a drawer next to the sink. She turned it on as the kitchen lost the gloomy light from the refrigerator.

"Let's find the car keys and get out of here," Sara whispered. Dottie nodded and they went through the kitchen. There was a key rack by the back door with a set of keys hanging from it.

"Look at that." Dottie pointed to a picture thumb tacked on a cork board above the key hook. She trained the light on it.

"Wouldn't you just know it?" Sara said. It was a picture of a man and woman holding hands. The woman was wearing a blue formal dress and the athletic looking man smiling down at her was wearing a police officer's uniform.

"Think it's one of the ones that's chopping up our rental?" Dottie said.

"Fair trade." Sara grabbed the keys off the hook.

"That you, honey?" A woman's voice echoed through the house. Her voice was slurred. Sara and Dottie froze. "Bring me a glass of water when you come to bed." They stood silent. Sara saw a kitchen radio on the counter next to a toaster. She reached over and turned it on. Bruce Springsteen and the E Street Band filled the kitchen, cutting off the sound Sara and Dottie made as they bolted out the back door.

"Boost me over the fence," Dottie said. "Sherman won't come for anybody else. Meet us at the front of the cemetery." Sara cupped her hands and Dottie scrabbled over into the graveyard.

Sara got into the car and pumped the accelerator as she turned it over. Her old Trooper always loved that.

The porch light came on. The door opened as she was backing out the driveway. Swell, she stole a cop's car. In seconds the Trooper was gonna be hotter than that Taurus ever would have been.

"Mike, wait," the girl at the back door shouted out.

Sara turned on the headlights. The woman was tall, slender, large breasted, and wearing some kind of see through thing that left everything exposed. She looked drunk and she didn't look like the woman in that photo stuck to the cork board. This was not the cop's wife. Certainly not his daughter. This cop had a Carole, too. Maybe she wouldn't be reporting the car stolen right away after all.

Sara worked the clutch and gears, first, second, third, getting the feel of the car. She took the corners quick and close, braking at the cemetery gate.

"How'd it go?" Dottie held the seat forward and Sherman jumped into the back.

"Men are such shits," Sara said.

Dottie got in and Sara pointed the car toward the road out of town.

CHAPTER SIXTEEN

IT HAD BEEN RAINING on and off for the last three hours. Thank the fucking Lord it finally quit, but there was no sign of Guthrie or the brats. He took a drag off his Camel, then tossed the butt out the window. For the thousandth time he questioned his decision to wait on the northern side of the cattle pens. She could have doubled back.

He squeezed his hands, imagining them on her tits. They'd be so white. And the nipples. He ran his tongue over his dry and cracked lips. He slipped a hand into his pants.

Guthrie had to find them.

He closed his eyes and tried to think. On the surface it looked like it was over, but he'd been checking the news on the half hour and had heard nothing. Sure as shit, soon as they were in the clear, they would be on the news. The whole world was worrying about Paige Radoslaw. They couldn't keep it quiet if she turned up. Press wouldn't allow it.

A rapping on the window startled him. He pulled the hand from his pants.

The door opened.

"Scared ya."

"I knew it was you." Rice clenched the wheel to keep from screaming his disappointment. Guthrie was back without them. That's not how it was supposed to play.

"Sure you did. You were supposed to be waiting back by the hotel, in case they doubled back."

"I figured they must've heard. They're gonna come this way." Rice took his hands off the wheel. It wasn't over. She was still out there. As long as it was still dark, there was still a chance.

"How do you know?"

"I feel it." Fuck, his balls ached, even though he'd whacked it earlier, it didn't seem to make no difference. His boner was rock solid, cocked and ready.

"I hope you're right. I don't want to lose that money," Guthrie said. That's all it was for the big fuck. The money. Fuck the money. There were more important things than money.

"All we can do is wait it out." Rice cracked his knuckles.

"You been waiting. I'm the one that's out there sloggin' in the rain."

"The rain's stopped. Besides, someone's gotta stay with the car."

"I don't know why," Guthrie said. "Seems with two of us out looking we got twice the chance to find them."

"We're gonna get 'em back." He shifted in the seat so Guthrie wouldn't see how stiff he was.

* * *

Paige shivered under the porch. She was cold and wet. Kelly was finally asleep. Paige didn't know how she did it. She couldn't even close her eyes for a second. It felt like it was almost morning. She had a kink in her leg. Hours must have passed. No way would they still be looking. They were long gone. Had to be.

She edged toward the crawl space. Her neck hurt like she'd slept wrong, even though she hadn't. By the time she reached the crawl hole she realized that her whole body ached. She wanted a hot shower. She needed one. Would she ever get one again?

"Hey, you're not going?" Kelly was awake. Paige felt guilty for disturbing her. She was just a scared kid. As long as she was asleep she wasn't shaking and worried about getting caught.

"Just outside to stretch my legs."

"I wanna stretch too."

"Okay. Go ahead. But keep your eyes out. Just in case."

"You think they're still out there?" Kelly said. "They can't still be after us."

"I don't think so. It's almost morning, but you should be careful anyway."

"Yeah, I'll stay close to the house till you're out."

Kelly inched forward. It seemed like she was taking forever. Earlier she'd been in such a hurry to get out. Paige guessed she wasn't as afraid of the rats anymore. She knew she wasn't. They were nothing compared to Guthrie and Rice.

"Oh yuck. I'm gonna have to crawl through where he peed." Kelly stopped.

"I'm sure the rain's washed it all away."

"Not," Kelly said. "I can smell it."

"Hold your nose." Paige laughed when Kelly, on her stomach and elbows, pinched her nose with her right hand, then wiggled out through the crawl hole. Once out, she stood and pushed the muddy piss filled dirt away from the front of the crawl hole with her feet.

"Now you won't have to crawl through it, too." She really was a good kid. For a second she flashed on Kelly not wanting to go over that fence, but then she had to wonder what she would have done herself if she was only seven years old.

Paige scooted through the mud and pulled herself out. The rain had finally stopped. There wasn't much light and Paige guessed it would stay gone till sunup. There were no stars. She brushed as much dirt off the front of herself as possible and smiled when she saw Kelly imitating her.

"So what are we gonna do now?" Kelly's clothes were filthy. Mud caked her hair and face. She looked like a television orphan. Paige reached a hand up to her own hair and realized that she must look the same.

"We'll head on to the cattle pens. The sun's gonna come up soon. There should be lots of people there taking care of the steers. They'll help." Paige flexed her toes, squishing dirt under them. She was glad she had tough feet. They didn't hurt a bit, not even where she'd pulled that splinter out.

"How about back where we first saw Guthrie? There was stores back that way, and that hotel."

"I think it's farther," Paige said. "Besides, Rice told Guthrie that's where he'd be waiting, remember?" She ran her fingers through her hair, pulling out some of the mud.

"Yeah." Kelly copied her again, using both hands to try and get the stuff out of her hair.

"They're probably gone, but if they're still waiting for us, that's where they'll be." She leaned against the building and pulled one of her feet up. She ran a hand along her calluses. The foot felt fine. She was a runner. The fastest kid in her school. She checked the other foot, feeling where the splinter had gone in. Just a twinge of hurt. Lots of miles left.

"Paige?"

"Yeah."

"I'm sorry I didn't go over the fence. If I woulda then we'd be home right now. You'd be back with your parents. I'd be with Sara and old Clay and Jerry would be in jail. Guthrie and Rice too."

"That's okay."

"Really? You're not mad?"

"No, I'm not mad. We came out okay in the end, didn't we? And besides, we learned how tough we are. We may only be girls, but we took a lot and we got away."

"Yeah, but I shoulda gone over the fence. I was a big chicken and I really hate chickens."

"They didn't catch us. That's all that counts."

"And the rats didn't eat us." Kelly said. "That

counts for something too."

"They didn't eat us because we stopped being afraid of them. Something happened under that porch. We stopped being chicken."

"Yeah, we got brave."

"Not exactly brave," Paige said. "Just not so scared. We got so used to being afraid that we got over it."

"I'm still afraid, kinda, but if I ever have to go over a fence again, I'm going."

"A little afraid is good, but a lot isn't. You can't think so good when you're really scared. You do stupid things."

"Like not staying up on that roof when we shoulda?"

"Yeah, like that."

"So, which way?" Kelly said.

Paige looked off into the dark. The round, irrigated rows seemed to go on forever. "Onions." The smell was powerful now, carried on a light breeze.

"Are we gonna trample through them again?"

"No. There must be a road that comes up to the house. Let's see." Paige started around the house, keeping close. The white paint was dirty, cracked and fading. More boarded windows. A dripping rain gutter. Spooky. There was a covered porch in front. Bigger than the one in back. Tall round columns held the roof above it. Big windows, also boarded. Real spooky.

"Driveway." Kelly pointed. It was cracked concrete. Not used in a long while, but it led to a one lane road. "Now we don't have to trample the onions, and no more walking in the mud."

"I think it goes to the cow pens," Paige said. "This must have been a rancher's house once upon a time. Maybe the guy that used to own all the cows."

"Think he died?"

"I don't know. Maybe. But maybe he moved to the city. No one wants to live in the country anymore."

"How come his kids didn't move in? It's a big old house. Someone should live in it."

"There's the rats." Paige shuddered.

"Yeah, them." Kelly shuddered too. Paige saw it.

They started down the road. Paige kept looking to the sky. Any minute she expected it to get lighter, but it didn't. It must not be as early as she'd thought. Kelly tugged on her arm and Paige took her hand.

The wind shifted.

"Yuck. What's that smell?" Kelly put her hand to her nose and pinched it like when she crawled through where Guthrie had peed.

"Cow shit. Lots of it," Paige said. "I've been up here with my folks. You should see it. There's about a million cows and they're all standing on this mountain of shit. They just eat and shit all day long and that mountain just keeps getting bigger and bigger."

"You're making that up."

"Am not and your nose is saying that I'm telling you the truth."

Kelly took her fingers from her nose and made a show of taking a big whiff. "Yuck again. You're not lying. That's poop alright. Pretty awful."

"Pretty awful," Paige said. "Just think of the poor cows. They stand in it all day long and then somebody turns them into hamburger."

"Big, big yuck. I'm never eating meat again."

"I thought you liked Mickey Ds?"

"Not anymore."

"That's what I said when I was up here. But after a little while I started back up again. I love hamburgers too much, so I try not to think about it."

After a bit they were at the pens. The cattleyard was between them and Highway 5. Paige saw the headlights off in the distance.

"You weren't lying. It's a lot of cow poop," Kelly said. The cows were milling about, like they too were waiting for the sun. The girls kept walking. The road wound around the penned in cattle, then turned away from them. "Look." Kelly pointed. "A real road."

"Yeah, and it's going to the highway. We're safe now." They turned left, spirits high.

* * *

Guthrie flicked his Zippo and lit a cigarette.

"You smoke too much," Rice said.

"You smoke."

"In moderation." He pulled one out of his pocket. Guthrie handed him the lighter. Nothing better than the smell of lighter fluid as flint sparked it to flame.

"Yeah, well I like cigarettes. Is it a crime?"

"No. But looking at you, the way you work out, you wouldn't think smoker. And you're a chimney."

"I hold my own. I'm not the one sitting in the car. I'm in shape. Great shape. I can go forever."

"I know," Rice said. He was agitating him. That was the last thing he wanted to do. "I'm not one to talk. I get out of breath going to the john. I was just making conversation."

"Just so you know I can hack it. Don't want no

one thinking I can't."

"I know you can, Guthrie. We're all counting on you." The dumb fuck was puffing up like one of them birds with all the feathers in its tail. He was so easy to manipulate. Just had to know the right buttons.

"Look out there." Guthrie had his hand on the door latch.

"Wait. Let them get closer. They gotta go right by here to get to the highway. That way you won't have to run as far."

"I told you I can hold my own."

"Yeah, I know, but there's two of them. What if they split up? Be a lot harder to catch."

"Right. I'll wait." But he didn't take his hand off the latch. Guthrie wanted those kids so bad his whole body was shaking and his head had gone red with anger. Rice couldn't let him hurt the cunt.

"After we get them, you're supposed to take the kid down to the boat so Clay can make the exchange." That was the first plan. Jerry and Clay could just go back to it. The cunt was his.

"I thought we were supposed to keep the big one alive?"

"Yeah, that's what I said. I meant for me."

"You mean so you can poke her?" Guthrie said.

"That's the reason. You got a problem with that?"

"No, you can poke the kid too for all I care."

"What, you think I'm some kind of pervert? You don't mess with kids. Not like that. What the fuck's wrong with you?"

"Just making conversation."

"Are you making fun of me?"

"Yeah."

"You just make sure you get the kid down south

alive and kickin'. I'll take the pickup down after I'm done with the cunt. I'll be about three hours behind."

"You need that long?"

"I'd like forever, but three hours will have to do."

"How you gonna kill her?"

"I'm gonna fuck her to death."

Guthrie opened the door. "I'd rather be out there chasin' after them, than in here listening to this shit."

"Let 'em get closer," Rice said. But they'd stopped. They'd recognized the car.

"Go."

"I'll get 'em."

* * *

"I'm hungry." Kelly said.

"Yeah. Me too. It won't be long now." Paige couldn't remember the last time she'd eaten. Yesterday, before her mom dropped them at the beach. She thought of Peter, glad that he'd gotten away. Would she ever have a story to tell him.

Kelly tugged on her arm. "It's their car."

Paige stopped. "Looks like it."

"They're never gonna give up." Kelly clutched onto Paige's hand.

"We're gonna have to make a run for the ditch. It goes back toward the cow pens." It was a good ways back to the pens. They should have sought help there, but the road looked so much better.

"Not the ditch again."

The car door opened. Someone was getting out. It was Guthrie.

"Come on!" Paige said and they took off toward the ditch.

Guthrie was out of the car now, running to

intercept them, but the road they'd been on ran northwest after it passed the pens, intersecting the highway at an angle. The ditch ran north and south along the highway, Guthrie was north and ahead of them. No way could he get in front of them before they were down in the ditch.

In seconds they were there. Kelly slid down on her buttocks. Paige jumped in behind her. The bottom of the ditch was full of water now, because of the rain. It went up to her knees. Kelly was splashing ahead of her, frantically charging through the water and the mud. Now they were running south, the opposite of the way they'd been going earlier when Guthrie was after them. Kelly stumbled and went down in the mucky water. Paige pulled her up.

"Come on, we gotta keep going."

"I'm going." And she was up, running and splashing again.

This time there would be no hiding. The sun would be coming up soon. So even though they were in the dark, the fresh-grave atmosphere of the ditch offered no safety. It would only be a matter of seconds before Guthrie came in after them. The water was up to Kelly's thighs, slowing them down. Guthrie would be able to go a lot faster.

Behind them, Paige heard the sound of falling dirt and tumbling rocks. He was sliding down the side. They heard him splash as he hit bottom and Paige wished they could see. Now she was ahead, pulling Kelly as they struggled to get away from the steady machine-like wheezing that was down in the coffin-like enclosure with them. He was way out of shape, maybe he couldn't keep up, but they couldn't take the chance, they had to get out of the ditch and get to safety.

When Paige judged they were below the pens, she started to climb, pulling Kelly up with her. Guthrie was coming fast. His wheezing increased in tempo and lowered in pitch. Paige felt it steamrolling toward her. Kelly pushed past her and was out. Paige slipped. Guthrie was so close, reaching for her leg. "Run, Kelly!"

"Take that!" Kelly screamed.

A large rock smacked into Guthrie's face. He stopped, staggered, fell.

Paige pulled herself out of the ditch.

The moon peeked through a hole in the clouds, but Paige didn't need the light, because Guthrie was too hard a target to miss. The ground was peppered with big rocks, like broken up concrete. She picked one up and sailed it into Guthrie's side as he tried to pull himself up. Kelly threw another, missed. Paige hit him a second time.

"Now! Run!" Paige wanted to get away while he was stunned. They turned and started all out for the pens, visible now in the full moonlight. Paige was afraid she wasn't going to make it. She was running flat out. She forced heart and muscle to give a little more. Then she got her second wind. Kelly must have too, because she was running right with her toward the wooden fence as the clouds aloft again blacked out the moon.

The rocks had slowed, but not stopped him. He was back there. Coming. She smelled the cows. Thousands of them. She inhaled it, sucking the odor deep into her lungs as she ran for the cattle pens.

"Gotta get in with the cows," Paige said. Kelly shot ahead, charging toward the pens. The kid was faster than she thought. They'd beat Guthrie easy. She risked a look over her shoulder as she ran. Somehow he'd gained on them and he was closing the distance. She heard his rumbling wheezing like stereo blasting from giant speakers. Any second he was gonna be on them.

"Help," Kelly wailed. Paige was fighting for breath. She tried to scream, but she couldn't, not and run at the same time. "Help," Kelly yelled out again. But Kelly could, thank God. Her screams pierced the night. Someone had to hear.

Close now. The ghost shapes of hundreds of beef steers were moving in the pens. Kelly's screams had them agitated. Kelly hit the fence first and she was on the ground, sliding under it without any urging from Paige.

"Help," Kelly yelled. Cows mooed and moved.

"Don't." Paige slid under the fence. "You're scaring them." She was on her feet, covered in mud and manure. Kelly grabbed her hand and started pulling her in among the animals.

They were in danger of being trampled by the nervous cattle, but right now she was more afraid of Guthrie. Did he come in after them? She was afraid to look as she followed Kelly. They made their way through the fenced-in herd, each step burying their feet in squishy manure as they climbed a mountain of the muck.

They headed toward the center of the pen, dodging between the animals, like winding through a maze. The cows began to settle down and Paige felt a tug on her arm as Kelly stumbled and fell. She pulled her up. Kelly was shaking. Paige pulled her into herself and tried to hug her fright away. Then, with the cattle quiet, they moved toward the other side of the pen. She wanted out before the cows panicked.

When they'd slid under the fence the danger outside was worse than the danger inside, but now Paige was thinking about what could happen inside and she didn't want to be crushed. She'd seen enough of those old cowboy movies to know what stampeding cattle herds could do.

The clouds overhead parted for a few seconds again, allowing a hint of light through the dark and Paige saw the other side of the pen only feet away. She made for the fence. There was a building in the background. She couldn't see what it was, but it had a light on. That meant people. Someone up. If she could only make it to there.

The cattle were quiet and that was a good sign. She allowed herself to breathe a sigh of relief as she reached her hand out to the fence.

"I see you." Guthrie's voice ripped through the night. He was among the herd. The cattle started to panic, pushing against each other, and them. Kelly's hand was ripped away when a frightened steer bumped into her.

"Paige!" Kelly screamed. Now Guthrie had her and he was dragging her into the swirling cattle. Then something banged into her head and Paige's world went black.

CHAPTER SEVENTEEN

"OKAY DAD, FILL 'ER UP. We'll be back in a bit."
Mike tossed the keys.

Malcolm Morrison snatched them out of the air.
"Don't you think you're pushing it, taking that car?"
He squeezed the keys so hard it hurt. Those two were
too reckless. One of these days they were going down
and Malcolm was afraid he'd be going along for the
ride, because neither one of them was a stand up guy.
When it came right down to it, they'd talk.

"It's Saturday morning. Shooting day. You know
that."

"One of you should stay in town," Malcolm said.

"Yeah, Dad, you said that, but nothing ever happens around here. Saturday morning's important to us." Mike had been calling him Dad ever since he'd married his daughter. Divorced a year now and he still called him that. Malcolm never liked it. Not then, not now.

"Yeah, nothing ever happens around here, but look what turned up," Malcolm said. "The most wanted car in the state and you hotwire it up so you can go off to the desert in it."

"Those women are long gone."

"What if you get caught in the car?"

"By who? We're the law." Mike was acting like they were the only two cops in the state. Didn't he understand they sent crooked cops to jail all the time?

"Just makes more sense to take the Cherokee," Malcolm said.

"She ain't running right. I told you."

"So. It's not like you're gonna be ripping up the desert with it."

"We got the Taurus. We're taking it." Mike got in. J.D. slid into the shotgun seat.

Malcolm shook his head. They were two stupid sons of bitches.

* * *

Sara pulled away from the cemetery, driving with the headlights off. She felt high, like when she used to smoke grass before she was married. It must be an adrenaline rush. She'd never broken into a house before, never stolen anything. Did burglars feel this way every time they got clean away? She tingled. If so it was a powerful reason to steal. You could get hooked on it.

She smelled the tuna casserole as Dottie took the lid off the Tupperware dish. Like a shot, Sherman's head was over the seat with his nose in the bowl. In an instant it was gone.

"Jeez," Sara said. "What a pig. We were supposed to share that."

Sherman barked from the back seat.

"He's hungry."

"What about us?"

"He's still growing."

"Looks all grown up to me. Never mind. Tell him we'll find something soon," Sara said. She was hungry too. "We'll stop at the first McDonald's or Burger King we see."

"He likes Wendy's."

"Oh, does he?"

"It's good to hear you laugh," Dottie said. "It shows that even in adversity you can keep your humor. That means you'll keep your head, too. Not panic or go off half cocked."

"I went off pretty half cocked when we lost the Taurus."

"Oh, I don't know. We have a car the cops aren't looking for."

"So now we can add auto theft to our list of crimes." Sara was still speeding from the adrenaline rush. "Are you all tingly inside, like you just pulled off the heist of the century?" She turned onto the road out of town.

"Yes, I guess I am. I kind of like it," Dottie said.

"Yeah," Sara said. "You get away with a small crime like that and you feel like you can do anything." She shifted up into third.

"I didn't feel like that after we got away from the

mall," Dottie said.

"Me either. Maybe because we were too scared. I wasn't that scared back there. Not in the laundry or breaking into that house."

"Does that mean we're getting used to living on the lam?"

"God, I hope not." Sara laughed. "Living on the lam. No one talks like that anymore." She clutched and tried to shift up into fourth. "Uh oh."

"What?"

"Won't go into fourth." She clutched and tried it again. "No grinding. It just won't go." She tried fifth. "No fifth either."

"What's it mean?"

"Broken linkage maybe. Something wrong with the trans, I don't know. The car's broke, that's the bottom line."

"Car coming ahead."

"I see it." Sara saw the lights far ahead. It looked like they might have pulled out of the gas station. There was a house on the right. Sara popped it into second. The tires chirped as the car slowed. She pulled over to the side of the road, passed the driveway and backed into it, all the way up to the side of the house. She stopped next to a curtained window that opened onto the driveway. "Let's hope we didn't wake anybody up."

A light in the house went on. "We did," Dottie said.

"That light's not too bright," Sara said. "Maybe it's a bedroom in back. Maybe someone just got up to go to the bathroom."

But another light went on and the light peaking through the curtains got brighter. "Guess that's not it," Dottie said. "Someone's up."

Sara shut off the engine and it became quiet. Sherman's panting seemed like a roar. Dottie rolled down her window. Crickets chirped through the night. A slight breeze rustled the leaves of the tall hedge that surrounded the house.

She wished that car would hurry up and pass. Maybe she was being overly cautious. Maybe she didn't have to hide from it. But maybe whoever it was knew the Trooper. She couldn't chance that.

All of a sudden light came through the window and illuminated the Trooper as someone parted the curtains. A face pressed against the glass, looking out.

"It's just a kid," Sara said.

"But I'll bet Mommy and Daddy are home," Dottie said.

"He can't see us," Sara whispered. "Too much light inside, too dark out here." But as if he'd heard, the boy put his hands to his head, like blinders, so he could see better. "Oh shit. He's raising the window."

He got it up and peered through the screen. "Hey, neat dog." The boy was about six or seven and was smiling wide. He was missing his two front teeth and kind of whistled when he talked.

"His name's Sherman." Dottie reached back and scratched the dog between the ears. Her face was only inches from the boy's.

"Hi, Sherman," the kid said.

Sherman barked.

"I don't believe this," Sara whispered. Why hadn't that car passed? Did they stop for something? This was taking forever.

"My mom won't let me have a dog," the boy said.

"Maybe when you get a little older," Dottie said.

"I hope," the boy said.

"Kenny, who are you talking to?" A woman's voice from somewhere behind the boy. Nervous.

"This lady and her dog," Kenny said.

"How many times have I told you not to make up stories." Mom didn't sound friendly. Sara saw her come up behind her son. Saw her put a hand to his shoulder.

Sherman barked again.

Mom screamed.

"Hey, it's okay," Kenny said.

"Henry, get the gun," Mom yelled.

* * *

Malcolm shuffled around to the front of the Cherokee. He looked around. No one. He opened the door, slid behind the wheel and started it up. He gave it a little gas. She sounded fine. Ah, well. He put it into drive and drove it up to the pumps. He shut it off and put the keys into his pocket out of habit.

He went around to the pump and pulled out the hose. He filled the two jerry cans hanging off the right rear first. Mike needed the extra gas, because he never believed the gauge. When the car sputtered, he filled it from the jerry cans, then came in for the real deal. The jerry cans full, Malcolm stuck the hose in the tank and locked it on. He jerked a couple of blue paper towels out of the dispenser while it was filling, then he pulled the squeegee from the bucket and started to do the windows.

Someday Mike was gonna go too far and they were all gonna get in a lot of trouble, but for now, Malcolm was enjoying the extra money. Besides, the boys only stole rentals from up to the hotel. Nobody got hurt. It wasn't like they took anybody's personal car. Rental cars and insurance companies got a little of their own back. It was only fair.

A car pulled off the interstate. Malcolm hurried back to the safety of his bullet proof booth. Couldn't be too careful.

* * *

"What is it?" Male voice screaming from the background. Loud, protective.

"Kenny, get away from the window." Mom going nuts.

"There," Dottie said. The car went by. Finally. "It's our Taurus. Must be those cops."

Sara popped the clutch and spun the tires down the driveway as the porch light came on. "That was close."

"That was sad," Dottie said.

"What?" Sara looked in the mirror as she went into second. The house was all lit up. She turned to look out the back window. Mom, Dad and Kenny were on the porch. She didn't see a gun. Kenny was waving.

"They won't let him have a dog. What kind of parents won't let a kid have a dog?"

"My parents never let me have a dog."

"Did you get along with them?"

"Not when I was little."

"See."

"Won't get much past forty in third. Two slow for the highway and we'd probably burn it up."

"What are we gonna do?"

"Just ride it out in the slow lane, I guess."

"Look there. It's that cop car," Dottie said. "And

no cops."

Sara turned into the gas station. A Corvette, low and sleek, passed them as they pulled up to the pumps. It was red, top down. A young man with bleached blond hair was driving. All tan and muscles. The passenger was an older woman. Not his mother, Sara guessed. It roared out of the station, shooting under the interstate and taking the southbound ramp.

"No cops came running out to chase after that 'Vette," Dottie said.

"Didn't see any."

"They took our car. Only fair we take theirs."

"That's the way I see it." Sara stopped next to the Cherokee. "See any keys?"

Dottie stuck her head out the window and looked into the Cherokee. "No, but I bet he has 'em." She pointed to the man in the booth.

"Let's ask." Sara drove over and got out. The man behind the glass looked ancient. The neon light above his head accented the liver blotches on his face and arms and made the blue-black veins on his drinker's nose stand out like rivers in a desert.

"Evening," Sara said.

"Back at cha," the man said. "What are you doing with Mike McKinna's car?"

"I borrowed it. My name's Sara and the woman in the car is my friend Dottie, but you know who we are, don't you?"

"I know."

"And your name is?"

"Morrison, Malcolm Morrison."

"Here's the deal, Malcolm. We're gonna leave the Trooper with you. That way Officer Mckinna won't be so mad 'cuz you gave us the keys to his police car."

Sara heard Dottie's door open and close, but she didn't take her eyes off the man in the booth.

"Can't give you the keys." Malcolm's lower lip was quivering.

Sara saw Dottie take the thirty-eight out of her purse. All they'd been through and she hadn't had to use it. Would she use it now? Sara saw the look on her face. Yes, she would. "So then you know we're not playing games here. I'm going to tell you something. I'm going to make it quick, because we don't have a lot of time. Everything you've heard about us is a lie. We've been framed. My little niece was kidnapped along with Paige Radoslaw. No one believes me and I'm trying to find her before it's too late."

"I'm sorry." His hands were shaking. Oh well, she'd tried. He picked up a phone.

"I wouldn't do that," Sara said.

He started pushing buttons.

Sara rushed around to the side of the booth, looking for the phone wires. Nothing coming from the sky.

"There," Dottie pointed to wires coming from the ground. They stopped at a junction box.

Sara grabbed them and jerked. Nothing. No give at all. "They're in too good."

"Let me," Dottie said. She pointed the thirty-eight at the wires and pulled the trigger. The sound was thunder-loud as it ricocheted back from the side of the booth. The neon light inside went out.

"Hey!" Malcolm yelled.

"Wrong wire," Dottie said.

Sara went back around to the front of the booth. "Okay, Malcolm, the keys or we start shooting." He looked different lit up only by the overhead lights outside. Kind of maniacal.

His eyes slanted when he said, "Bullet proof glass. You can't do anything to me. And pretty soon someone's gonna come off the highway and you'll be in deep shit."

"Last chance, Malcolm," Sara said.

"No."

Sara jumped into the Trooper. She revved it up, backed it up and faced the booth.

"Shoulder harness," Dottie yelled out.

* * *

"You can't do this!" Malcolm shrieked as she pulled on the harness and latched it into place. The headlights came on. He put a hand up to block out the light. She hit the brights. She revved the engine again. "Stop!" He jumped back as the car slammed into the front of the booth.

The sound was deafening, like he was rolling around inside a thundercloud. The neon tube popped, raining glass. The phone jangled and flew from the little desk, hitting him in the head as he slammed into the back wall. A couple of field mice ran out from under his desk, by the place where he rested his feet. One of them scurried across his leg in an effort to get away. In a daze he watched as they squeezed under the door at a full tilt run and were gone.

No way were they gonna get the best of him. Not tonight, not while he could still draw breath. He pushed himself up. One hit and the inside of his booth had been turned to dust and debris, but it held. She wasn't getting in. Not a chance.

He looked out through the bulletproof glass. She

was kinda slumped forward, but the harness had saved her from crashing into the wheel. She looked dazed. Good. But then her eyes cleared and focused on his.

"I don't believe this," he muttered. "She's gonna do it again."

He stepped back to the back wall as she put it in reverse and moved back. Their eyes were locked together like they were having good sex. Maybe that's the way a killer sees his victim. And there was no doubt, she was a killer. She was gonna do him sure as shit. That asshole Mike never should have messed with her car. Mess with a tiger, you get eaten.

"You're crazy," Malcolm hollered.

"I know." He couldn't hear, but he saw the words on her lips. She never took her killer eyes off him. Just bore into him. So intense.

"Oh, shit," he wailed. The wheels were spinning on the slick concrete. Black smoke flew from the tires, the smell assaulting him before the car caught traction. "Wait," he yelled, but it was too late, the screaming tires found purchase and the car shot forward like a striped ass ape. He pulled himself away from the lock her eyes had on him. One of the headlights was out, steam hissed out of the radiator. His world was moving in slow motion. He sighed. He was going to die.

The car hit. His desk flew from the wall. The booth shook on its foundation. The wood ceiling screeched as the wooden beams and slats ripped. He was knocked on his ass again. He hurt. He pushed himself against the back wall and pushed himself to his feet.

Both headlights were out now. Miracle of miracles, the thick bullet proof glass held. The booth was still basically intact. He sought her eyes. She was leaning forward in the harness, head down. Was she hurt? She didn't move. Was she dead? For an instant he hoped so, but quickly regretted it. She was taking every bit the beating he was. She wanted those keys real bad.

A car pulled off the interstate. One of those Jap cars. A Toyota maybe. He watched as it drove up to the pumps. Saved. Surely the women would go now. A man got out. Started toward the booth. Stopped.

"What's going on here?"

"Gas station's closed," the old woman said. Her hands were at her sides, but she had that gun in one of them. Malcolm saw it. The man from the Toyota saw it.

"What are you doing to that man there?" Mr. Toyota said.

"Nothing you want to know about," the old woman said. Something growled, then Malcolm saw the biggest damn dog he'd ever seen in real life. Mr. Toyota saw it too. He backed up. "This man here is cheatin' on my little girl," the old woman lied. "He ain't getting any less than he deserves. You wanna get involved, you're gonna wind up like him."

The dog growled again.

"You're not gonna kill him?" Mr. Toyota said.

"No, but he's gonna wish he was dead. There's another gas station up the road. You should go there."

"Come on, Jim. Let's just mind our own business," a woman said from the passenger window of the Toyota.

"Your wife?" the old woman said.

"Yeah," Mr. Toyota said.

"Smart lady," the old woman said. Her dog

growled again.

"I think so." Mr. Toyota got in his car and took off.

"What's wrong with people today?" Malcolm wailed. He was shaking. His world was coming apart and nobody was gonna help him. Mike and J.D. were off shooting their damn guns and there was no way anyone else was gonna help.

He looked up at the woman behind the wheel. "The key," she mouthed.

Malcolm shook his head no. The front of the car seemed welded to the booth, but she spun the wheels in reverse, again stinking the place up with the smell of burnt rubber. She was in first now, wheels spinning in the other direction. This was the final charge. He knew it. She knew it. One or both of them was gonna die. She wasn't gonna give up. He'd seen it in those eyes that had no bottom.

The car was moving as he threw his hands up in the air. The tires screeched as her foot stomped on the brakes. She had lightning reflexes. Then he remembered that she was a race car driver. Took guts to do that. She must be very good.

* * *

His hands were up. She blasted the brakes and spun the wheel to the right. The Trooper fishtailed toward the side of the booth, but she had her foot back on the gas and only struck it a glancing blow as she pulled away from it. Clear, she shifted to neutral and was once again on the brakes.

Dottie was at the door, helping her out of the Trooper. Sherman licked her hand. "Good dog." Sara staggered over to the booth. "You okay?"

"Yeah." He nodded.

"We're in a hurry now. The guy in that car might get the cops and we wanna be gone."

"Sure," he said. He tried the door. The latch clicked, but it didn't open. He stepped back, lowered himself and gave it a kick. The door flew open. She saw a lot of anger behind the kick.

"The key." She had her hand out. He stuffed a hand into his dirty jeans and pulled out a key ring. He tossed it to her and she caught it easily.

"You know anyone named Guthrie?" She didn't know why she asked. Instinct.

"Yeah, Guthrie Dunn. Watchman over to Orsmond Oil where they got all them fancy wells."

"How far?"

"Not very. He's got a kind of house, well more a cabin. He lives out in the middle of all them wells."

"You know the way?"

"Yeah. You can cross the interstate and do the rest of the way overland if you don't want anyone seeing the car. Little over a mile maybe, something like that."

"Come on. You're coming with us." Sara went to the Jeep. Malcolm stood fast. "I don't think you understand," Sara said. "You don't have a choice. I need to get to that cabin as quickly as possible and I'll roll over anything that gets in my way. Give me your word you won't be any trouble and you can ride with your hands free. Don't and I'll use a pair of your friend's handcuffs. I don't have any keys though, so I don't know when you'd get them off."

"Every cop in the state is gunning for you." He started toward the car.

"Yeah." She opened the back door.

"What the hey. There's gotta be more to life than pumping gas and selling hot auto parts."

"For the record. I told you the truth," Sara said.

"I know."

"How?"

"You got heart. I saw it in your eyes." He got in the back seat. Sherman jumped in after him.

"Don't eat the man, Sherman." Dottie climbed in the front.

CHAPTER EIGHTEEN

RICE JUMPED OUT of the car. Guthrie had the kid. The cunt was down, rolling under the fence. Rice ran through the muck. The steers were milling about, upset by Guthrie, but they were stepping around the cunt. She was half in the pen and half out.

He was wheezing louder than Guthrie by the time he made it to her body. She looked dead. No, the tits were rising and falling with each breath. His tits now. His boner had gone soft during the run around the pens, but it was going hard again. He grabbed her muddy feet and pulled her out from under the fence.

She was unconscious, but she looked asleep.

Something had whacked her in the head. Did she trip and get smacked by a hoof? Guthrie's fist? He bet on the fist. It'd be just like that hermaphrodite to try and waste her behind his back. Deny him what was his. Jealous, that's all it was. Some guys could get it up. Others couldn't. He wouldn't trade with the muscle bound donkey for all the boys on the planet. Young ass is no good if you can't get it hard. Better to have AIDS than to be like Guthrie.

Where was he? Rice stole a quick look around. No one in sight. Did he have a minute to pull it out and pound it? Sure. His hands were going to his zip when he realized they were all muddy. He'd foul the pants. Guthrie would see. Have to wait. He had all the time he wanted with the cunt now anyway.

He thought about calling out for the big fuck to carry her to the car, but he was afraid he'd hurt her beyond repair. Besides, he wanted his hands on her as soon as possible. Right away. Now. He bent and squeezed a breast. Soft as he'd thought. He squeezed the other one half expecting her to cry out.

Not a peep. Zonked. Good for now. No screaming. No crying for help.

The sky was going gray off in the east. The sun was trying to come up. Daylight soon. He had to get her to the car before anybody came. He moved around her body till her head was laying between his feet, then grabbed her by the wrists and dragged her toward the car.

It was slow going. He had to stop and rest twice. It was hard work. Too tired during the rest stops to play with the body. He wanted to do more than squeeze tits. Besides, no fun squeezing them if she wasn't awake to enjoy it.

He saw the car. He stopped for a third time. Guthrie was standing by it with a hand on the kid's neck. She was stone quiet. Probably afraid Guthrie would snap the life outta her if she opened her yap. He probably would too.

Rice grabbed onto her wrists again. The boner was gone now. He was gonna need a little rest before the morning activities. That's alright, he'd recover quick.

"You took forever. Place is starting to wake up," Guthrie said.

"I'm here now. Let's move."

"You guys are gonna get it. My aunt's gonna turn you guys to toast."

"Shut up, kid," Rice said.

Guthrie opened the trunk. "Gonna tie her?"

"No, she'll stay out. Besides, where's she gonna go?" The big fuck just stood there watching him. "You wanna help me here? I can't get her in by myself. And don't hurt her."

Guthrie scooped her up like she was air and dropped her into the trunk. She landed hard. Good thing she was out, she'd have screamed. Guthrie slammed the lid.

"Not gonna put the kid back there?"

"Last time we left them together, they got away. She rides in the back seat." Guthrie handed him a short length of rope, then pushed the kid toward him. "Do 'em behind her back."

Rice spun the kid around and tied her hands. No boner now, thank the saints. He didn't mess with kids. Didn't want the kid to think he was anything but normal.

Guthrie got behind the wheel, started the car and

revved it up like a teenager at a stoplight. He backed up, turned around and floored it.

"Hold down the speed. We don't want to draw the cops."

"I know all the cops around here. No one's gonna stop my car. We're drinking buddies."

"I'll bet."

"Was that a chop?"

"No, I just meant it made sense you drinking with the cops, you're so alike and all."

"Yeah." He had a smile on his face, ear to ear. Big fuck. Just push the right buttons.

Guthrie pulled the Chevy onto the interstate with his foot on the floor. They only had one off ramp to go, but he'd get it up to a hundred before they reached it if he could.

"So kid, tell me about your aunt," Rice said. "The one that's gonna toast me."

"She's just gonna, nothing to tell. You won't see her till she's on you. Then it's gonna be too late for you."

"So she's pretty tough?" He stole a quick look out the window. He wished the fuck would slow down, but he could never ask. It would mark him as weak. Couldn't have that. Better to keep talking to the kid. Keep his mind off the way the asshole was driving.

"She's tough. You gotta be tough to be a race driver. She's gonna get you. Then she's gonna toast Clay and Jerry."

"So you know about them?" Rice said. Guthrie glanced over. He was a dumb fuck, but even he realized the kid just signed her own death certificate. He doubted the kid would live very long after the call to Hawaii. Old granny would get one crying, tear jerking phone call, then curtains for little big ears Kelly. Stupid kid, shoulda kept her mouth shut.

"Yeah, and once Sara finds out, they're history."

"Maybe she ain't gonna find out," Rice said.

"I'll tell—" The kid shut up. Maybe she finally realized what she'd done. Maybe she just didn't want to talk anymore. No difference. It didn't matter. Guthrie was slowing down, getting ready for the off ramp. Safe.

And soon the cunt would be naked.

* * *

"Hey, Sherman." Malcolm moved closer to the dog. He wrapped an arm around the great head and put the dog in a headlock. "You're a big one, aren't cha boy?" He rubbed his knuckles in between the dog's ears. He loved dogs. All shapes and sizes. Dogs take you like you are. They just loved you. Sherman growled as Sara started the car, kind of a low rumble that matched the purring of the Cherokee's engine.

"You don't mean it, big guy," Malcolm said. Sherman stopped, but the engine kept on. It sounded fine. There was nothing wrong with it. Mike just wanted to take that Taurus out for a ride. A kid playing with what he shouldn't.

"Go under the interstate." Malcolm kept the dog in the headlock and continued his knuckle massage. "After a couple a hundred yards you're gonna take a right and head out off road. It'll look like you're driving off onto the moon, lots of rocks. You'll have to take it slow for the first bit, till you run into the first of the wells, the one painted up like Goofy. There's a dirt road just past it. Follow that and you'll wind up at Guthrie's."

She pulled it into drive and Malcolm released the dog. "Friends?"

Sherman barked.

"He usually doesn't take to people," the old woman said. Malcolm looked up at the woman. They were separated by wire mesh as the back seat was designed to transport felons. She didn't look so old now. Dottie, yeah, that was her name. She wasn't any older than he was.

"Dogs like me, Dottie. Always have. They know I don't mean them or theirs any harm. I'm not afraid of them and they're not afraid of me. Right, Sherman?" He scratched behind Sherman's ears and the dog barked again.

They were going under the interstate. He heard the whine of a big truck's tires as it roared overhead. "You can turn anywhere along here. Don't look for a road or tracks, you won't see none."

She turned. The sun was coming up to the right of them, bathing the clouds in a bright pink. "See the wells up ahead?" They were off in the distance, horse's heads bobbing up and down.

"I see them." Sara picked her way through the rocks.

"Only fifteen or twenty minutes of this, then if you know how to drive on a dirt track you can fly."

"I can drive on dirt," Sara said.

"I heard that about you on the TV," Malcolm said.

"How come they didn't bring the dirt track all the way to the road?" Sara said.

"I guess no one wanted to move all these rocks. Besides, you got access from the next exit up by the hotel, so it wasn't really necessary." Malcolm could see where someone might want to go charging through the rocks if they were in a hurry, but not this woman. She was a pro all right. She was taking the rocks at just the right speed. Any faster and they'd be tearing up the tires.

Sherman barked. The dog seemed to be having a hard time keeping his balance as Sara wound through the rocks.

"Down boy," Malcolm said and the dog dropped on the seat, laying his head in Malcolm's lap. "You got a good dog, Dottie," he said.

"I'm beginning to wonder. He's not supposed to mind anyone but me."

"Dust cloud," Sara said. "Car moving along that dirt track. Fast."

"There's binoculars in the glove box." Malcolm leaned forward, hands on the wire mesh, straining to see through the oil wells and the dust cloud.

Dottie popped the glove compartment open and took them out. "Old Chevy, moving quick."

"That'd be Guthrie," Malcolm said.

Sara added power, bouncing the Cherokee over the rocks. The right rear tire went with a hiss. "Flat. Damn. I know better." She shut it down and was out of the car in a flash. Dottie too. Sara pulled the back door open on her way to the rear of the car as there were no door handles on the inside.

"Let's be quick," Sara said.

"I've rotated these tires dozens of times." Malcolm had the jack out in seconds and was jacking the car as Sara was loosening the lug nuts. She was efficient.

"They've pulled up to a house," Dottie said. "I can just see between two of those stupid wells."

"Can they see us?" Sara said.

"Don't know," Dottie said. "Maybe the car."

"Guthrie won't think nothing even if he does see it. He'll just think it's Mike and J.D. out shooting. They do it every Saturday. Sometimes here, sometimes way over to the other side of the interstate."

"Who put these on?" Sara was struggling with the last lug nut.

"They're getting out of the car," Dottie said. "Two men, one young and big, one older and thin, sick looking."

"Sometimes I don't know my own strength. Stand on it," Malcolm said.

"The big one is pulling something out of the trunk. Oh, Lord. It's a person. Too big to be your niece, it must be Paige Radoslaw."

Sara stood and jammed her foot down on the tire iron. The lug nut gave with a screech.

"They're taking the girl into the house. One of them is dragging her. Damn, I can't see any more. Hold it. The big one's getting back in the car."

Sara twisted off the lug nut, then pulled off the tire.

"He's leaving," Dottie said. "Alone."

Malcolm looked off into the distance. The dust cloud was flying toward the interstate.

"Kelly, did you see Kelly?"

"No," Dottie said. "She's probably inside."

"Get that spare!" Sara yelled.

Malcolm had it right behind her, ready to go.

* * *

Rice looked down at the girl on the floor as he heard

Guthrie's tires spinning in the dirt. He was in an awful damn hurry to get away. Good. Two's company and he didn't want no crowd.

He bent over to pick her up. Fucking ape could've at least helped him get her onto the bed. The midget poodle barked. More a yap than a bark. Why the fuck didn't he take the fucking thing with him? Shit.

"What do you want?"

It ran over to its empty water dish.

"Fuck."

It barked again.

"All right!" He picked up the dish and filled it with water. "There!" The dog started lapping like it had just come in off the desert. Something about the fucking thing made him laugh. Cotton ball fluff on the end of its tail. A faggot's dog. Perfect for Guthrie, but cute.

He turned back to the cunt. He could do her on the floor, but the bed would be better. He grabbed her under the arms again, dragged her to the bedroom, across the throw rug and on to the bed. He stepped up on it and pulled her up. He got off the bed. "So nice." He planted a kiss on those lips. Nothing. Where was the boner?

He ran his hands over the tits. Squeezing. So firm. So soft. Heaven. But no boner. He rubbed his cock. Flaccid. He unzipped and pulled it out. It dangled between his legs. Useless.

He fisted it and started jerking. Nothing. Limp, limp, limp. Motherfuck. He turned back to the girl and dropped to his knees. He massaged the tits again. Ran his hand up and down her body. Rubbed his palm over her cunt. It felt like he knew a cunt would. It had been so long. He put his other hand to his cock. Still limp. Fuck. This couldn't be happening. It wasn't fair.

He grabbed her shorts. Was about to pull them off when he stopped himself. He pulled his hand away and stood up. He backed away from her, one hand still jerking on the limp dick. Reflex action. Years of training. The hand was doing its part. What was wrong with the dick?

He leaned back against the far wall and stared at the cunt. Maybe it was because she was unconscious. Yeah. If she was awake it would work.

He went outside to get the hose. He turned the water on and it reminded him of being hosed down in prison. All those naked men. Oh, fuck it was happening. In seconds he was fisting a stiff and rigid cock.

"Yes, oh yes." He dropped the hose and dropped to his ass on the porch. His hand never left his boner. He lay back, jerking, jerking, jerking, then he was shooting. Hot damn. Then the shock ran through him. He was a faggot. He couldn't get it up for the cunt.

And even if he could, he'd just spent himself. He bent the end of the hose, shutting off the flow and dragged it into the house.

Once he got the clothes off the cunt and had her hosed down it would be different. He'd be stiff again. He'd fuck the shit out of her. It was gonna be okay. He wasn't no faggot.

* * *

Malcolm admired the way Sara pulled the dead tire off and tossed it aside. There was a lot of strength in those slender arms. He rolled up the spare.

"Let it down." Sara spun on the lug nuts as he

released the jack. He started to put it away. "Leave it." Sara got back in the car. Dottie piled in back with Sherman. Malcolm jumped in as Sara was cranking it over.

She picked her way over the rocks. So slow. But not much further to the dirt track. She was one efficient lady. He'd never seen a flat changed so fast. And she was determined.

"There it is." Dottie pointed to the dirt track ahead.

"I see it," Sara said. Then they were on it. She pulled the trans into low. Dirt and rocks shot out from the tires as the rear wheels sought traction. They found it and all of a sudden they were flying. She upshifted to drive and Malcolm knew this woman hated automatics.

"You'll have to slow down soon," Dottie said.

"Why?"

"We can't go charging in. He might hurt the kids."

Sara slowed immediately.

"You can get closer," Malcolm said. "That oil well behind the house makes a hell of a racket. They won't hear us unless we drive right up on them."

"You sure?" Sara said.

"I've been in there. Guthrie worships Mike and J.D. At least once a month we all come over and get drunk on his beer. Not me. I'm old enough to know that getting yourself falling down drunk is pretty stupid. But Guthrie and the cops, they get pretty tanked.

"Those aren't the only cops that visit Guthrie," Sara said.

"No, his brother and another come up pretty

regular. Your husband, the one on the TV. That's the other one, I'm guessing."

"Yeah," Sara said.

"That sucks," Malcolm said.

"Yeah," Sara said. "It sucks."

"We should stop here," Malcolm said.

Sara braked. "It's getting light now," She said. "You two circle around to the left. I'll take the right."

"You know how to use a gun?" Dottie said. Sara gave her a look. "Dumb question. You take it. We'll have Sherman." Dottie handed over the thirty-eight.

Malcolm didn't understand it. These women just assumed he was gonna help. And what he didn't understand even more was that he wanted to.

* * *

Rice pulled the hose into the bedroom. Something nagged at him. She looked healthy. What if she woke up? She'd fight. He dropped the hose, not caring that water was spraying all over the floor. He looked around for something to tie her up with. Then he saw it. The phone cord. He hurried out to the kitchen and got a serrated bread knife. Sharp. He ripped the phone out of the wall. He cut off the cord, then cut it in half.

Back in the bedroom he tied her hands to the headboard, but he didn't have enough cord to do her feet. He wanted her tied down good. It was the best way. Besides, she could kick out if he didn't do the feet. He pulled the sheet out from under her and tore it into strips. Then he pulled her legs wide apart and lashed her feet to the foot of the bed.

He picked up the knife. So easy. He could cut her throat right now and nobody could stop him. An icy hand seemed to be tickling the back of his neck. The hairs on his arms stood up as if electricity was running through him. He could do anything he wanted. She belonged to him.

He tossed the knife onto the floor and picked up the hose. "Time to wake up." He was breathing fast as he hit her with the water. Immediately dirt and muck started oozing off the bed onto the floor. After a few minutes he started obsessing. How clean could he get her?

He covered the end of the hose with his thumb, making the spray harder. The shorts were white once. Could he make them white again? He worked in close. He stopped. He needed soap. Back in the kitchen. Dishwashing liquid. He poured it over her shorts, scrubbing, cleaning.

Now the tee shirt. He stepped back, squeezed the bottle over her, soaping her all up. Hosing her down. She was his. He scrubbed. Then there was no more soap. He kept at it with the water.

* * *

Paige felt like she was drowning. Sputtering, trying to suck air. She opened her eyes. It was raining. She was in the rain. Her head hurt. She tried to touch it, but she couldn't move her hand. Then she saw him. Rice, and behind him a little dog. It all came flooding back. The ditch, the rain, the cows. Running.

She turned her head away from the rushing water and it stopped.

"Finally awake. Good." He was standing above her. My God. His zipper was open and his thing was hanging down, a wet noodle between his legs.

He followed her eyes. "Fuck." He grabbed his

thing. He jerked on it. "It's your fault!"

What was he talking about? The room started spinning. She was dazed. He bent over. Why? Oh my God. He had a knife. "Your fault," he said again. She tried to roll away from him, but couldn't. Her feet must be tied up.

"Please," she said, voice a whisper.

"Your fault. Gonna cut you."

The little dog growled.

* * *

Rice stopped. Quiet now. The dog was looking toward the window. The hairs on the back of its neck were up like a cat ready to fight. Someone was out there. He peeked out the window. The fucking Hackett woman. The aunt. Coming up the back. How in the fuck had she found him?

He went to the bureau and started pulling open drawers. Guthrie always had a lot of guns around. Second drawer, Star nine millimeter automatic. Good gun. Made in Spain. He hefted it in his right hand. It felt good. Then he remembered the forty-five in the kitchen. Two guns were better than one. He went and got it. He set the Star down on the counter by the sink and felt the weight of the bigger gun. Too heavy, so he jammed it between his pants and the small of his back. Just like Magnum, he thought as he made his way to the door with his finger on the Star's trigger.

He stepped outside, then slipped behind the bobbing oil well. Fucking thing, Big Bird sucking oil out of the ground. Stupid big yellow bird.

She was close now. So smart. Stupid bitch hiding behind the pickup. She had a gun in her hand, but it wouldn't do her any good. He raised the Star automatic, pointing it at the back of her head.

"Bang, you're dead," he said.

"Kill," someone said and out of nowhere a giant bear thing sank long teeth into his gun hand, ripping at the hand, pulling him down as he jerked on the trigger.

CHAPTER
NINETEEN

NOT A BEAR. Big fucking dog. Big. It howled when the gun went off. Rice howled too as its fangs ripped flesh. Fuck. He grabbed a look at the thing that used to be his right hand as he reached behind his back for the forty-five with his left.

Eyes on the beast, fingers wrapped around steel. Where was the woman? He yanked his head around. Got her. She was turning, leading with the gun. Wait. Man coming. He jerked the gun free, still stumbling, he brought it around and fired.

Missed and the man was going for the Star auto on the ground. No fucking way. Fucker has the gun.

Fucker's toast. He pulled the trigger. Watched the ground in front of the man explode as the gun kicked high and to the right. Bring it back. Take your time. Squeeze the trigger. This time he was ready for the kick. The man spun around with the blast. He was hit. Blood erupted on the guy's left side, but he was coming back around. He wasn't out.

Rice was about to pull the trigger again when something slammed into his right side. He jerked his head toward the woman as his whole body shuddered. He started to bring the forty-five around when he felt a blow to his chest. Fuck. The man on the ground was firing the Star. He pulled the gun back to the fucker. Another hit in the side. Another. Another. Fuck, he was being hammered.

The fucking woman. She had to go. Slam, slam. Two from the Star. The fucker. Rice pulled the trigger, again, again and again. He was firing wild. The small part of his mind still capable of rational thought knew it, the rest of his being didn't care. Another hammer blow to the side.

A pounding in the chest. From the Star. How many could it hold? Another kick to the chest, he stumbled. Blood, his. The thought jackhammered through him. Three more quick kicks to the chest, splitting him open. But he was still standing. Fuck them. The world was going dark. Would he see the tunnel? That light?

"Fuck!" He fell forward into the dirt.

Then he had his answer. No.

* * *

Malcolm was empty. Sara Hackett was, too. Malcolm was lying in the dirt. He tossed the gun aside and struggled up onto his ass. He put a hand to his left bicep. It came back covered with blood. The bullet went clean through, but he didn't think the arm would ever be the same, a lot of the muscle was gone.

He tried to move it. Couldn't. It hurt. Bad. Like the bone was nicked. Big gun, big wound. It was gonna get worse real quick. He'd been shot before. He knew the drill and he wasn't looking forward to it.

Dottie went over to the body and kicked it. "Dead." That woman. Didn't balk an inch at the gunfire. Stood there unafraid. Any woman he'd ever met would be running for the hills. She was something. The Hackett woman, too.

"The kids?" Sara dropped the thirty-eight and charged the house, Dottie right behind her. Hope they're okay. Whoever would've thought it of Guthrie? Still, he was out here by himself all the time. Hard to figure people.

"Come here, boy." Malcolm forced himself to his knees. Sherman trotted over. Malcolm inspected his mouth. A little bleeding, but the animal was going to be okay. "You are one lucky dog." Malcolm rubbed him between his ears, then with a hand on his back, he tried to stand. Nausea. Maybe vomit. He held it in. Not in front of the women. Forget about standing right now. Shock maybe. Yeah, shock.

Sherman licked his face. His arm hurt like a mother. Lots of blood, red, not dark. That was good. He clamped his hand over it to staunch the flow. Soon those women would be out of the house and then he could worry about it.

"Just me and you, boy. They got more important things to take care of right now." The dog moved close. Malcolm sat. The dog sat next to him.

* * *

"Sweet Jesus." Sara stared at the girl tied to the bed. She seemed awake. Dazed. Filth oozed off her body. Her white tee shirt was black, except for her breasts. That part of her was white, the spot between her legs, too. The monster had been pawing her. Soaping her down. It was like he'd tried to clean her, but only the sex spots.

"We have to get her out of there." Dottie picked a knife up off the wet and filthy floor. The hose was still going, jumping around like a scalded snake, hissing water in all directions.

"Right." Sara grabbed the hose, clamping off the flow as Dottie cut the girl loose. What was he going to do? Rape her or kill her? What had he already done? Would the girl ever be the same?

"We have to get her cleaned up. Find her some clothes." Dottie stroked the girl's hair. She held her hand up. "Smells like shit."

"It is," Paige Radoslaw said, her eyes more alert now.

"Find the shower." Dottie had a hand behind the girl's back, helping her up.

Sara dropped the hose, got up and found the bathroom. "Over here." She turned the shower on, adjusting the spray to warm.

Dottie brought the girl in, an arm around her waist. "Come on, honey, you'll feel better in a few minutes."

Sara knew they were doing the absolute wrong thing. They should take her straight to the hospital. They should preserve the evidence in case of a rape. But nobody was going to be prosecuting that man out front. Besides, the girl came first.

"Hands up, kiddo." Dottie helped her off with the tee shirt. "Now the shorts."

"I can do it." The girl pushed them down and stepped out of them. "So dirty," she mumbled. Then, "You're Kelly's aunt, aren't you?"

"Yeah."

"She said you'd come."

"Is she alright?"

"In the cattle pens. Trying to get away. Cows pushing, afraid." She was still kind of dazed, shaking.

"Are you okay? Did he do anything?" Dottie said.

"No. I don't think so. One of those cows kicked me in the head. I didn't wake up till just before you came." Sara felt Dottie's sigh. She sighed too. The bastard had been playing with the child's body, but she'd never know. Thank God. Sara helped her toward the shower. The girl stopped beside the tub and met Sara's eyes. "We were trying to get away. Guthrie caught her just before I got hit in the head."

"We'll find her." Sara desperately wanted it to be true. "But right now we're more worried about you." The girl looked so lost. Sara's heart went out to her.

"I'm okay." Paige stepped over the rim and under the spray. Water splashed out of the tub. The welt on her head was surrounded by a dark bruise. It had to hurt.

"You're sure you're alright?"

"Yeah." Paige took a bottle of shampoo from a rack under the shower head. "I'll be fine." She gave Sara a small smile, then drew the curtain. "Toss me my shorts. I'll clean them with the shampoo." She sounded rational.

"No," Sara said. "We'll find you something dry.

She didn't want the girl to see the white patch on the shorts. "Take as long as you need. Get really clean." Then to Dottie, "Why don't you check on Malcolm and Sherman while I try and find her something to wear."

Dottie left and Sara started going through drawers. Everything was too large. She could wear one of Guthrie's oversized sweatshirts, no problem, but she needed pants of some kind. She was about to give up and wash the dirty shorts when she saw the duffel bag. She dumped it out and discovered the smaller man's clothes. She picked out a faded pair of Levi's, a sweatshirt with cut off sleeves and a pair of high topped tennis shoes.

Dottie was back in the house. She started opening drawers in the kitchen. "This guy was into guns. Lots of ammo." She pulled boxes of shells out of a drawer by the sink and set them on the counter. "Hey, thirty-eights." She stuffed the shells into the front pocket of her jeans. "This is what I need." She pulled a couple of dish towels out of the next drawer down. "His wound's pretty bad." Then she was up and heading for the door.

"How you doing, Paige?" Sara was back in the bathroom.

"I've got a headache, but I'm okay. I don't think it's a concussion." Paige shut off the water and opened the curtain.

"You know about concussions?"

"Sure, I ride. Jumpers. I've taken a few falls. Concussions twice. I think I'm okay." She saw the clothes. "Those belong to Rice?"

"If that was his name, then yeah, they were his."

"Were his?"

"He's dead."

"We're supposed to love everybody. That's what they say in church. But I'm glad he's dead. Is that a sin?"

"I don't think so."

"Do I have to wear his clothes?"

"It's all there is."

"Okay." Paige dressed quickly.

Outside, Sara found Dottie with the towels wrapped around Malcolm's bloody arm. What a strange man. So obstinate at first, then he risked his life saving hers. And he had saved her. Without him that man would only have had one target. He took the bullet meant for her.

"Why?" she said.

"Why what? Ah, why did I help? Is that it?" Sweat ringed his forehead, dripping off his hair. He needed a shave. One of his front teeth was chipped. He had a lazy eye and that drinker's nose. He was gaunt like he didn't get enough to eat. Pale like he never went out in the sun. And he had those horrible liver spots on his arms and face. He was the most beautiful man Sara had ever seen.

"Yeah," Sara said.

"I don't know. After I gave Uncle Sam my twenty I just sort of settled for less. You ladies gave me a glimpse at what I coulda been."

"You are a hero," Dottie said. "No coulda been about it." She picked up her thirty-eight and dusted it off.

"Not really. I just figured my hand was a better place for the gun than his. Who knew he had another one? Who knew he'd start shooting at me? I was just lucky."

"Bullshit," Dottie said. "You're a hero. That's the plain truth. Period." Sara saw fire in Dottie's eyes.

"Yeah, well they said I was a hero in Vietnam, too. That didn't get me very far."

"You a good mechanic?" Sara said.

"The best."

"I race cars. All over the world. I need someone with tools that can travel. Hero preferred. Pay's good."

"I can travel."

"Job's yours." Sara watched Dottie load the thirty-eight as she talked.

"What about Kelly?" Paige said.

"We'll have to call the police," Sara said. "We don't have any choice now." She looked at Paige. She looked like an average California kid in those faded Levi's and sweatshirt. The black high-top tennis shoes gave the ensemble sort of a just thrown on look. A kid on the way to the mall. "There's something I have to tell you and I don't really know how to say it."

"What?"

"Your father's dead. I'm sorry."

"How?"

"I think my husband did it." It hurt to say. Would Paige blame her? Sara didn't know if she could stand that.

"Your husband, Clay?" Paige's lower lip was quivering. She bit it.

"Yeah."

"My dad had these rent-a-cops that were supposed to watch us," Paige said. "But me and Peter always gave 'em the slip, so he was gonna hire the real thing. Two cops named Clay and Jerry. They were gonna quit the police department and watch us full time." Her eyes were misting up. It was as if she was talking to someone who wasn't there. Sara wanted to take away her hurt, but she couldn't. Nobody could.

"That must be how he got the idea to kidnap you. And either your father figured it out or came to the house madder than hell at his security. One or the other. Maybe they had a fight. Maybe he accused Clay. Who knows? But Clay killed him. I'm pretty sure about that."

"But why did they take Kelly?" Paige asked. Her lip was quivering again. She couldn't stop it. She was going to cry.

"Because her grandmother is wealthy and would pay a fortune to have her back."

"What a creep." The tears started. Then she was in Sara's arms and Sara hugged her in close. "I should call my mom, she's probably really scared."

"I think that's a good idea."

"But I don't want to go back into that house."

"You don't have to, darling," Dottie said. "The phone won't work. He used the cord to tie you up." She put the gun in her purse.

"We'll call as soon as we get to a phone," Sara said. She turned to Dottie. "Let's load up and get out of here." Dottie helped Malcolm into the back. Sherman piled in next and she climbed in and closed the door after herself. Paige took the shotgun seat and Sara slid behind the wheel.

"Follow the dirt track straight out," Malcolm said. "In five minutes we'll be at the interstate. There's a truck stop and a hotel there. Lots of phones."

They were halfway to the overpass when Sara saw the dust cloud. "Someone coming, burning up the road."

"Lots of folks come by to look at the wells," Malcolm said. Then, "Better pull over, this one's in a hurry."

Sara pulled to the side of the road. The last thing she wanted was a head on out here in the middle of nowhere. It was a Jeep Wrangler. Top off. Really kicking up the dust. The driver slowed when he saw the police car, but he didn't stop. Then he was alongside. Sara locked on to his eyes when he passed.

"Jerry!" She dropped it into low, stomped on the gas, cranked the wheel hard to the right, spinning the car around. "It's Jerry."

"What?" Malcolm said from the back.

"Guthrie's brother. We've got him trapped. The road dead ends. No place for him to go."

"What are we gonna do if we catch him?" Paige said.

"We'll think of something." Dottie pulled the gun out of her purse.

The car was sluggish with all the weight, but it was a police car. Lots of power. Jerry's street model Jeep wouldn't be any match for it. They were gaining on him when Jerry made a hard right, going off the road and heading into the sea of oil wells.

Sara downshifted to low and pulled the wheel to the right. The car fishtailed and Sara had to fight the wheel to keep it in control.

"Yikes!" Malcolm said.

Sara glanced into the mirror. Malcolm was pressing the towels against the wound. His face was paper-pale. He was in pain. "You can swear," Sara said.

"Not in front of the kid." They were bouncing over caked earth. It was a smoother ride than her

Montero, but then she wasn't in the back seat with a bullet wound in her arm.

"I've heard it all. Say what you want," Paige said.

"Shit! Satisfied?" Then, "There's a dirt track up ahead, it leads through the oil wells to the foothills. Comes around behind Guthrie's. He must figure if he cuts across he can lose you in the hills. After a bit they change into mountains. Big trees, some houses, lots of places to hide. He could even pick up a road that gets him back on the interstate if he knows the area."

"How far to the dirt track?"

"Coming up quick. Make a right by the Road Runner."

"Okay, Malcolm. I'll let you out there. You guys can stay with him. I'll come back for you."

"No, I can make it," Malcolm said.

"Sorry. No arguments. Too much weight." Sara looked ahead. The sky was clear. It was early but it was already hot. She saw the Road Runner pumping oil and hit the brakes. "Quick, Paige get that back door open. It's a police car so they got no handles on the inside." Sara jumped out of the car and pulled open the door on the left. Malcolm got out, followed by Sherman.

* * *

Paige jumped out of the car, grabbed onto the door latch and pulled it open. The old woman jumped out.

"Here," she thrust the gun into Paige's hand. "Get in." She pushed her toward the car. "Go on."

Paige stared into the woman's shining gray eyes. Her head hurt where she'd been kicked. It was getting worse. She was so tired, but she couldn't quit. They still had Kelly.

"Hurry," the woman said.

Paige jumped into the car.

"Get out." Sara sounded hard.

"No." Paige clutched the gun to herself like a doll. "I'm staying." She fought tears. She sounded like Kelly at the fence, but this was different. That man was one of the kidnappers. They killed her father.

Sara shoved it into low. "Can you use that?" She still had her foot on the brake.

"I can. My father made sure we could shoot."

"You're the navigator. Watch ahead for hazards, tell me when the road's gonna turn before it does." Sara released the brake and put her foot to the floor. "And for Godsakes get rid of that. Put it in back or something."

"I'll hold onto it." She pulled her harness on and clicked it into place as Sara swung the cop car to the right. Then a quick left between a pair of bobbing zebras.

"Come on, Paige. You were supposed to tell me about that turn. Watch where we're going."

"The road goes left. Just after a giraffe." Paige took a quick look at Sara. She had her eyes on the road ahead. Full concentration, like Peter when he was playing those stupid computer games. They flew around the turn and she felt herself being pushed into the door by the centrifugal force. Sara was driving like a mad woman.

"Can you see him up ahead?"

"No, yes. There he is. I see the dust behind him."

Sara looked up, then back to the dirt track.

"There's some more wells up ahead. Giant bugs. I can't see what the road does." Paige thought Sara was going to drive right into the bobbing bugs. "Sharp right!" Without the shoulder harness she'd have been thrown into Sara as she took the turn.

Sara's hands were working the wheel as the car spun around. For a second Paige thought they were going to roll over. Then they were sliding off the road, but Sara's foot never left the floor. Dirt and dust flew from the tires as Sara struggled the car back onto the track. Then they were on it.

"The road goes straight now," Paige said.

"I see, thanks." Then, "You gonna shoot him?"

"Maybe," Paige said. The car was flying now. "How fast we going?"

"Real Fast," Sara said without taking her eyes off the dirt track." They were talking loud, but not yelling. "It's hard to shoot a man."

"You did."

"He was shooting at me."

"Yeah, well I can do it."

"You're only a kid."

"But I grew up a lot in the last couple of days." Paige's head really hurt now. "If I have to, I can do it. You just catch him."

"Maybe you should give me the gun." Sara was driving with only her left hand on the wheel. She reached over with her right for the gun.

"No!" Paige said. "I'm not running anymore." She pulled the gun to her breasts. "Don't even think about taking it." She scooted close to the door, as far away from Sara's outstretched hand as she could get. She turned away and looked out the window. The world started spinning, like she was inside a washing machine looking out. She turned back forward and it stopped. Maybe she had a concussion after all.

"Okay." Sara put her hand back on the wheel.

"We're gaining," Paige said.

"Yeah, we'll catch him before the hills."

Paige leaned back into the headrest. She watched the speedometer as the needle jumped around ninety. Then it started to move up. Ninety-five. A hundred. She'd never been this fast in a car before. She shifted the gun to her right hand and pushed the hair out of her eyes with her left. They were gaining on the cloud of dust ahead.

The road went up into the foothills. The Cherokee was faster on the grade. Then they were close. Going so fast. All the windows were open and it seemed like a storm was rushing through the car. So loud. It felt like her head was splitting open. Would he pull over? Then what would they do? Could she really shoot him? She shivered, because she knew she could.

"I'm going to shove him off the road." Sara clenched the wheel, yelling to be heard above the roar of the wind. Sara moved right up on his rear. "He should be shitting right now." She ran right into him, then tapped the brakes. The Jeep ahead started fishtailing, but after a few seconds he got it back under control.

"He's better than I thought." Sara mashed the accelerator to the floor again.

Paige barely heard Sara. Her head was screaming. She thought it was going to explode. The guy in that car. His fault. She should be home with Peter. Kelly should be safe with Sara. They had no right. They were policemen. They were supposed to be better than that. They were almost up to his bumper again. Sara was going to ram him again, harder this time.

But that wasn't good enough. Paige stuck her

right hand out the open window, pointed the gun ahead and started pulling the trigger.

"Whoa!" Sara stomped on the brakes. "Stop!"

But Paige kept firing and the Jeep in front fishtailed again, out of control. Good. She'd hit it. And it started to slide sideways. It was going to roll.

"Hang on!" Sara pulled the wheel to the left to avoid the collision, but she wasn't quick enough.

Paige dropped the gun and pulled her arm inside just before they slammed into the side of the other car. Metal against metal screeched through her brain. Then an explosion from the back of the car.

"We're on fire!" Paige screamed.

CHAPTER TWENTY

SARA KEPT HER FOOT PLANTED on the brakes with the wheel turned into the slide. The car was still on the road, but it was going sideways up the hill. She had no clutch to work, no gears, just the sluggish automatic. She added gas, regained some control. Jerked the wheel back to the right. Forty miles per hour. Engine screaming. Work the brakes.

"Road turns right," Paige shouted, but Sara had all she could do just keeping the car going straight. They shot off the road, accelerating down the hill. "Look out, there's a ravine!"

"What ravine?" Sara looked ahead. No time to

stop. She took her foot off the brakes and stomped on the gas.

"What are you doing?"

"Hold on!" It was just a gully. She'd jumped hundreds. But not in an automatic and not in a car on fire. She instinctively wanted to work the clutch. She hit the brakes just before the gully, pulled her foot off. Airborne, wheels spinning.

They slammed into the other side with the rear wheels grabbing only air. But the car plowed through the earth powered by forward momentum until the wheels hit the side of the gully, digging in and all of a sudden they were up and over.

Again Sara stomped on the brakes. She felt the heat. She grabbed a quick look behind. It must have been the jerry cans. One or both. What a stupid place to hang them. The back of the car was flaming. She'd never heard of anything like it. It shouldn't be happening. But it was.

"Tree!" Paige screamed.

Sara jerked her head back around. Big tree. Foot off the brake, back on the gas, wheels seeking traction, accelerating away from it. Not in time. The back of the car slammed into it. Oh, Lord. If that tank ruptures. Foot back on the brake. Slowing. "Get out," Sara yelled.

This time Paige obeyed. She had her door open. They were still going down hill. Quick look at the speedo. Ten miles per hour. "Now!" Sara opened her door and jumped away from the car. Paige was already out, pushing herself from the ground. "Stay down!" Sara yelled.

Paige dropped.

Sara dropped, facing away from the car, arms over

her head, waiting for the explosion.

Waiting.

Waiting.

Waiting.

She turned around. The car was barreling down the hill. The black and white Cherokee was covered in yellow and orange. A burning Halloween display off in the distance. But no explosion. Sara stood. Paige did too. They watched as the flaming car reached the bottom and rolled to a stop.

"God damn it, Paige. Who said anything about shooting?"

"I wanted to get even."

"Yeah, well, I guess he had it coming."

"Sorry. If I didn't do it, we wouldn't be here now." She looked like she was going to cry again. This wasn't the time or place to comfort her, but she'd been through a lot and she needed it.

"Hey, come here." Sara hugged her. "You tried to shoot one of the bastards that kidnapped you. He deserved it. You just screwed up. If you start apologizing for that, you'll be saying you're sorry for the rest of your life. I screw up all the time. I never apologize for it. I move on and try to do better."

"Yeah, but maybe he knew where Kelly was. I wasn't thinking."

"That was stupid. Don't apologize for being stupid either."

"What do you apologize for?"

"Almost nothing. You do something bad you know you shouldn't. Then you can say you're sorry."

"You screw up all the time? Really?" Sara broke the hug and looked into Paige's liquid eyes.

"Yeah, I do. It's because I'm always trying new

stuff. Anybody can work at Wal Mart, come home and watch TV till he goes to sleep. That guy's never gonna screw up. People like you and me, we're gonna do it all the time, because that's what you do when you live. You try something new. You screw it all up, learn from your mistakes and do better."

"You think I'm like you?"

"How many times did you try to escape?"

"Twice."

"So you screwed up the first time and tried again?"

"Yeah, I guess I did. And I stayed away a lot longer. I could've made it too, but—"

"But what?"

"Nothing."

"But you had Kelly with you and wouldn't leave her. That's it, isn't it?"

"Uh huh."

"Yeah, kiddo, you're like me. And we're not through yet. We'll just keep plugging away till we get her back and the bad guys are all in jail."

"Or dead," Paige said.

"Yeah, or that." Sara put a hand to her eyes and looked at the sun. "I guess Jerry's long gone and we have a long walk back. But at least we don't have to go up that hill. We'll go the same way the car did, then cut to the left and pick up the road."

"We should go up and see what happened," Paige said. "I think he wrecked the car. It looked like it was gonna go over when we went off the road."

"Alright." Sara started up the hill. Paige trekked along next to her.

"Look." Paige pointed.

"I see it." The Jeep was on its side. "Come on."

Sara started running. Paige matched her stride for stride.

* * *

Paige's head still hurt, but it was a dull ache now. Maybe she didn't have a concussion. Maybe it was nothing. Just a shock from being hit on the head that was wearing away. They reached the top at the same time. Sara ran to the Jeep. Paige stopped. She didn't know if she wanted to see a dead man. One that she'd killed.

"Over here," a man's voice called out. Paige turned. He'd been thrown clear. Oh, God. His face, the flies. She turned away. Stomach muscles clenching. Hard to breathe. No air. Vomit. She doubled over, grabbed her knees, gagged and retched.

"It's okay, honey." Sara was behind her, holding her.

"Look at him. I did it." Paige wiped her mouth with the back of her hand, then wiped it on the Levi's.

"Don't think about it."

"But look at him." Paige trembled.

"You wait here." Sara started toward the man.

"No, I'm coming." She took Sara's hand and turned to face him.

"I can't feel my legs." His voice cracked. He was crying. Tears mingled with all that blood. He was trying to shoo away flies with his left hand, but he couldn't keep them off his face. His right arm lay useless at his side. It looked broken.

Paige studied him as guilt bathed over her. He was on his back, his right leg bent at an ungodly angle, the upper bone in the right leg had snapped and was poking out. Blood poured out of the wound.

He'd been thrown clear, but he'd landed on his face at high speed, his body slowed down only by the friction of flesh against rocks and hard ground. She shivered. It was her fault.

"Where's Kelly, Jerry?" Sara dropped to her knees and started to examine him.

"I didn't want this. Clay's gone off the deep end. He's not himself."

"No shit." Sara looked over his leg. "Compound fracture of the femur. We've got major blood loss here." His other leg looked okay. Paige clenched her fists as Sara squeezed it. "Can you feel that?"

"No."

She squeezed his hip. "That?"

"No."

"You're in pretty bad shape, Jerry." Sara unbuckled his belt. He wore a pocket knife in a leather case attached to it. It fell at his side when Sara pulled the belt off.

"Tell me about Kelly."

"Sara, I'm bleeding to death."

"I'm working on that. Tell me about Kelly." She took the knife out of the pouch and made a couple new holes in the belt. The sharp knife easily cut through the leather.

"What are you doing?" Paige asked.

"Making a tourniquet." Sara wrapped the belt around Jerry's upper leg and cinched it tight. Almost immediately the blood stopped flowing out of the wound.

"How bad?"

"You're gonna lose the leg. Your back's probably broken. That arm looks pretty bad."

"You're not pulling any punches."

"We've known each other too long for that. Besides, you've already figured out about the back."

"Yeah, I guess I have."

"Are you in any pain?" Sara moved from his leg and cradled his head in her lap.

"My face kind of tingles, but other than that, no. Isn't that something? If it wasn't for the damn flies, it'd be almost peaceful."

"They're gone now," Sara said, gently shooing them away.

"Thanks," Jerry said.

"Why'd you run?"

"Stupid. Panic. I don't know. When I saw you I knew it was all over. I just wanted to get away. I should have known better."

"Now, tell me about Kelly."

"Clay called me on the car phone as I was coming off the interstate. Just before I saw you. Guthrie called him from that truck stop. He said that Paige was dead and that the kid knew all about us."

"Is he gonna hurt her, Jerry?"

"I hope not. I never wanted any killing." Jerry coughed, there wasn't any blood and after a few seconds he was able to go on. "I'm glad Paige isn't dead. I want you to know that. It was supposed to be a simple deal. We take Cyril's kids, he pays us thinking we're gonna make the exchange for him. Guthrie brings back the kids and everyone lives happily ever after. But Carole showed up pregnant and all of a sudden Clay starts blowing it hard. He had Rice snatch Kelly without even telling me and it all went down hill from there."

He coughed again. This time blood came up and Sara wiped it off his lips with her fingers. He tried to force a smile and Paige cringed, because it looked grisly. Blood coated his teeth. He didn't have long. Paige found her heart going out to him, despite what he'd done.

"Maybe you shouldn't talk," Sara said.

"I want to tell you."

"Okay."

"That kid in her belly was driving him nuts and when you helped her get away his mind sorta went south. Radoslaw walked in on him when he was pouring the gasoline in your house. The poor son of a bitch couldn't think how to explain away what he was doing, so he shot the man. Stupid. He killed one of the most famous men in America and he thinks he's gonna get away with it." Sara met his gaze. One of his eyes was bloodshot and didn't seem to be tracking, the other was filming over.

"Hasn't he? The whole world thinks I did it, thanks to those juicy tidbits you gave me."

"Cops aren't as stupid as people think. You called the FBI late at night and asked for the Special Agent in Charge. You got a kid with half a brain. Tom Montgomery's the SAC. He knows people. He would have believed you no matter how much we tried to incriminate you. That was a dumb idea, and it just puts the blame back on us, because sure as shit you'd a told Tom how you found out about the condom in the pocket crap.

"He already half believes you had nothing to do with any of it anyway and he hasn't even talked to you. Just that Spider kid from down the street and some black ex-con who came forward saying he burned up a store in the mall because he believed in you. Once you were caught, Tom would have believed you, too. Guaranteed, every cop in California is after Clay. You too, for sure. But the FBI knows he's guilty, probably me too by now."

"Talk to me about Kelly." Sara pulled her hair back. It was slick with sweat.

"You don't have much time. He's gonna kill the kid right after she talks to her grandmother tonight."

"What?" Sara said and dread chilled Paige to the bone.

"Five-thirty her time. Eight-thirty here. Soon as he hangs up the kid goes overboard."

"Overboard where?"

"He's on the boat. He thinks it's the perfect hideout. And apparently it is, because no one's found him yet. Maybe cops are stupid. Everyone knows about that boat."

"Time now?" Sara said.

"No watch," Paige said.

"Me either." Sara pulled a cheap digital off his wrist. "Sorry. I'm gonna need it."

"That's alright," he said as Sara stood. "Can you keep my name out of it? For Janet. It'll kill her."

"Sorry, Jerry. There's a dead man back at your brother's place. Cyril Radoslaw's been murdered. And it's not over yet. I couldn't keep your name out of it even if I wanted to."

"I had to ask." Then, "If my car phone still works you can call 911, maybe stop Guthrie before he gets the kid to Clay. He's driving an '82 Chevy. License plate is easy, seven letters. His name G-U-T-H-R-I-E, Guthrie.

"Check the phone," Sara said.

Paige ran to the Jeep. It was lying on the driver's side and it looked like it had rolled several times. For a second she thought about the burning cop car and she wondered if this one could catch fire, too. She smelled gasoline. The top was off. It was easy to reach in and grab the receiver.

It was the same kind of phone that was in her father's car. The thought almost brought tears to her eyes again, but she pushed them away. She had to worry about Kelly now. She checked the phone. Dead. She pushed the power button. Nothing.

"Phone's history."

Sara came over to Paige, almost whispering, "We've got a long run. Three, four miles, maybe more. Are you in shape?"

"Yeah," Paige said. "I'm a runner." The pain in her head was gone now. She looked side to side. Nothing moving that shouldn't be moving. "But we're not gonna just leave him, are we?"

"You've got no choice." Jerry had heard. They turned toward him. Paige fought back a second wave of nausea. He looked so broken staring up at them like that.

"He's right. It's eight o'clock, twelve-and-a-half hours before Clay calls Hawaii. Maybe if we can get to a phone, we can stop Guthrie before he gets off the interstate."

"Don't even think about calling anyone," Jerry said. "It's a lot farther than you think. You can't catch Guthrie before he gets to L.A. If Clay finds you called the cops, he'll kill the kid, sure as shit. He's got a scanner with him, too. More important, your boat's the last one on the dock. He'll be watching. No chance to approach before dark. He'll know. And there's no guarantee he'll have the kid with him anyway. Guthrie could have her someplace else. If he doesn't get the right signal, he could kill her."

"Would he do that?" Sara said.

"Oh yeah, he would," Paige said. She picked up the knife and started to cut the legs off the Levi's, turning them into shorts.

"You've got something he wants," Jerry said. "He might trade."

"What are you talking about?"

"You know where Carole is."

"He's that crazy?" Sara said.

"He is." Jerry said. "You want Kelly back. Go alone, offer a deal. He might go for it. He's not rational enough to think you'd turn him in the second you get Kelly back. Right now he hates you. He blames you for taking his unborn child. He calls you an aborter. But that could change. Show him how he can have Carole back. It's your only chance."

"Thanks, Jerry. I know you didn't have to do this."

"It was a bad idea from the get go." He coughed. It didn't sound good.

"Yeah. See ya."

"Don't run, Sara." He coughed again. "It's more like ten or twelve miles, not five or six. You got no water, so take it easy. A fast walk and a fast car might get you to the marina on time."

"That far? You sure?" Sara said.

"And it could get hot around midday, even though it's winter. Maybe eighty or eighty-five. Try running any distance in that heat without water and you'll kill yourselves." He was still trying to keep the flies off his face.

"Then we better get started."

"You better fix your jeans," Paige offered the

knife.

"Good idea." Sara took it and turned her jeans into shorts, too.

"Sara?" Jerry's voice was a whisper now.

"Yeah?"

"Tell Janet I'm sorry."

"I'll do that, Jerry."

"Good luck." He closed his eyes.

"Come on, Paige. We've got a long way to go." Sara tossed the knife aside and led off down the hill. At the bottom they had flat land all the way back to the interstate. They started off at a brisk walk.

"What did he mean? 'Tell Janet I'm sorry'?" Paige said.

There was a gunshot.

"Oh."

"We'll go as fast as we can," Sara said, "but if Jerry's right about the distance, it'll take us five or six hours to get to that truck stop on the interstate, if we make good time. It takes four hours to drive from here to Long Beach, so we won't get to a phone before Guthrie gets to Clay."

"But we have enough time to get there before eight-thirty," Paige said. "Right?"

"We have time, we'll make it," Sara said.

They talked while they walked, getting to know each other. Paige told Sara about her hopes and dreams. How she'd always wanted to be a pilot when she grew up. How she wanted to take lessons, but her father wouldn't let her. But now she was more into music. Her ideal life would be to manage a rock band, at least up to two days ago. Now she didn't know what she wanted to do.

Sara told her how she'd been racing ever since she

could remember. She'd been a tomboy growing up, loving cars better than life. She also talked about how her parents were killed in a helicopter crash. Talking about it caused Sara to choke up and Paige cried. She wished she could see her own father one last time. She wished she could have said goodbye.

The time seemed to race by. Till noon. Then they were too tired to talk. They just kept heading east toward the interstate. Paige had never been so thirsty. Her face was sunburned. Her lips were cracked. She was covered in sweat, feeling dizzy, and just when she thought she couldn't go on any more, Sara said. "Look, the Road Runner."

"What time is it?"

Sara looked at the watch. "Two-fifteen."

All of a sudden Paige felt better. Like she could go on forever. "Let's run," she said and she took off. Sara matched her stride and incredibly they closed the distance between themselves and Malcolm and Dottie in ten minutes.

Dottie saw them coming. She welcomed them with a smile and a wave. They were panting, sucking air through parched lips. "This way." Dottie led them to a spigot in front of the shed near the oil well. She turned the water on. "Take it slow."

After they'd each had a little to drink, Sara cranked the spigot up and dunked her head under the cool spray. Then Paige did the same while Sara told Dottie and Malcolm about Jerry, Guthrie, Clay and Kelly. When Paige finished running the water over her hair, the big dog was there, wanting a drink. She stood aside for him and scratched behind his ears.

"It's about an hour to the truck stop on the interstate," Malcolm said. Somehow Dottie had torn those towels into strips and had managed to wrap them around his wounded arm. "Who knows how long it'll take you to beg, borrow or steal a car. Then it's four hours to Long Beach. It doesn't look good."

"Then I better get going," Sara said.

"Why don't you call Kelly's Grandmother in Hawaii and tell her? Maybe she can stall your husband," Dottie said.

"What if Guthrie is the one talking to Estelle," Sara said. "I'd be afraid of what he'd do if he smelled a problem."

"He'd kill her," Paige said. "I know. He tried to kill me."

"Can you fly?" Malcolm asked.

"What do you mean?" Sara said.

"A small plane. A Piper Cherokee 140. Can you fly it?"

"I don't have my license yet, but I've done my cross-country. A solo flight from Long Beach to Santa Maria and back. The only thing I've ever been up in is a Cessna 150. But I could fly a Cherokee if I had one."

"You didn't happen to notice the landing strip out behind the Mobil did you?" Malcolm said. "The one with the 140 parked by the end of the runway."

"No."

"Belongs to my ex-son-in-law. The one that took your Taurus. You know, the cop. You took his car, might as well take his plane, too. There's a key to it on his key ring." Malcolm was holding his bad arm against his chest as he made the motion of a key turning with his good hand.

"The keys are back with the burnt out car," Sara said.

"Ah, but they're not the only keys." He reached down to one of those Yo-Yo kind of stainless steel key chains on his belt. He pulled the keys out a couple of feet and let them go. They shot back to the belt.

"If you can fly a Cessna, you can fly the Cherokee. The low wing doesn't make a bit of difference. She works the same. Mike and J.D. don't usually get back from their shooting excursions till around four or five, so if you hustle you could be long gone before they get back. There's just a couple of bothers with the plane."

"What?" Sara said.

"The battery's dead and she's only half full. Paige could hand prop it. It's not a problem. You turn the ignition on and it'll fire right up when she pulls the prop through the compression cycle." He turned to Paige. "You grab the prop at the top and pull her down, and make sure you follow through, like in baseball. You understand?"

"Yeah, like when I'm swinging for a home run. I don't stop at the ball. I swing the bat all the way around, through the ball. You want me to keep going down, so I get more power in the pull, but also so I don't get my hands or my head cut off."

"Exactly."

"Don't worry, Malcolm. I'm not stupid." Sherman was by her side. He licked her hand and she scratched him behind the ears again.

"I didn't think you were."

"Exactly how much fuel is there?" Sara asked.

"Probably enough, but you'll have to watch it. If you don't think you can make it all the way to Long Beach, land at Van Nuys. You should be able to get a car there."

"Right behind the Mobil?" Sara said.

"Yeah, and don't worry about us. It's a long walk, but I'm not losing any blood. We'll be fine. Now take off, you two."

Sara hugged Dottie and impulsively Paige dropped to her knees and hugged the great dog. Then they were off and running.

Chapter Twenty-One

THEY RAN THROUGH THE WELLS because it was quicker than following the winding road. Sara was breathing hard, sucking in air like she was coming toward the end of a marathon. Paige seemed to be in better shape. Youth. Then they were at Guthrie's. They passed the cabin, running over the rocky terrain beyond. Sara stumbled and went down.

Paige stopped. "You okay?" She offered her a hand up.

"I think so." Sara tried taking a few steps, putting a little weight on her ankle. "Sprained I think." She was limping. She looked at the watch. Quarter-to-three.

"We don't have that far to go. Lean on me." Paige laced an arm around Sara's waist and Sara did the same. They started toward the road, with Paige taking the weight off of Sara's bad foot. All they could do was to keep on going.

Twenty minutes later they were at the road that went under the interstate toward the Mobil station and the town a mile or so beyond. Sara never wanted to go back there.

"Okay, I think I can walk now." Sara put weight on the foot. Pain, but it wasn't going to kill her. "A slow jog, maybe." She started off. Each step a fire bolt up the leg. Then they were under the interstate, then at the Mobil Station. Sara was panting, Paige looked like she could go ten more miles.

"Jeez," Paige said, "what happened here?"

"I was in the Trooper." Sara struggled the words out between breaths. "Malcolm was in the booth. The police car was over there." She pointed. "I wanted the keys. Malcolm was locked inside and wouldn't give them to me."

"So you attacked him with the car?"

"Yeah."

A van pulled off the interstate, turned into the gas station and drove up to the pumps. A man got out, surveyed the damaged booth and the wrecked Trooper, got back in his truck and left without a word.

"Come on." Sara started off, walking, the pain not as bad. "The landing strip is supposed to be out back." They went around the station. "There it is." The runway paralleled the interstate. Behind it was acres of cultivated earth. Sara hadn't noticed it earlier, but now she inhaled the smell.

"Onions," Paige said.

"Crop dusters." Sara was looking at two yellow biplanes parked at the end of the runway. And next to them the Piper Cherokee. There was a hanger that bordered on the gas station. It was open and deserted. "It's spooky."

"Maybe no one works on Saturday," Paige said.

"Is that all it is? It seems like I've been running forever."

"Me too."

"I haven't slept in so long," Sara said. "I must be running on adrenaline."

"I feel like I just drank a zillion cups of coffee," Paige said.

"You're too young for coffee."

"I'm Polish, there's no such thing as too young for coffee." Paige started toward the plane. "It's smaller than my dad's."

"Your father had a plane?"

"Yeah, a Piper Arrow. They're bigger, faster and they have retractable landing gear."

"I thought you said your father wouldn't let you take lessons."

"He wouldn't, not with a real instructor, but I've flown with him a lot. We used to go out to the desert and land on the dry lake beds."

"Did he ever let you handle the controls?"

"All the time. He even let me take it off. It's not hard, but he never let me land it."

"So you can kind of fly from the right?"

"Kinda, but I'm not real good. I'm sorta all over the sky. That's why I wanted to take lessons. He wasn't a very good teacher. He yells a lot. Not 'cuz he's mad, it's just his way. She was crying again.

"I wish there was something I could do to make it better." Sara hugged her. "But there isn't and it's so sad."

"Come on." Paige broke the hug. "Let's get going."

"Are you sure you can do this?" Sara said.

"I've never hand propped a plane before, but I've seen it done. Once when we were out in the desert the Arrow wouldn't start. Dad propped it while I gave it the gas. It didn't look that hard and this is a smaller plane, so it should be easier."

"You're kind of a tomboy yourself, aren't you?"

"For sure."

"Paige—"

"No. I know what you're gonna say and the answer is no. You're not leaving me here. I'm going."

"I'm not the best pilot. It could be dangerous. I just can't take the responsibility."

"It's not your responsibility. It's mine. Besides, you said yourself you haven't had any rest. I can fly from the right so you can catch a nap. You need me. They still got Kelly and I'm not quitting till we get her back. Then you can ditch me, but not till then."

"I'm not trying to ditch you."

"Good."

"But—"

"Why don't you just get in so we can get going?" Paige went to the tail and moved the ailerons up and down. Then she moved the rudder. She did it without thinking. She was used to being around airplanes. She checked the flaps on the left side on her way to the front of the plane, not even aware that she was preflighting the aircraft. "Come on, get in. We don't want to be here if somebody decides to come along."

Sara unlocked it. Unlike the Cessna, the Cherokee only had a door on the right side, so she had to climb over the copilot's seat. She strapped herself in and checked the unfamiliar controls. She found the master switch and turned it on. No steady hum telling her the electronics were coming to life. The battery was really dead. She set the mixture for full rich, then flashed Paige the thumbs up signal. Paige pulled the prop down. It started up, first try. Sara watched her check the flaps on the right side as she came around. She climbed up on the wing and an instant later was strapping herself in.

"Come on," she said. "We're outta here."

Sara checked the flaps from the inside by flipping the flap switch up and down. She rotated the yoke, checking the ailerons, moved the foot pedals, checking the rudder, then she looked at Paige. "Foot hurts a little when I work the pedals."

"Want me to take it off?"

"No, I will."

"Then get the carb heat," Paige said and Sara turned it off. The girl knew her stuff. "Fuel gauges," Paige said and Sara checked them. Both tanks were about half full. "Oil pressure." Sara checked it and saw that it was in the green. "Brakes on and bring it to about a thousand," Paige said. Sara pushed on the brakes, and pulled out the fuel control knob till the tach needle climbed up and settled at a thousand RPM. She looked at the wind sock. A slight wind was blowing right down the runway. She checked the gauges under power, then backed it back to idle.

"Okay," Paige said. "We're good to go."

"Your father teach you all that?"

"Yeah."

"I guess his yelling really paid off, because I woulda forgot the carb heat. Thanks."

"See, you need me."

"Yeah, I guess I do." Sara taxied to the end of the runway. She ran her eyes over the controls, then made a last check of flaps and rudder.

"Come on, you're ready."

Sara stomped on the brakes and pulled the throttle all the way out. Then released the brakes. The plane responded, shooting down the runway like a horse given its head.

"Start your roll at about seventy or seventy-five," Paige said.

Sara kept her concentration on the runway. She'd never flown in a low wing airplane, everything was so different. For a second she thought about aborting the takeoff.

"You're doing fine," Paige said. Thank God for her calm voice. "Call out your airspeed."

"Fifty, fifty-five."

The plane started to shake. "Hold the nose down," Paige said. "And keep calling out the airspeed."

"Sixty, sixty-five."

"Ease back a little," Paige said, and Sara obeyed, gently pulling on the yoke. The girl was a lifesaver.

"Seventy," Sara called out.

"Pull back a little harder," Paige said. She sounded just like a flight instructor. Just like Carry Ann.

"Seventy-five," Sara said.

"Go for it," Paige said.

Sara pulled back on the yoke. "Eighty, eighty-five." She pulled back more, keeping the back pressure on it, the familiar tingling sensation shooting through her as the plane left the ground.

"Feel the rush?" Paige said.

"Yeah," Sara said. She relaxed the pressure a bit, guiding the plane, flying the plane. They'd taken off to the south so Sara climbed to fifteen hundred feet and flew over the highway, letting the interstate be their guide.

"Pretty neat," Paige said.

"You're good," Sara said.

"That's what my dad always did when I took it off."

"How'd you know the takeoff speed?"

"I didn't for sure. But I knew it'd be a little slower than the Arrow, so I kind of guessed." Paige looked over her shoulder in the back seat. "What's this?" She reached over and grabbed onto something, bringing it up front. "A backpack. Maybe somebody's lunch or something. I'm starved."

"Me too." Sara felt like she hadn't eaten in a month.

Paige opened the pack and pulled out a flare gun, five charges, a hiker's GPS and two liter bottles of water. "It looks like he thought he might crash." She twisted the top off one of the bottles and took a long drink.

"There's a lot of empty land out here," Sara said. "You could see a flare forever after dark."

"Drink?" Paige handed her the bottle.

"You want to take the controls?"

"Yeah, sure. Just a second." Paige put everything back in the pack, except the water. "Ready?"

"The plane's yours." Sara took a long drink as

Paige took over the aircraft.

"Handles like a dream," Paige said.

After a few minutes Sara said. "You're not all over the sky. You're doing fine."

"Yeah, this is easier than the Arrow."

"I was born to race cars in the dirt. I'm one of the best in the world. You were born to fly. You're a natural."

"Really?"

"Take it up to five thousand and follow the road." Sara settled back as Paige eased back on the yoke. The girl really was a natural. Perfect coordination between rudder pedals and yoke.

"You don't really like flying, do you?" Paige said.

"You can tell?"

"If you love it, you grab every chance you can at the controls, like I just did."

"I guess I just like my wheels on the ground."

"So why fly?"

"There's this wonderful woman. Carry Ann Donovan. She used to be my co-driver. She was really into racing. But planes more than cars. She quit off road and bought a flight school. Condor Aviation at Long Beach Airport. She kept nagging me to buy in with her. So I finally decided to do it. I didn't really want to, but I didn't think I could raise Kelly right if I was racing all over the world."

"And if you own a flight school you should be able to fly?"

"Exactly."

At five thousand feet Paige said, "This is the part I love. It's like you're with the angels." Her lower lip was quivering again. She was quiet for a bit, then, "My dad never hid anything from me. I knew all about him. They say he made the money to get into his software business by loan sharking. It's true. He started out small and made loans to people that needed it. He charged high interest, but he made loans that banks wouldn't. And he knew who he was loaning the money to and what it was for. He never took a man's house away, or his car. Sometimes he got rough when someone wouldn't pay. But he never hassled someone that couldn't pay. There's a difference."

"You loved him a lot?" Sara said.

"Like the earth loves the sun. He was loud and gruff and yelled all the time. It's the Polish way. But he loved me and Peter so much. Maybe he was loud, but he never hit us and he was always there whenever we needed him." She flashed Sara with a look. "There's no way you're ditching me. I'm gonna stick with you till we get Kelly back. And then I'm gonna get even."

"What are you talking about?"

"Just promise me you won't try and ditch me." There was fire in her eyes.

"I promise," Sara said, "but after we get Kelly away from them, it's a problem for the police. I won't ditch you, but you gotta promise me that you won't do anything stupid. Otherwise I'll dump you the second we land."

"Okay, I promise too. Nothing stupid. We find Kelly, then call the cops."

"The FBI," Sara said.

"Okay, them."

Sara looked out the window. It was so different seeing the wing. In the Cessna it was like she was floating. Nothing between her and the earth when she looked down. She looked beyond the low wing at the cars moving up and down Highway 5. They looked like the Hot Wheels toys that Kelly liked so much. Little cars racing on tracks. Kelly wanted to grow up and race the big cars, just like her Aunt Sara. Shit, I might want to get a little even myself, Sara thought.

She checked her watch. Three-forty-five. Under five hours, but enough time. How could Estelle change the plan and agree to pay for just Kelly? Did she believe that Paige was dead? Sara shivered a little. What would she do if she was in Estelle's place? Loving your granddaughter and not knowing the other girl at all. What a decision. She could hardly blame Estelle.

"Why don't you close your eyes for a bit?" Paige said. "If I get into any problems I'll wake you."

"I couldn't," Sara said. They flew along in silence for about an hour. Sara's foot throbbed. She was lucky Paige could fly from the right, because working the pedals would kill her. How in the world would she ever walk once they got it on the ground? Could she even land it?

"Close your eyes. Get some rest," Paige said again. "It's another hour and a half at least till we get to the pass. I'll wake you. Honest."

"I couldn't sleep."

"Okay, then don't, but we're flying straight and level. The gauges are good. Nothing's gonna happen."

"Alright, just for a bit." Sara closed her eyes and after a few minutes fell asleep.

"Sara, time to wake up."

"What?" She felt a hand on her shoulder, shaking

her. She opened her eyes to the steady drone of the airplane and it all came flooding back. "Where are we?"

"Over LAX at twenty-five hundred."

"Jesus, Paige, you were supposed to wake me." She knuckled the sleep from her eyes and looked out the window. There was a 747 taking off right below them.

"You were sleeping so sound. Besides, I've flown over here a lot with my dad. We're gonna start a climb back up to five thousand as soon as we pass the airport."

"How'd you get clearance?" Sara was talking to Paige, but she couldn't take her eyes off the big jet below. It was probably going two hundred miles an hour when it lifted off, but it looked like it was going so slow as it struggled to leave the ground.

"I used the radio. Hey, I've done it before. My dad hated talking on it. I did it all."

"Isn't that against the law?"

"We're talking about my dad. Laws were for other people."

"How's the fuel?"

"We might make it."

"What?" Sara looked at the gauges, both pinned on empty. She was wide awake now and had to fight to keep the anger out of her voice. "What happened to we land at Van Nuys if we were low on fuel?"

"Too late, passed it. Besides, Long Beach is closer to where we gotta go."

"What if we don't make it?"

"My dad always said to think positive."

Sara kept her eyes on the gauges as Paige initiated their climb. Any second she expected the engine to die, but the drone continued, the prop kept turning. "Okay, turn a little to your left. We'll head out toward Compton, just in case." They could almost glide to the small uncontrolled airport, so if they ran out of fuel she could land there.

"Kinda hazy," Paige said.

Sara looked up. Clouds covered the sky and it was a typical hot and hazy L.A. day. She watched the cars, stalled in the rush hour traffic below and wondered why she lived in Southern California. Well, once she got Kelly back she'd be moving. She'd promised Estelle, but she wouldn't mind Hawaii. Not at all.

"You don't have to be nervous. We're gonna make it," Paige said.

"I'm not nervous."

"You keep shifting your eyes from the fuel gauges and the ground. I'll bet you're plotting places to land."

They were over Compton Airport now and Sara sighed as she looked down at the small runway.

"See, we're gonna make it," Paige said.

"I'll take the plane now." Sara was still a little angry as she slipped her hands on the yoke. The engine coughed and Sara shoved the power in, turning the plane into a glider.

"What?" Paige said.

"We're gonna need what little fuel we have left to taxi off the runway." Sara picked up the mike and thumbed the push to talk button. She read the number off the plaque on the dash. "Long Beach Tower, this is Piper Cherokee Four-three-one-six-tango, coming into your downwind at two-five-right to land."

"Number three after the Bonanza, One-six-tango."

"You're not gonna land back there?" Paige said.

"It's basically a deserted field. No way to get a car and it's almost five-thirty."

"So we're gonna glide into Long Beach? That's a long way."

"We'll make it," Sara said.

"Okay, let's trim it up for our best glide ratio," Paige said. Sara was impressed. Paige wasn't fazed a bit. She worked the trim control and in a few minutes they were in a controlled descent.

"Pattern altitude is a thousand feet, we might come in at a little less," Sara said.

"I'll cross my fingers," Paige said.

A few minutes later they entered their downwind at nine hundred feet. Too low.

"One-six-tango is number two after the Bonanza on a long downwind," the tower's voice over the radio said.

"No way," Paige said.

Sara picked up the mike. "This is One-six-tango, requesting permission for a practice power off landing." She didn't want to tell the tower they were flying on fumes. She was afraid if she told them it was an emergency he might pay a little better attention to her numbers. She didn't know if Malcolm's son-in-law had come back from his shooting session yet and reported the plane stolen.

"There's a plane in front of you One-six-tango, about to turn base."

"I can have it on the ground and off the runway before they get anywhere near the numbers."

"When do you want to turn base?"

"Now, I'm gonna do a side slip." She handed the

mike to Paige, shoved her left foot forward, giving it full left rudder as she cranked the ailerons to the right, cross controlling the aircraft, keeping it in control as she went into the slip, dropping fast.

"I didn't give you permission," the tower said.

"But you were gonna," Paige said into the mike.

Sara kept the nose pointed to the right, toward the runway. They were dropping at two hundred and fifty feet a minute. She stayed in the slip, pushing the yoke forward.

"Going down a little fast," Paige said.

"It'll be fine." Sara added more pressure on the yoke, increasing the rate of descent even more.

"You ever done this before?" Paige said.

"Couple of times. Carry Ann showed me how."

"You sure you have it?" Paige said, loud. The ground was coming up fast.

"I hope." Sara pushed the yoke in more. Nose down, the cross controlled plane started spinning around. They were facing forty-five degrees to the runway. Paige started to reach for the yoke on her side of the plane. "Hands off the controls," Sara said. Paige pulled her hands back like they'd been burnt.

Two hundred feet from the ground and Sara started to ease off the left rudder. A hundred and fifty, the plane was almost all the way around and she released the left rudder altogether. A hundred feet and she added a little right rudder and eased off the pressure on the ailerons, straightening them a little.

"Oh, fuck," Paige said.

Fifty feet from the ground and Sara eased off the right rudder and straightened the ailerons. She was flying straight and level, only a hair's breath to the right of the runway. She eased the plane to the left

KEN DOUGLAS

and at ten feet she was over the center line. At five feet she started her flare, squeaking it in smack in the center of the four thousand foot runway.

"Beautiful," Paige said.

Sara eased the power out as they were taxiing off the runway.

"Contact Ground Control on one-two-zero-point-eight, One-six-Tango."

Paige grabbed the mike, "Roger, Tower. Thanks very much for your cooperation."

"I should send you to jail." But Sara heard the chuckle in his voice as the Bonanza behind touched down. "You really were too close to cut him off," the tower said.

"We won't ever do it again, promise," Paige said. Then she switched to ground control.

Sara pulled into the guest parking at Condor Aviation as the plane coughed and died.

CHAPTER TWENTY-TWO

SARA LOOKED OVER at the parking spaces by the flight school office. "Damn, Carry Ann's car isn't here. I was sorta hoping—"

"What are we gonna do?" Paige said.

"There's only a few cars parked in front of the flight school and I don't know any of them. I'd be afraid to go inside without Carry Ann there. They might be civic minded and call the cops. So I guess we'll have to go over to airport parking and see if someone in a hurry left his car unlocked."

"You're gonna steal a car?"

"I can hotwire anything."

"How you gonna get past the parking lot guy?"

"I'm gonna drive real fast."

"Neat, let's go." Paige slung the backpack over her shoulder, pushed the door open and climbed down the wing and Sara scooted across and followed her out. It was only a short walk to Donald W. Douglas Road, the road that looped around to the airport off of Lakewood Boulevard, and they started toward it.

"Hey, stop!" Sara yelled.

"What?" Paige said.

"Hotel van." Sara said as the Marriott Hotel courtesy van stopped for them. "Come on." The automatic door opened and Sara stepped into the back. "Beats walking," she said to the driver, getting a smile from him in return.

"Now what?" Paige said.

"It'll take us to the Marriott. No parking lot attendants. Easier to get a car," Sara whispered. She checked the time. Six-fifteen.

The van made the loop around to the airport, picked up three other passengers and their luggage and was turning right on Lakewood when two police cars came screaming off the boulevard, sliding around the turn into the airport.

"Looks like they found out about the plane," Paige whispered.

"Looks like," Sara said.

The shuttle bus made the next left and minutes later pulled up in front of the Marriott's reception area. Sara and Paige were first on, last off, waiting for the others to off load their baggage. She felt like screaming, but finally they were out and she was chasing after Paige, limping toward the parking lot.

"Look."

"Beautiful," Sara said. "1960 Sunliner, a classic. Dottie would love it." The convertible was painted candy-apple red, had the top down, a *Just Married* banner on each side and tin cans tied on a rope to its fenders.

"Yeah, it's a great car. Look at the trunk," Paige said.

Sara did and right under a third *Just Married* banner was a set of keys hanging off a key inserted in the lock. "Looks like they were in an awful hurry to get to their room."

"We're in a hurry, too." Paige tossed the backpack into the back seat.

"Get the cans." Sara grabbed the keys as Paige untied the ropes. She pulled off the sign on the trunk and Paige was taking the banner off of the passenger side as Sara pulled the one off the driver's. She checked the watch. Six-thirty-five.

"How long to get to the Marina?" Paige said.

"Twenty minutes," Sara said. She did it in fifteen. She parked in the marina lot, in a spot close to where her forty-five foot sloop was tied up. It was dark now, but it was Saturday night. A lot of people were around the boats. Others were going and coming from the seaside restaurants and the pricey stores.

"Which boat?" Paige said.

"*Wave Dancer*, Over there. Oh shit!" Sara stood on the seat. "It's gone."

"Gone?" Paige stood on the seat, too.

"It's supposed to be over there." Sara pointed to an empty berth at the end of the dock. "Come on." She sat back down and got out of the car. Paige vaulted over the door, landing on her feet. Sara started down the dock. A boat was coming in. *Sweet Jane*, a thirty-six foot schooner, Jim and Marie Larsen, good friends.

"Hey, Sara, you want to catch our lines?" Jim Larsen said. She didn't. She was in a hurry. But out of habit she grabbed his bow line when he tossed it and she cleated it off. Then she was at the stern. She caught the line and cleated it too. "Saw *Wave Dancer* out at one of the oil islands."

"Which one?" Sara said.

"Oh hell, I can never tell which is which. The one just south of that tall blue apartment building, the Ocean View Towers." The three manmade oil islands. *Grissom*, *Chaffee* and *White* were named for the three Astronauts that had been killed in the Apollo One fire years ago. They had false facades covering the drilling structures and artificial waterfalls that were lit up at night. They were a favorite anchoring spot for weekend sailors, but were usually deserted during the week.

"What are we gonna do?" Paige said.

"It's not far. I can swim out to it from the Towers."

"You wanna tell me about it?" Jim was a retired circuit court judge and a news junkie.

"You mean about what you've been seeing on television?"

"Hey, Sara we're in a hurry, remember?" Paige said. She turned to the judge. "Mister, my name's Paige Radoslaw. If you've heard about Sara on television, then you've heard of me."

"I have," Jim said.

"Then you better believe me when I tell you Sara didn't kidnap me. She rescued me right when they were about to kill me. Now we gotta go or they're gonna hurt Kelly. Bye."

"What?" the judge said.

"Can't talk, Judge. It's all true."

"I should call the police." He stepped off the boat.

"You do that and they'll kill Kelly," Paige said.

"It's five-to-seven. In an hour it won't make any difference. Call 'em now and you're killing her," Sara said.

"Come on, Sara!"

"Doesn't look like the girl's kidnapped," the judge's wife said.

"Were gone," Sara said. She limped after Paige who was behind the driver's seat with the engine running by the time Sara reached the car.

"Which way?" Paige backed out of the parking space and was headed toward Ocean Boulevard. No way was she old enough to drive, but Sara needed a few seconds breather. Besides, Paige looked like she knew what she was doing, and she'd flown that plane, after all.

"Make a right. It's about a quarter mile down Ocean, maybe less."

Paige stepped on the gas. It was a three speed stick on the column. She shoved in the clutch as she made the turn onto Ocean, cutting off a pickup truck. The guy in the truck honked his displeasure, but Paige ignored him. She revved the engine and popped the clutch with her foot on the floor, laying about twenty feet of rubber on the street.

"Good way to dump the transmission."

"We in a hurry or what?"

"There," Sara said, "the tall blue building." The Ocean View Towers was a nineteen story building that overlooked the beach. Lisa used to live on the top floor. Like the name of the building implied, it had a great view.

"Nowhere to park." Paige stopped, double parked and pulled on the emergency brake. She reached into the back and grabbed the backpack. She didn't even shut off the engine.

"You can't park here, we're blocking all the traffic." But Sara was talking to air. Paige was already out of the car.

"Let's go." Paige was around to Sara's side of the car. "You're too slow, put your arm around me." The pickup Paige had cut off was stuck behind the convertible and he was honking again. They ignored it as Sara and Paige started toward the door.

"How do we get down to the beach?" Paige said. Ocean Boulevard paralleled the long beach, but they were three or four stories above the sand and sea below.

"We have to go through the building. There's an underground garage. We can take the elevator down."

Paige helped Sara to the lobby. The door was locked. "Now what?"

"Buzzer." Sara pushed it. In seconds a guard was at the door.

"You got your key?" He was in his sixties and Sara didn't remember him from when Lisa lived in the building.

"Emergency." Paige pushed herself in past the guard who was busy staring at the cars on Ocean all backed up behind the double parked convertible.

"That your car?" he said, but Sara had already pushed the down button and the doors were opening. "Hey," he said, but he was too slow. They were inside the elevator with the doors closing before he was able to get to them.

The doors opened into the well lit parking garage. "That way." Sara pointed to a door on the far side of the garage. Paige helped her to it. "Wait," Sara said. She checked the watch. Seven straight up. "Gimme the pack." Paige handed it over and Sara pulled out the flare gun. "Can you use this?"

"Of course."

"Okay, listen and no back talk. I'm gonna swim out to the boat and check to see if Kelly is there." Sara took Jerry's watch off her wrist and handed it to Paige.

"I should go, your foot—"

"No! I can swim no problem. I can be out there in ten minutes easy. I've done it lots of times. If Kelly's out there I'll come right back and we'll call the cops. So, give me ten minutes each way and ten to find out if she's there."

"What if she isn't or if you can't find out?"

"Then I'll have to board and talk to Clay. You know, try what Jerry said. Try and convince him I'll tell him where Carole is if he doesn't hurt Kelly. If it looks like I'll be able to persuade him, I'll blink the anchor light."

"And if you can't convince him?"

"If I'm not back here by 7:30 and you don't see that light blink, start shooting that thing off. Light up the sky above the boat. Keep shooting till you're out of charges. And scream like hell. Yell rape. That should get the cops here real quick."

"This is a stupid plan," Paige said.

"Yeah. Let's go." Sara opened the door. On the other side it was dark and eerie. She saw the lone anchor light out at the small man made island. Clouds covered the sky.

Paige helped her to the water's edge where she kicked off her shoes and pulled off the thick running socks. She curled her toes in the cool sand. *Wave Dancer* was the only boat anchored in front of the closest island. No wonder. She could hear Bob Dylan's twangy voice drifting across the water. Maybe that had been his intention. Drive off the neighbors. No. He just played it loud because he could. He was a cop. He didn't care about anyone else.

She turned to Paige. "Remember, 7:30. If I'm not back, fire the flare and get the cops." She gave her a quick hug.

"I really like that song," Paige said.

"*Corinna, Corinna,* The eleventh song on the *Freewheelin'* album and the only one he didn't write. Clay's into real early Dylan. He's puts that in the CD player every night when he goes to bed. Leaves it on repeat."

"All night long?" Paige said. "The same CD? Every night? He is crazy."

"Yeah, I shoulda seen it a long time ago, but we sorta had our own lives. I just didn't know it." She hugged Paige again. "Time's running out. I gotta go."

"Desperation Moon," Paige said.

"Kelly told you about that?" Sara looked up. Sure enough there was a sliver of sky where the moon was trying to poke its light through the clouds.

"Yeah, she did," Paige hugged her tighter. "I love you, Sara. And you tell Kelly I love her, too."

"I love you too, kiddo." Then she broke the hug and jogged into the sea. Her ankle hurt like fury, but she was still able to put weight on it. Maybe not tomorrow, but it was tonight that counted.

The cold, mushy sand sent shivers up her bare legs as she splashed into the water. She dove into a wave, thankful that the breakwater kept them small, and started swimming out toward *Wave Dancer*. Halfway there she stopped to catch her breath.

Treading water she looked ahead to the boat. How could she have been so blind? The great life she'd been living was all a lie. She thought back to when she was dating Clay. She was just starting to become known on the off road circuit. They used to joke about it, how one day she'd be on all the talk shows and he'd be her number one supporter. He was gonna move up in the ranks, become captain one day. They had a future. They wanted kids. Kids. How could she have known he'd wanted them so badly? How could anyone want them that badly?

Bob Dylan started singing about all those roads a man had to walk down. Uh oh. Two songs had gone by, the CD had started over. She didn't have much time. She started back toward the boat, water flat and calm.

She saw a glowing cigarette fly over the side when she got close. Had Clay started smoking again, or was it Guthrie's? She swam toward the aft end. Whoever tossed the cigarette overboard had gone back down below. The swim ladder was down. Who'd been swimming? Clay hated being in the water. Did it mean that Guthrie was on board? Was he a swimmer?

She started up the ladder. The music was a lot louder out here. Maybe Guthrie wasn't on board. She moved through the cockpit without making a sound, but it wouldn't have made any difference, Bob was into the last verse of *Blowin' in the Wind* as she stepped out of the cockpit and moved behind the companionway hatch. She was afraid to look through it. Afraid she might be seen.

"How about some rock and roll?" someone yelled out. It had to be Guthrie. That meant that Kelly was on board. It went quiet and for a few seconds silence reigned. Then Bob Dylan's scratchy, raspy voice filled the night again. This time he was singing about being tangled up in blue. Clay had put on *Blood on the Tracks*. His idea of Rock and Roll, Bob Dylan with backup.

She hadn't actually seen Kelly, but she must be on board. She'd heard that other voice. Surely Jerry and Clay hadn't let anyone else in on their get rich quick scheme. She didn't know for sure how long she'd been on the boat, maybe five minutes, tops. Ten to swim out. She might have fifteen left before Paige shot off the flare. She should get in the water and get back, because if Paige let off that flare the cops would lose the element of surprise.

She was about to slip back in the water when someone below cranked up the volume even louder. Had to be Clay. Damn him. *Wave Dancer* was her boat, not his. Was he trying to blow out her speakers? Something inside of her snapped. It was such a little thing compared to everything else he'd done, but it was the back breaker. She wasn't going to shore. She wasn't leaving without Kelly.

Sara didn't think the speakers would take it for very long, but she didn't care anymore, because now they were hiding whatever sounds she might make on deck. She stepped out of the cockpit, walking softly to the main mast, where she undid the snap shackle on the spinnaker halyard. She held the line firmly in

hand, as she unwound the other end of it off the drum
of its winch and moved back to the cockpit, where she
wrapped it around the drum of the starboard side
power winch and snugged it into the self-tailing jaws.

She grabbed a look through the companionway.
Kelly was laying on the starboard settee. Her hands
were tied behind her back. Her feet were tied. There
was gray duct tape across her mouth, but she could
see, and her eyes went big when she saw Sara looking
in.

Sara put a finger to her lips and Kelly closed her
eyes.

"How much you think we can get?" Sara heard
him over the music, because she was only inches from
the back of his head and he was shouting. Clay must
be in the forward cabin, or the head. She got a
glimpse of Guthrie's back. He was tall and big boned,
with a close cropped military style haircut, not at all
like Jerry. He started to turn. Sara pulled her head
back quicker than an eel strike.

She sat behind the hatch, ignoring the cold as she
fed the line through the snap shackle, making a
sliding loop for a noose. Then she waited. She needed
a way to make one of them come out. Then it'd be
one on one with the other one. Could she take either?
She was mad enough. But she was also dead on her
feet. She hadn't slept in so long.

"Gonna piss." Not Clay's voice.

She made ready with the noose, but waited as he
came out. What if he turned? But he didn't. He
stepped out of the cockpit and went to the aft rail. He
stood with his knees touching the lifelines. She
couldn't hear the zipper come down because of the
music, but that sliver of moon caught the stream of

urine, making it glow.

She stepped up behind him. He was still pissing into the night when she shoved him overboard. Then she pulled up the swim ladder and dashed back to her place behind the hatch.

"Help!" Guthrie's scream pierced the night. Louder than Bob Dylan.

"What?" Clay yelled. His head was out the hatch. That beautiful wavy hair she'd loved so much. She dropped the noose over it, jerked the rope around his neck, then stepped on the deck button, activating the power winch. Clay's scream was cut off with a gag as he shot upward.

Guthrie struck out for the beach.

"So long, Clay," Sara said, eyes on her husband riding up toward the spreaders, swinging and kicking while Bob Dylan sang about a simple twist of fate in the background. Clay's tongue was hanging out of his mouth, his eyes were bulging, his neck was broken and he was dead, his kicking feet just didn't know it yet.

She went below and pulled the tape off of Kelly's mouth.

"I knew you'd come, Sara."

"Easy now. It's not quite over." She needed a way to let Paige know what was happening and to warn her about Guthrie possibly headed her way. "It's okay, baby," she said. Then she turned on the spreader lights and flooded the deck and the hanging dead man in light.

* * *

Paige shifted her eyes from the bobbing anchor light to the watch. It had a luminous display that stayed lit for a few seconds when she pushed a button on it. Bright blue with black numbers. Seven twenty-nine. One minute. She hated it that Sara hadn't come back.

A few more seconds. She pointed the gun toward the sky above the boat, then the light on its mast lit up and she saw the hanging man. Seven-thirty. She held her fire, straining her eyes out into the night. The desperation moon showed just enough light for her to see there was a swimmer in the water. Sara?

No. She clutched the backpack tightly in her left hand and stepped backwards, holding the flare gun in her right.

He was close to the shore now, struggling to stand. Guthrie. The winds aloft parted the clouds some and they locked eyes as he walked out of the water. It was up to his waist, his thighs, his knees, dripping off his clothes. He was a creature coming out of the dark, lumbering toward her.

He was on the sand.

"Stay back."

He started toward her.

"I mean it! Stay back." She shouted, but he kept coming, eyes piercing hers. She dropped the backpack and held the flare gun out in front of herself, gripping it with two hands, steadying her aim.

He roared, like an animal. Then charged.

She waited till he was ten feet away, then pulled the trigger.

He screamed as the flare slammed into his chest. Then he collapsed on the sand.

Paige didn't wait around to know he was dead. She kicked off her shoes and took off toward the water and in seconds was in it, swimming toward the boat.

* * *

Sara wanted to untie Kelly right away, but no way was she going to let her see Clay swinging by the neck below the spreaders. She went to the cockpit, eased the halyard out of the self-tailing jaws of the power winch and lowered the body till it was a couple of feet off the deck. She grit her teeth, then pushed the body over the lifelines, lowering it till its feet were dragging in the water. She grabbed a fistful of the dead man's shirt and held the body up while she removed the halyard. Then she dropped it into the sea. The cops would hate it. They'd have a thousand questions. Tough shit. Kelly didn't have to see, that's all that counted right now.

She went below, turned off the spreader lights and shut off the stereo.

"Did Paige get away?" Kelly asked as Sara started to untie her.

"Hey, the boat!" Paige's voice drifted up from outside.

"Why don't I go help her aboard and you can ask her yourself?"

EPILOGUE

SIX MONTHS LATER Malcolm squirmed in his tuxedo. Dottie squeezed his hand. The wedding dress made her look thirty years younger, tight at the waist, hemmed at the ankles, satin and silk with a veil that looked Arabesque. Dottie and Malcolm were getting married at sea. *Wave Dancer* was too small for the ceremony, but nobody cared.

Sara gave over the helm to Paige. The sun blazed high in the summer sky, there was a ten knot wind, gusting to fifteen, but only baby swells as they were inside the breakwater. Other boats were out on this breezy Saturday. Several had sailed close by. Sailors and their wives waved at the barefoot men in black tie and the women dressed like Dottie, only without the veil and in pink instead of white.

"Okay, keep turning to starboard till you feel the wind on your face, then hold it there," Sara said.

"Aye, aye, skipper." Paige spun the big wheel to the right. If she was nervous, she didn't show it, but after all she'd just gotten her pilot's license, so this should be a piece of cake to her, Sara thought.

"Okay, we're in the wind," Paige said.

Lisa stepped out of the cockpit with Peter on her heels. He looked older in his tux, and he'd cut his shoulder length air. He was so young, but he was the man in his family now and he looked it. At the mast Lisa took the main halyard out of the self-tailing jaws of the winch and handed it to Peter.

"Here she goes." He started hauling on the halyard.

"Way to go, Peter," Paige shouted as the sail climbed the mast, billowing and flapping behind it.

"Alright, crank it tight," Lisa said when the sail was at the top.

"Got it." Peter wrapped the halyard around the winch three times, then snugged it in the jaws.

"Good." Lisa handed him a winch handle and Peter slapped it into the winch and ground the sail up tight.

"Hang on," Paige yelled and she turned the wheel back to port as Sara sheeted in the sail. *Wave Dancer* healed over and picked up speed, slicing through the water.

"Gonna unfurl the jib?" Kelly asked as Lisa and Peter scooted back to the cockpit.

"I don't think so. The minister went down below

pretty quick, I think he might be getting seasick,"
Sara said. The minister was an old friend of Dottie's
and hadn't wanted to perform the ceremony at sea,
much less on a small sailboat, but Dottie usually got
her way when she put her mind to it.

"He looks like Rice," Kelly said.

"No he doesn't." Sara wished Kelly could just
forget about all that. She'd had nightmares for
months, but she hadn't had any lately and for that
Sara was grateful.

"The minister's not looking too good," Estelle
said, coming up from below. "We should get
Malcolm and Dottie married while he can still stand.
Besides, the sooner we start, the sooner we can cut
the cake. I'm hungry."

Sara smiled, she was getting used to Estelle's
bossy behavior and kind of getting along with her
now. It was something they were both working on,
liking each other for Kelly's sake. Lisa, on the other
hand, got along with Estelle like she was her own
grandmother. That helped a lot.

And it helped that she'd finally found a buyer for
the house, because the insurance wouldn't pay for the
repairs. They believed Clay started the fire. Sara
believed it too, but she was just so tired of dealing
with carpenters, plumbers and electricians. She could
hardly wait to get back on the racing circuit.

"I'm hungry too," Kelly said.

"You're always hungry," Sara said.

"Yeah." Then, "Wait till you see what Grandma
and Lisa did to my room. It's all pink with baby blue
balloons painted on one wall and a pink elephant
mobile hanging above my bed."

"Neat," Sara said. Kelly was living in Hawaii with

Estelle. But it wasn't so bad. Lisa had rented a two bedroom apartment on the beach with a view of Diamond Head and Sara spent a lot of time there. They were gonna buy a house as close to Estelle's as they could as soon as the sale of the Huntington Beach place went through, so even though Kelly was living with Estelle, Sara would see her often. She was going to be a part of her life.

"What's up with this minister," Jake said. "If he don't hurry up I'll perform the ceremony myself. I was one of those Universal Life Science Minister's back during the peace and love days and it's still legal, so if the right honorable down there can't cut it, I can get this show on the road." Jake was sitting in the cockpit, wedged between Sherman and the bulkhead.

Sherman barked, then slurped the side of his face.

"Stop with the fucking tongue."

"Watch your language, Jake." Jane was sitting across from her husband, next to Lisa.

"Then tell him to watch his tongue."

"He's a dog," Jane said. "He doesn't understand. Besides, he likes you."

"Oh, he understands alright."

Sherman tongued the side of Jake's face again. Jake grabbed the big dog in a headlock and knuckled rubbed him between the ears and everyone laughed. Jake was faking his anger and they all knew it.

"Leave the dog alone, Jake," his wife said.

"Sherman can take care of himself. Can't cha, boy." Greg rubbed the great dog's stomach.

Sara laughed. In the three years she'd been shopping at Lucky's, she'd never known Greg was going to law school at night. Now he worked for the Public Defender's office in Long Beach. She had dinner with him on occasion and she enjoyed listening to him as he told her about his cases.

Sherman slobbered on the back of Jake's neck.

"You cut that out, dog."

Sherman barked.

"Hey, Spider," Jake shouted down below, "push that minister up here 'fore this dog drowns me."

"Coming," Spider said and to Sara it looked like he actually was pushing the minister up from below.

"Why don't Dottie and Malcolm come back here," Paige said.

"Good idea." Dottie took Malcolm by the hand and led him behind the wheel as Paige moved around to the front of it.

"Places." Jake stood and helped guide the seasick minister into position. Then he moved next to Malcolm as Sara moved next to Dottie. Peter stepped out of the cockpit and hung onto the port shroud, Spider grabbed onto the starboard one. The rest of them linked hands in the cockpit behind the minister.

Malcolm caught Sara's eye. He winked and for a second she pictured Clay's face at her own wedding. He was a striking man, they'd truly been in love, or so she'd thought. Then she pictured Clay as she'd last seen him, face down in the water. Dead of a broken neck.

It had been a problem for several police departments and the FBI, but in the end they'd all decided it would be best for all concerned if no charges were brought against Sara. The authorities in Long Beach were only too glad to hand everything over to the FBI. Likewise the departments up north that had to deal with Rice's and Jerry's bodies. And as far as the FBI was concerned, Sara was a hero who foiled a kidnapping. The fact that she and her gang, as they'd become known in the press, had killed the kidnappers only raised the gang's status in their opinion. And of course no one told the FAA about her illegal flight across half the state.

She took a deep breath as the minister started to speak.

"Ladies and gentlemen, we are gathered here—"

The Bootleg Press Catalog

Ragged Man, by Jack Priest
ISBN: 0974524603
Unknown to Rick Gordon, he brought an ancient aboriginal horror home from the Australian desert. Now his friends are dying and Rick is getting the blame.

Desperation Moon, by Ken Douglas
ISBN: 0974524611
Sara Hackett must save two little girls from dangerous kidnappers, but she doesn't have the money to pay the ransom.

Scorpion, by Jack Stewart
ISBN: 097452462X
DEA agent Bill Broxton must protect the Prime Minister of Trinidad from an assassin, but he doesn't know the killer is his fiancée.

Dead Ringer, by Ken Douglas
ISBN: 0974524638
Maggie Nesbitt steps out of her dull life and into her dead twin's, and now the man that killed her sister is after Maggie.

Gecko, by Jack Priest
ISBN: 0974524646
Jim Monday must rescue his wife from an evil worse than death before the Gecko horror of Maori legend kills them both.

Running Scared, by Ken Douglas
ISBN: 0974524654
Joey Sapphire's husband blackmailed and now is out to kill the president's daughter and only Joey can save the young woman.

NIGHT WITCH, by Jack Priest
ISBN: 0974524662
A vampire like creature followed Carolina's father back from the Caribbean and now it is terrorizing her. She and her friend Arty are only children, but they must fight this creature themselves or die.

HURRICANE, by Jack Stewart
ISBN: 0974524670
Julie Tanaka flees Trinidad on her sailboat after the death of her husband, but the boat has a drug lord's money aboard and DEA agent Bill Broxton must get to her first or she is dead.

TANGERINE DREAM, by Ken Douglas and Jack Stewart
ISBN: 0974524689
Seagoing writer and gourmet chef Captain Katie Osborne said of this book, "Incest, death, tragedy, betrayal and teenage homosexual love, I don't know how, but somehow it all works. I was up all night reading."

DIAMOND SKY, by Ken Douglas and Jack Stewart
ISBN: 0974524697
The Russian Mafia is after Beth Shannon. Their diamonds have been stolen and they think she knows where they are. She does, only she doesn't know it.

TAHITIAN AFFAIR: A ROMANCE, by Dee Lighton
ISBN: 0976277905
In Tahiti on vacation Angie meets Luke, a single-handed sailor, who is trying to forget Suzi, the love of his life. He is dashing, good looking, caring and kind and it looks like her story will have a fairytale ending. Then Suzi shows up and she wants her man back.

BOOKS ARE BETTER THAN T.V.

THE BOOTLEG PRESS STORY

We at Bootleg Press are a small group of writers who were brought together by pen and sea. We have all been members of either the St. Martin or Trinidad Cruising Writer's Groups in the Caribbean.

We share our thoughts, plot ideas, villains and heroes. That's why you'll see some borrowed characters, both minor and major, cross from one author's book to another's.

Also, you'll see a few similar scenes that seem to jump from one author's pages to another's. That's because both authors have collaborated on the scene and—both liking how it worked out—both decided to use it.

At what point does an author's idea truly become his own? That's a good question, but rest assured in the rare occasions where you may discover similar scenes in Bootleg Press Books, that it is not stealing. Writing is a solitary art, but sometimes it is possible to share the load.

Book writing is hard, but book selling is harder. We think our books are as good as any you'll find out there, but breaking into the New York publishing market is tough, especially if you live far away from the Big Apple.

So, we've all either sold or put our boats on the hard, pooled our money and started our own company. We bought cars and loaded our trunks with books. We call on small independent bookstores ourselves, as we are our own distributors. But the few of us cannot possibly reach the whole world, however we are trying, so if you don't see our books in your local bookstore yet, remember you can always order them from the big guys online.

Thank you from everyone at Bootleg Books for reading and please remember, Books are better than T.V.

KEN DOUGLAS & VESTA
IRENE
WANGARAI, NEW ZEALAND

CPSIA information can be obtained at www.ICGtesting.com
Printed in the USA
BVOW031341250712

296132BV00001B/9/A